DANGEROUS DESIRE

Scotia could only watch, hardly daring to breathe, as Ian captured one of the tendrils of her hair that had escaped her tight plait during battle. He twined it about his finger. "Scotland might have forgotten how lucky she is to have you, but I have not." His voice deepened to a husky whisper.

Before she could react, he leaned down and placed his lips against hers. His kiss was swift, but it set off a wistful yearning deep inside her. When he drew back she was tempted to grab his shirt and pull him close again. But she could not lose herself to her desire, no matter how desperately she might want to. That could get her killed....

The WARRIOR TRAINER

GERRI RUSSELL

LEISURE BOOKS   NEW YORK CITY

A LEISURE BOOK®

January 2007

Published by

Dorchester Publishing Co., Inc.
200 Madison Avenue
New York, NY 10016

ISBN 0-8439-5825-1

The name "Leisure Books" and the stylized "L" with design are trademarks of Dorchester Publishing Co., Inc.

Printed in the United States of America.

Visit us on the web at www.dorchesterpub.com.

*To women warriors everywhere
who fight every day to better their lives,
overcome great obstacles, and work tirelessly
to make the world a better place.*

*To the bravest warrior woman I know, my mom.
You are my guide, my strength, my inspiration.*

ACKNOWLEDGMENTS

The saying goes that "it takes a village to raise a child," but in my experience I have also found the saying holds just as true when it comes to publishing a book. I'd like to take a moment to thank my "village," those people who have made it possible for me to follow my dream into publication.

Chuck, the hero of my heart, you are proof that reality is better than fiction. Pamela Ahearn, the most amazing, supportive, and savvy agent on the planet, you have my undying gratitude. My critique partners: Pamela Bradburn, Teresa DesJardien, Karen Harbaugh, Heather Heistand, Judith Laik, Nancy Northcott, Gina Robinson, and Joleen Wieser, you helped me keep the faith for so many years, the words "thank you" hardly seem big enough to encompass what that has meant to me. To *Romantic Times BOOKreviews* magazine and Dorchester Publishing for sponsoring the American Title II competition. Leah Hultenschmidt, thank you for seeing something special in my entry and for helping to make my dreams come true. And finally, to each and every person who voted for me. Thank you from the bottom of my heart for believing that *The Warrior Trainer* deserved a chance to become a published book.

AUTHOR'S NOTE

As long as I can remember, rocks have intrigued me. It didn't matter if it was a simple white pebble on the beach or the monolithic stones at Stonehenge. I was equally fascinated. It was the study of stones, their origins and history, and the people who owned them that led me to the discovery of the Stone of Destiny. And once I heard the tale of the Stone and the warrior women who guarded it, I knew it was a tale that had to be told.

Tales about the origin and purpose of the Stone of Destiny, also known as the Stone of Scone, have been handed down over the centuries. Its influence has spanned two continents—first as a holy relic, then as a national treasure.

Coveted and fought over by the Egyptians, the Greeks, the Spanish, and the English, the Stone originated in the Middle East and was then brought to Egypt, where it was thought to be the pillow upon which Jacob had his famous dream about a ladder to heaven. Eventually, the relic made its way to Greece, where it was placed under the guardianship of a warrior woman and master of martial arts named Scotia.

When her husband died in battle, Scotia decided to lead her people to the Isle of Destiny as foretold by a Hebrew prophet named Moses. After months of travel, they arrived in a remote land just north of present-day Ireland. They named their new country Scotia, after their queen, and the new rulers were called Scoti.

For generations, the Stone of Destiny was used to inaugurate the high kings of Scotland. It came to represent a sense of nationhood to the Scottish people. As long as they possessed the Stone, they held their freedom against English rule.

But when England, under the rule of Edward I, invaded Scottish lands, the task of protecting the Stone grew more and more difficult. Edward's army would stop at nothing to find and possess the stone, exerting its domination over the Scottish people.

And thus our story begins….

Prologue

Scotland, 1308

The ominous thunder of hooves echoed through the village of Glenfinnon. Four men on horseback, each with a weapon in one hand and a torch in the other, charged forth with one purpose in mind—to destroy the small village and everyone in it.

For three months now, the Four Horsemen had resurrected their roles as the apocryphal riders, rampaging through Scotland.

"Where is the warrior woman?" the White Horseman growled as he brought his horse's hooves down on one of the villagers, crushing him. The others nearby scattered right and left, grasping for survival.

"Yes, run away. It makes the chase more thrilling," the White Horseman taunted. For days, months, even years he and his fellow Horseman would continue their quest for the Stone of Destiny and the woman who protected it. Then the Stone, and the legendary good fortune it brought, would belong to England. His king would reward him handsomely.

The relentless hunt had driven them to the edge of this tiny village near the coast. Like a force of fury, the White Horseman shot forward, ready to kill. His bow sprang, launching an arrow into the chest of his enemy.

Today was a day for revenge, and a day for answers. Someone must know where the Stone and the Warrior Trainer were hidden. And someone would talk, or they would all die.

The White Horseman reloaded his crossbow, then kicked his heels into his horse's side, urging the beast forward. With a swing of his torch, a dry thatch roof caught fire. A whoosh of sound and light were followed by the crackle of hungry flames.

A child's screams cut through the piercing cries of war and death. A little girl, no more than eight, raced out of the burning house, her yellow skirt on fire. Tears streaked down her cheeks as she batted at the flames, feeding their ravenous tongues instead of dousing them.

Easy prey. The Horseman reined his mount to follow the child. She would die, just as they all would, merely because they were Scots, savage barbarians, and different from their English superiors. Three more steps and the child would be his, crushed and lifeless. He charged forward, a surge of euphoria taking root in his veins. He held the power of life and death. Death was what the Scots deserved for withholding such a valuable treasure as the Stone. Once he had it in his possession, he could carry it into battle for England wherever he went. And he would never lose.

One more step. One last petrified scream. A pull on the reins brought the horse's hooves up, ready, primed, when a dash from the side startled the horse. The beast nearly toppled over. A woman raced toward the child, batting at the flames before thrusting her out of the Horseman's way, to the safety of the nearby woods.

Rage, hot and hard, roared through him. He turned his horse again, this time toward the woman. She ran away from the woods—no doubt trying to save her child's life. He would show her. After he finished with the mother, he would go after the child.

The White Horseman chased the woman at a full gallop, overtaking her in a few steps. At her side, he reached down from his horse, grasping a handful of her thick, black hair through her homespun snood. Her face twisted in pain, but she did not cry out, merely let him drag her alongside his horse by her hair. The woman was brave. But would she be brave enough to tell him the truth? He slowed his horse, then stopped.

She struggled against his grip, which held her suspended, lashing out at his hand in her hair. "Let me go!"

"Perhaps, when you answer my questions, I might feel more merciful," he said with a sneer.

"What questions?" She stopped flailing her bruised and battered arms.

He jerked her face toward him. A sense of power shot through him at the fear that paled her mud-streaked face and shadowed her eyes.

"Where is the Warrior Trainer? Where is the Stone?" he asked, giving her body a light shake to add emphasis to his words.

"I doona know what ye mean." Again, she tried to wrench free of the hand in her hair.

"Tell me now!" He shook her harder, until her teeth rattled in her head, reveling in the surge of power his dominance over her brought.

"What stone?" she gasped, as her body sagged forward.

He pulled her roughly back to face him. "The Stone of Destiny. I know it still resides in this godforsaken land."

"Have you not heard?" Steely resolve replaced the fear in her eyes. "Your king stole it years ago, to the shame of us all."

The Horseman sneered. "A monk from Scone told us that Stone was a fake—after we cut off each of his fingers and toes." He smiled at the stark fear glittering in her eyes. "We know the real Stone remains here, guarded by the woman warrior." He watched his victim closely for signs she knew more.

"Nay." Tears spilled down her cheeks, leaving white streaks as they washed away the grime. "'Tis not true."

The Horseman thrust the woman to the ground, no longer willing to listen to her lies.

The woman scooted over tree branches and rocks that should have impeded her progress, but did nothing to slow her down. Fear had an amazing effect on these worthless creatures. The Horseman raised his bow. "I will find the warrior woman and the Stone, if I have to kill every Highlander to do so."

She gained her feet and broke into a run. He gave her just enough distance to taste her freedom before he took aim. With a single shot, he stole her future as payment against the debt the Highlanders still had to pay. Then he turned his horse to the woods to pursue the child. No one made a mockery of England, nor of him, and lived to tell the tale.

No one.

Chapter One

Ian dismounted outside the gatehouse of Glencarron Castle and looked around as he patted his mount's sleek neck. The morning mist had rolled back across the Highlands, leaving a startling blue sky as a backdrop against rugged green peaks that dropped dramatically toward the sea.

The waves, lapping at the shore below, sounded like a constant whisper—not the rhythmic beat he heard in his village of Kilninian. The whole place seemed peaceful and quiet. Too quiet for a place where a mighty warrior resided.

Ian tied his horse in a copse of heather nearby and searched the outbuildings and the towers for signs of inhabitants or guards. The entire place looked deserted, further proof of his suspicions that the Warrior Trainer was only a myth, despite his foster father's words to the contrary. He should turn back now, return to the clan that needed him to keep them safe, and stop wasting his time. But the promise he had made to his father to learn to fight in the ways of the ancients kept him moving toward the gate. He had come all this way. He owed it to his father to see it through, trainer or no trainer.

As Ian approached the wrought-iron gate, the soft sounds of voices and the lowing of cattle could be heard. "Greetings!" he called. He was about to shout again when a thin old man, leaning heavily on a cane, shuffled toward him from the gatehouse.

"What do ye want?" The man peered up at Ian through the iron bars with hazy, watery eyes.

Ian's frown deepened. "I seek the Trainer."

"What's that ye say?"

"I seek the Trainer," Ian shouted, enunciating each word.

The man pulled back and stared at Ian with a mixture of surprise and irritation. "No need to shout, laddie. I'm no' deaf."

Ian bit back an annoyed reply. "Please," he said. "My need is urgent."

The old man hobbled away and soon the bellow of a horn cut through the air. Moments later, shuffling sounds came to Ian from the battlements as fresh-faced youths with arrows and swords peered over the ramparts, their attention focused on him. And yet he did not feel threatened by their presence. Instead, he felt an odd sense of relief that there was someone, no matter how young, protecting the castle and the mythical Trainer.

The rattling of chains and the creaking of wood sounded as the gate slowly lifted from the ground. As soon as he was able, Ian slipped under the portcullis, then moved to the old man's side to help him lower it again. "Where can I find the Trainer?" he asked.

"She be in the keep."

So she was real after all. "I must see her."

A puzzled expression moved across the old man's face. He sighed as he waved Ian toward the keep.

Ian offered his thanks, then hurried across what appeared to be a seldom used outer bailey and into the inner courtyard. Servants carried pitchforks filled with hay toward the stables, where cattle awaited their meal. The bang and rattle of a hammer striking iron punctuated the air with a constant beat. Women strolled across the expansive courtyard carrying loaves of fragrant, yeasty bread from a brick oven near the kitchen shed.

As he strode past, he could almost feel the gazes upon him like fingers—some urging him forward, others holding him back. He ignored them with the same skills he had developed against his own clan when they stared at him. He was accustomed to being an outsider. When he made it to the great door, he gave it a confident rap with his gauntlet-covered fist. "I have come to see the Trainer," he announced, and instantly a hush fell over the courtyard.

"Put yer weapon down if ye want to enter here," a man ordered from behind the door.

Ian narrowed his gaze. "I will see the Trainer before I give up my weapon."

"Then ye'll not see the Trainer this day."

Give up his weapon? "What kind of warrior will only see unarmed men?"

"'Tis my rule, not hers. Now put yer weapon down or go away."

He just wanted to get this task over and done with. Once he fulfilled his obligation to his father, he could hunt down the Four Horsemen and exact his revenge. Family honor demanded no less.

With a grunt of frustration, Ian drew his claymore from the scabbard at his back and set the weapon at his feet. "I am unarmed."

The door creaked open and a wizened old man with white hair stared at Ian from beneath bushy white eyebrows. "Yer dagger, too."

Ian complied, but kept his gaze trained on the ancient creature before him. He might be disarmed, but he was far from defenseless. "I must see her now."

The stooped man moved aside and signaled for Ian to enter. He searched the cavernous space before him. Except for the fire that crackled in the hearth at the far side of the chamber, the room was empty.

"What purpose have ye here?" The wizened man stared up into Ian's face as though he were searching for something.

Ian fixed his attention on his adversary, revealing nothing in his calm, steady gaze. He had no secrets to share with anyone here.

Yet he could not help wondering what secrets the legendary warrior had hidden in her keep. For she must have a truly dark reason for staying so concealed. All Scotland had assumed she'd died twelve years ago when the Four Horsemen had ravaged their country and conquered the Abbey of Scone.

Then three months ago, news of her survival began to circulate among the clans. He had heard the tale and dismissed it as wishful thinking, some fantastic story fabricated to bring the clans hope for survival from the chaos the Four Horsemen created. Fantasy or reality, that hope had driven him here, to her.

But Ian had no time to ponder the Trainer's mysteries. He had come to train quickly, then leave. He tamped down his growing irritation at the delay. "I have no time to waste. I will see the Trainer now."

The man's expression instantly darkened. "So ye've come to fight."

"Aye."

"Another fool then," the old man muttered as he

turned away, walking toward the hearth. "If ye must see the Trainer, come this way."

Ian followed the old man through a doorway at the side of the great hall and into another chamber. A single candle stood in the center of the room, leaving a ring of dark shadows everywhere he looked.

"Wait here."

Frowning at the further delay, Ian turned to demand entrance, but the old man had disappeared into the shadows. Even so, Ian sensed he was not alone in the room. As his eyes adjusted to the darkness, he saw a shape hidden in the shadows at the top of the stairs. All his senses sharpened, alert to the danger. "Show yourself."

"What murdering deed brings ye here?" The female voice sounded old and gruff, not what he had expected from the Warrior Trainer.

He had no intention of murdering anyone except the Four Horsemen, and they would feel his justice, painful and swift, for attacking his clan and murdering his brother Malcolm. He would seek justice against the man responsible as soon as he satisfied his duty to his father.

"Step into the light," Ian ordered as he moved closer to the stairs, trying to make out the shape above him. A robust silhouette reflected against the hazy gray of the room.

"The darkness serves my purpose," the figure replied in a low, almost imperceptible tone.

Seconds clicked by and silence hovered in the room. Ian's body tightened, intuition flared. Something was amiss. His hand moved to his sword only to come away empty, and he remembered too late that his weapons remained outside. "Why should a woman fabled to be the greatest fighter in all the land have to hide in the darkness against an unarmed man?" he asked, seeking the shadows in the room for an answer.

"I'll ask the questions here."

The voice quavered ever so slightly. Why?

"What is yer purpose here?" she said. "To fight like all the rest?"

The faint glow of a candle lit the room from behind Ian, but he did not turn around to see where it came from. Instead, he could only stare at the illuminated vision before him. An aged female with stark white hair stared back at him in fear.

Ian relaxed at the lack of threat. "'Tis not possible. An ancient woman . . . the Trainer?" he said.

"Were ye expectin' someone else?" The creature, the Trainer, appraised him warily.

There must be a logical explanation. This stooped crone could not teach him any skills he did not already possess. Yet his father had been convinced the woman could teach him special fighting techniques from foreign lands—ways of moving his body, anticipating his foe, of weilding a sword that would help to defend himself and his clan against the Four Horsemen. Martial arts, his father had called her ways. Ian was still skeptical.

"Why are ye here?" she repeated, remaining where she stood.

"To train with the Warrior."

Her face brightened. "To train? Not to fight?"

"Aye," Ian drawled out the word as he narrowed his gaze. What manner of deception existed here? The woman wore her steel breast plate on her back and a back plate on her breast. A couter covered her right elbow, but not her left. A gauntlet covered her left hand, yet she held her sword in her right. Either she had dressed in haste, or she was not who she claimed to be.

"Are you the Train—"

"Burke, cease!"

Ian turned to see a black object hurling toward him. Pain exploded against the side of his head and a sickening thud reverberated in his skull. Ian gaped at the grinning old man who clutched an iron kettle.

That vision stayed with him as the light receded and darkness swallowed him.

Chapter Two

"I told ye to halt!" Maisie exclaimed as the huge man slumped to the floor. If her instincts were right, he was the one they'd been waiting for. As promised, Abbus had finally sent him, a warrior worthy of continuing the lineage of Scotland.

"I tried, but the kettle was already swingin'," Burke said, offering her an apologetic shrug.

"Did ye have to use the kettle?" Maisie marched down the stairs, her hastily donned armor rattling with each step. When she reached the downed man's side, she frowned at her stooped helper, who was no taller than her shoulder. "Scotia might not like him if his head is bashed in on one side."

"'Twas the only thing I could find to hit him with," Burke replied.

Maisie tsk'd. "Never send a man to do a woman's job— at least not in this castle." She bent down beside the big and well-muscled man. He was dressed in a plaid of red and green and blue and white—definitely a MacKinnon, as had been agreed upon years ago between Abbus Mac-

Kinnon and Scotia's mother. It had been many years since she'd seen the likes of the clan MacKinnon near Loch Glencarron. She poked a finger into the large muscle on his upper arm, then smiled when it did not yield to her assault. "He's a bonny lad, and the first to come knockin' on our door in search of real trainin' in a fair long time."

"He could be here to deceive us, like the last one who came askin' for trainin'." Burke shuddered as he set the iron kettle on the ground and knelt beside their prize. "I say we throw him out."

"Faugh! This young man is here to help us, not harm us, ye fool. He'll do just fine. Or have ye forgotten how many moons have passed since our girl came into her twenty-fifth year? She must fulfill her duty and produce a girl-child soon to follow her as the Warrior Trainer, or we'll have failed her mother and all of Scotland."

Burke released a heavy sigh. "The man who fathers her child should be her choice, Maisie, not ours, and not her mother's." A look of regret settled in his tired gray eyes. "We have manipulated her life for far too long. She deserves the freedom to make her own decisions."

"Doona ye have even a wee bit of the Scottish soul in ye? 'Tis not her choice, but her duty to continue the line of trainers as her ancestors did before her. Scotia must submit to this man as 'twas arranged by their parents years ago. And to ensure she takes this lad to her bed, we will help her." She rubbed her gnarled hands together in excitement. "We must plan carefully."

"Ye're a daft woman, ye are. When has Scotia submitted to anyone? Or are ye forgettin' the fits she gave us while growin' up? Ach!" A smile of fondness undercut Burke's words. With an effort he got to his feet, cursing his ancient bones as he did so. "I say we let the bloody fool go before Scotia learns of our plan and has our hides as well as his."

13

Maisie ignored Burke's ramblings and grasped the fallen warrior by his arms, attempting to drag him across the flagstone floor. Long ago her strength had been great enough to easily move the large man, but now she was older and weaker. "Ye could quit yer blatherin' and help an old girl," she gasped as she continued to slide the man toward the bedchamber on the right. "I'm not as young as I used to be and he's a lot heavier than he looks."

Burke offered her a toothless smile and remained where he stood. "Serves ye right for messin' in other people's business, Maisie, old girl."

Ian woke to a throbbing in his temple. He tried to flex his shoulders, but found his hands were secured behind his back. He frowned, then regretted it when the movement brought a sharp pain to his head. It was bad enough that he, a formidable warrior in his own village, had been defeated by two antiquated biddies. But did they have to restrain him as well? Such things never happened to him. He was far too careful and clever for that. At least he had thought so until now.

He pulled at the ropes that bound his wrists together. They gave ever so slightly. He tugged again. The binding separated more, giving him the room he needed to wiggle his hands free. His captors might be sly, but they could learn a thing or two about tying knots. A moment later he released the bindings at his feet, then made his way to the door of what appeared in the darkness to be a bedchamber.

He should have been grateful they had not taken him to the dungeon. Ian allowed himself a sly grin. He knew now that neither of the ancients could be the Warrior Trainer. For some reason they were protecting their mistress. And Ian wanted to know why.

He opened the door cautiously, peering into the corridor beyond. Shadows lurked in the unguarded hallway, creating pockets of darkness along the gray stone walls. He stepped out of the room, then paused while he willed the throbbing in his head to subside.

Since the pain was not obedient to his wishes, he ignored it and crept quietly along in the shadows toward the staircase. He could see no one.

It would be easy to descend the stairs, head for the door, and leave. *Leave.* The thought grated more than he expected it to. If he left now, he would have to accept defeat. The Four Horsemen would go unpunished, perhaps even return to his village to destroy his clansmen. Worst of all, how would he face his foster father again, knowing he had failed to do as he asked? He must stay to fulfill his duty.

Ian set his jaw. To start, he would find the real Trainer. He slipped down the stairs, then paused, taking time to survey the unfamiliar surroundings. His plan was simple. Find her, demand her help, learn whatever secrets she harbored about fighting, then return to his clan. Time was of the essence if he was to avenge Malcolm's death and save his people.

Using the shadows as a shield, Ian crept into the great hall on the left. The room was neat and orderly, with the chairs pushed against the wall, tables free from clutter, and the rushes freshly laid. Here was evidence of a well-kept home.

Four young women stood near the hearth, one of them stoking the fire. Their backs were to him, and for that Ian was grateful as he picked his way across the hall, heading toward the corridor on the other side. Once inside the corridor, two doorways flanked the right and left side. He checked them both and found them empty before moving on to the doors farther down. After he checked the sixth chamber and found nothing, a stab of irritation shot through him. How many more rooms could there be in the main part of the keep? Already he had turned three corners, leaving only one side of the castle left to explore.

He continued down the corridor until he came to yet another doorway. He tried the latch and the door opened easily to reveal a much larger space than the others. This room stretched upward, topped off by an elaborate vaulted ceiling that gave the chamber an open, airy feeling similar to the church near his village. But this was no church. Swords, axes, pikes, daggers, and various pieces of armor lined the walls, their highly polished metal gleaming beneath the light cast from a series of arched windows at both sides of the room.

So many dangerous weapons—military strength worthy of any warrior. Except this warrior was female. He tensed at the thought. Women were meant to hold babes in their delicate and nurturing arms, not weapons of destruction. Perhaps she had not yet met a man who incited her to change?

Ian smiled at the thought, but he was not here to pursue anything other than training. Once his commitment to his foster father had been satisfied, he would leave this castle and its mysteries behind.

He strode to the wall of swords and reached for a lethal-looking blade. But the touch of cold, sharp steel against the front of his throat stilled him.

"Move and I shall give you a wound you shall wear to your grave," a husky voice threatened from behind.

Ian inclined his head only enough to communicate his agreement. He let his arm drop from the sword, cursing himself for not grabbing it sooner. "Are all the residents in this castle as friendly as those I have met so far?"

A second dagger pricked the flesh just below his ribs, causing a sharp pain. So much for humor.

His irritation quickly shifted to intrigue. What kind of woman was this trainer of warriors? No woman had ever spoken to him with such authority before. And there was no denying she was a woman. Her body pressed against his back—a combination of strength and hard metal wrapped in the soft scent of heather.

"If you release me, I shall do as you ask," he said.

The blade against his chest disappeared and the one at his throat eased. In that instant, he twisted out of her grasp. He meant to move away, but the sight of her held him captive just as tightly as her arms had done. Aye, she was definitely female. Even though her upper body was concealed behind a brigandine covered in faded red velvet, the plated armor did little to hide her curves. Her lower half was concealed by an assortment of leather and metal armor, yet the curve of her hips teased the soft red fabric of her skirt. But none of those things entranced him as much as the sight of her long, thick, sleep-tossed hair. It appeared dark in the uncertain light, perhaps red, perhaps brown. Locks of untamed curls spilled over her shoulders, teasing the edge of her chest armor as she returned her dagger to a sheath at her waist. An odd combination, that wild, feminine hair against the cold, masculine armor.

"You are the Trainer?" Ian asked, trying to conceal the slight breathlessness that stirred in his chest.

"I should be the one to ask who you are, trespasser." She drew a long, thin length of leather with two small weights at each end from her belt.

"Ian MacKinnon of the clan MacKinnon." He kept his gaze on her weapon—a weapon that had the capability to render him immobile if he chose to attack. But would she use it? Or was she playing some sort of game?

"Why are you here, Ian MacKinnon?"

A devilish part of him wanted to find out if she was half as tough as she appeared. He took two steps toward her.

She swung the two ends of the leather in a circle at her side, filling the distance between them with a threatening burst of air.

A false move on his part and he was certain she would wrap those leather strands about his neck before she let him anywhere near her. So much for testing her. Ian paused. "I seek the Trainer."

She snorted inelegantly. "You are a poor liar. If you had come to see the Trainer then why would I find you in this chamber stealing a sword instead of in the great hall preparing to make your introductions?"

"I was not given a choice," he said, suddenly feeling impatient at the time he wasted sparring verbally with this woman. If she was the Trainer, why did she not just acknowledge it and they could move forward with the training? Ian folded his arms over his chest. "Had I the choice I would beg pardon and ask to speak with you."

"And you think that would have gained you an audience?" She swung her weapon in a slow, methodical circle.

"I had hoped it would serve my purpose as well as anything else."

"If your only purpose is to fight me, then you are a fool."

In an instant the leather strands snaked around his arms. Two heavy weights struck his chest, forcing the air from his lungs. The powerful throw sent him off balance. He tried to move sideways, to twist himself free of the bonds, but she was too quick. She caught him in the stomach with her foot and sent him sprawling on his backside.

Slowly she stalked toward him, a tigress on the prowl. She straddled him with her leather-covered legs, then sat on his chest. She stared at him calmly, her face still and strangely sad, her mouth unsmiling, her green eyes so solemn he wondered if she ever smiled.

"You wanted to meet the Trainer?" she asked. "Consider yourself introduced. Now that the pleasantries have been observed, you may leave."

Chapter Three

"I will not leave until I get what I came for," the MacKinnon said. "Release me."

The blond man gazed at Scotia with a calm, unnerving stare. Despite the fact she sat atop his chest, something about his gaze pinned her there even as a surge of warmth flooded her cheeks.

Unnerved, she stood, then stepped back from him, hoping the distance would hide her fluster. He was only a man. She drew a slow, even breath in an effort to regain her composure. Since she could first wield a sword, she had battled and trained a hundred men. What made this one different from the others? What about him made her blush?

She studied him, measuring and appraising. An air of barely suppressed danger surrounded him. She saw it in the taut line of his shoulders and the grim line of his mouth. He had the look of a man prepared to take on the world and bend it to his will, no matter the consequences. Yet she sensed a vulnerability in him as well, something she could not quite define.

"There will be no battles today," she said impatiently,

suddenly angry at herself for having such ridiculous thoughts about a stranger who had entered her keep, a man who was still a threat.

He untangled himself from the cords of her weapon and stood, neither approaching nor withdrawing. "I have not come to do battle with you, but to train with you."

Scotia started at the words before she caught herself and masked her reaction. She could not allow herself to hope. *To train with you.* The words played over in her mind despite her efforts. It had been twelve of the longest and most difficult years of her life since she had heard anyone outside her castle utter those words.

The last warriors, a father and a son, had come to train with her mother and herself when she was thirteen. The son, a youth of fifteen, had been resentful of her age back then. But he soon learned that skill mattered more than age. The father had taken his knowledge and had joined forces the forces fighting the English. The son had remained with her. And over the years had become her most valued warrior, Richard.

But what of this warrior before her? What were his true intentions?

Fleeting emotion, subtle and reserved, flickered over his aquiline features. Fear? Desperation? Scotia studied him, searching his gaze for some clue of his true intentions. Could she believe him? Or was this some new ploy devised to get her to lower her guard, then strike when she was more vulnerable? It was a deception none of the challengers who had come to battle her for her title had tried yet. "Why should I believe you?"

"I give you my word. I am here only to train."

Again, the unexpected. Why did he not just draw some hidden weapon from his person like all the others? "What good is your word?"

21

"As good as the MacKinnon name," he said with a confidence that belied the sudden shadows in his brown eyes.

Hope started to unfurl within her, but she stopped it before it could flutter into full array. She had to be certain. So much was at stake—things even more precious than her honor or her life. She searched through her memories and recalled hearing from one of her scouting parties of the recent devastation many clans had suffered. Was his clan one of those who had been affected? Could what he claimed be true? And if so, was Ian MacKinnon's presence here a sign that some small measure of faith in the Warrior Trainer's ability to help them had returned to the clans? "Why come to me?"

His gaze remained focused, intense, determined. "My foster father is convinced our clan needs your help to save our people from the Four Horsemen."

"Your foster father. But not you." Perhaps he was not so different after all.

A flicker of challenge ignited in the cool depths of his dark eyes. "I . . . need your help." A silent moment passed between them. "Please."

The simple word hit her like a blow through her armor. Others who had come to challenge her had bullied, leered and demanded her help, but none had said *please*. She took a step back, retreating from sudden vulnerability, then froze as he dropped to one knee before her and bowed his head.

"I beseech you." Though his face remained impassive, his words sounded thick, as though spoken with some of the same deep emotion that flowed through her. "I humbly beg to be taught by the Warrior Trainer. I swear on the life of my foster father and the honor of my clan that I speak the truth."

Scotia looked away. She no longer deserved such respect, had not since her mother's failure to help the country fend off Edward I's invasion of Scotland. It was a time the Scottish people had yet to recover from, and the reason she believed her countrymen stopped coming to train with her. And perhaps why only challengers came to greet her now—challengers eager to steal from her the only thing she had left: her title as the best fighter in all the land.

At least no one had yet discovered her true secret. The Stone was safe, hidden away, the connection between the Warrior Trainer and Guardian of the Stone lost in the obscurity of the past twelve years.

Slowly, carefully, she met his gaze. It was her duty to train warriors, as her ancestors had done before her. Mindful of her true obligations, Scotia nervously pulled down the edge of her brigandine, then stifled a wince of pain from the gash her latest challenger had inflicted on her shoulder. Refusing to give in to the injury, she adjusted the leather gauntlets at her wrists. Shoulders back, assuming her warrior stance, she said, "I will train you, MacKinnon."

"Ian." Relief filled his gaze, but so did pride as he stood. "I am here to learn. But I will warn you now, this is the only time I humble myself before you."

Scotia bristled. She had not asked him to kneel before her. No one ever had before. "There is more than one way to be humbled." Turning her back on him and the odd jumble of emotions he set off in her, she pulled the hemp cord near the door. The bell had barely begun to chime before Maisie and Burke stumbled into the room. It was obvious by the chagrined looks on their faces they had been listening at the door.

"The MacKinnon will be staying with us for a while."

He interrupted. "I will learn quickly."

Scotia ignored him. "Please show him to the back chamber." She turned around, grateful that her usual control had settled over her once more. "We begin on the morrow."

"We begin now." He took two steps toward her, then stopped when her hand moved to her sword.

"We train when I am ready, or we do not train at all."

Incredulity flared in his expression, then it was gone. His gaze hardened, but he offered her a small bow. "As you wish."

"Come with me." Burke motioned toward the door.

The MacKinnon spared her one last searching glance before he turned and followed Burke from the room.

Scotia kept her spine stiff and straight as her mother had taught her, as she taught her own men. *Meet your enemy with fearlessness. Never show your feelings.* She thought about her own advice. Nothing about her had changed physically in the last few moments, but inside something felt different.

She only wished she knew what it was.

"At last someone has come to train, not battle ye for yer title as the best fighter in the land." Maisie picked up the weapon the MacKinnon had disentangled himself from, then handed it back to Scotia. "Is it not a day to celebrate?"

"Not yet," Scotia answered, finally allowing herself to relax as she wound the weapon into a loop and attached it to the belt at her waist. "I do not trust him yet."

Maisie frowned. "Ye would refuse to train him?"

"Nay, I cannot and stay true to my name. But there is something about him, Maisie, something I do not yet understand. He seems overly impatient to learn. Does he not understand these matters take time, patience, and practice?"

" 'Tis his age and his desperate situation, I fear. They used to send the young 'uns to yer mother for a reason. They were easier to mold, easier to tame." Her gaze moved toward the door. "This one has already tasted success on the battlefield. 'Tis a wound to his pride that he is here."

Scotia moved to the wall where she had found the MacKinnon. With a sigh she reached out and removed her mother's sword from its mount—the sword he had almost taken. "Then why did he come? He said his father sent him, but there has to be more than that."

"I'm certain he has his reasons," Maisie said as she joined Scotia near the wall. "Just as ye have reasons to rejoice in his presence here."

Scotia spun to face her castellan. "Just what do you mean by that?"

"Do ye not find him handsome?"

"He is as handsome as any other man." Even as she said the words she knew they were a lie. The image of his brown eyes—hardened and knowing one moment, the next searching and troubled—tugged at her in a most disturbing way. She shook her head in disgust, willing the feeling away.

" 'Tis providence that brought this man to yer door, love."

Scotia stilled, as did her heart. "What are you saying, Maisie?"

"That he is here to father yer child. That ye should take advantage of this situation that may never present itself again."

Scotia refused to allow her face to reveal her shock, though it reverberated through her entire body. Summoning a composure that had been ingrained in her since childhood, she replaced the sword on the wall without even the tiniest betraying clink of the metal.

Produce a child to continue the line. She knew her obligations. The words alone had the power to slice right
through her, raising up the guilt that had festered inside
her since she had come of age. How could she bear a
child? How could she willingly open herself up to the vulnerability pregnancy would demand? Her body could
never support a child when the whole of her life was
filled with conflict and aggression that was even more violent than her predecessors had experienced. Nor did she
possess the warmth and patience necessary in a mother.
Apart from all of that, she could never force a child to
endure the same aloof and loveless existence in which
she had grown up.

Yet sometimes she longed for a babe to hold, wished
her life could have another purpose besides training. At
the thought, she stilled. Such desires were not for her.

"How can I have a child, Maisie? What kind of destiny
would I leave to her?" Scotia asked with a hitch in her
voice. The armor that shielded her emotions slipped,
leaving the usual hollow, desolate sensation that always
followed.

Maisie's gaze filled with compassion, and quite suddenly her age sat heavy on the features of her usually
carefree face, deepening the lines that shadowed her eyes
and forehead. She had weathered many changes since
the reign of Scotia's mother as the Warrior Trainer. Now,
in this uncertain age, Maisie had slowly fallen victim to
the inexorable crush of time.

"A girl-child must be conceived. The legacy of Scotia
must continue with ye bearin' a female child just as yer
mother did and her mother before her. The Stone must
have a new guardian, or the soul of Scotland will crumble
beneath us all," Maisie said with a mixture of sadness and
exasperation.

Scotia longed to turn away, to ignore the plea as she always did. Yet she forced herself to remain strong as she boldly met Maisie's gaze. How could she communicate all the uncertainties she had about her inability to love or be loved by another? "Give birth to a child only to have her slain by those who challenge me? Nay. I could never be so cruel."

The old woman's gaze softened. "I understand yer fears, love. But doona ye realize ye have no choice? Scotland is dependin' on ye."

Scotia closed her eyes, willing the darkness to erase the hurt the words brought. She had spent her whole life performing her duties for her country. Her love for Scotland was the one emotion she had never been forced to block. Knowing her obligations, yet knowing just as well she could never fulfill them, was a slow-bleeding wound.

Yet somehow she had managed to continue on despite the incredible burden of her own sense of failure. Even so, her efforts had cost her much. Gone was the curious, mischievous girl of her youth. In her place was a cool, remote warrior who never lost her temper and rarely smiled. But control and bravery could not keep the despair at bay. Hope for the future—a future where she could once again be for Scotland all that her ancestors had been before her—seemed lost. She could not bring a child into her world with its heavy responsibilities and loneliness. But if she did not, who would carry on as the Warrior Trainer?

Refusing to bow to despair, she spent her days continuing to hone her already flawless skills. She forced herself to train harder, building muscle in her arms and legs that would help her outmatch her male opponents. She had learned how to hide herself and her femininity behind the plated armor she always wore, never removing her battle gear even for sleeping, even for bathing. It was the protection, the edge she must keep. If challengers caught her unprepared, it could be the end of her.

All because of the Stone. Perhaps it was time to reveal the Stone's location and let the entire country take over the responsibility of protecting the priceless artifact. Scotia opened her eyes. That kind of thinking would only cause further warring with England.

A better choice for the safety of the clans might be to hide the Stone in some secret cache unknown by even Burke or Maisie so that when she died the location would disappear along with her.

Scotia groaned. Why did everything have to be so complicated? "A tempest rages inside me, Maisie. I need more time to consider the possibilities."

Pain flickered across Maisie's face. "That young man may not stay long. Besides, I promised yer mother—"

Scotia held up her hand, cutting Maisie off. "Some promises are meant to be broken."

Maisie shook her head. "Nay, child," she said in a stern yet gentle voice. "In this ye are wrong. The forces of Mother Nature are stronger than ye can imagine, claimin' her victims no matter how hard they resist."

Scotia released a heartfelt groan. "I shall never be such a victim, of that you can be sure. I can protect myself against anyone and anything. Forces of nature . . . Truly, Maisie, do you not understand me at all?"

A hint of a smile sparkled in Maisie's tired gray eyes. "At times, I know ye, love, better than ye know yourself."

Scotia crossed her arms over the plated metal of her brigandine and winced at the pain the motion brought. "I came down here to try to loosen the muscles in my shoulder, not to discuss a baby." She extended her arm, then rotated it in small circles forward. "Your herbs helped the bleeding, but the stiffness remains. That challenge against Brodie Haldane cost me some of my agility."

"'Twas the wound he inflicted upon yer shoulder that did that."

"Aye, but I cannot let it slow me down."

Maisie's smile faded. "Are ye certain 'tis the new wound and not the old one that bothers ye, love?"

The muscles in Scotia's shoulder tensed despite her efforts to control them. After all these years, the mere mention of the arrow in her back had the power to overcome all her training. He had almost killed her. The White Horseman had nearly won. Her current injury was nothing compared to the wound he had inflicted on her that night.

She forced her muscles to relax despite the memory, and tried to steady the wild cadence of her heart. She drew a deep breath, feeling a peacefulness flow into her again, banishing the tumult, blurring the memories she wanted desperately to forget. "Only new injuries can hurt me now, Maisie."

"We could try a wrap of setewall to ease the pain," Maisie said gently.

Scotia shook her head. "If I am to train our impatient visitor on the morrow, I need to strengthen my arm, not dull the pain."

Maisie opened her mouth to speak, but Scotia silenced her with a look. "I shall train him, Maisie, but I have no more use for him than that."

Chapter Four

In her training chamber the next morning, Scotia studied her student. He stood with his feet apart, balanced on the balls of his feet, his sword in hand, his eyes watchful. Good traits for a warrior. Yet he carried his weight more on his right foot than his left and his broad shoulders pushed forward, obvious weaknesses. He would attack like a charging bull, all muscle and force, and she would best him. Scotia hid the satisfaction she could feel creeping up inside her. He would learn his mistakes before their session was through.

"Are you ready?" Impatience flashed in his eyes.

They were always so impatient to begin. The battles she had fought outside the castle walls in her youth had taught her that men on the verge of war often surged into a fight without thinking, planning, or anticipating their foe. The MacKinnon seemed eager to follow that same pattern.

Scotia nodded, then offered the MacKinnon a brief salute with her sword. "*Alba gu brath,*" she said in Gaelic: Scotland forever.

As she had predicted, he rushed forward, cutting and slashing as he advanced. Scotia parried his blade, then with a jab from her uninjured shoulder sent him to the ground.

He hit the stone floor with a soft thud, quickly rolled to his feet, and lashed out again.

The man fought well, but not well enough to best her. Scotia leapt sideways. She sent her blade whistling past his head, avoiding injury, but taking a few wisps of hair as it sailed by.

The MacKinnon's eyes went wide. "Are you trying to kill me?" he said, his tone filled with both irritation and surprise.

"Nay. I am trying to teach you. Just like I taught all the others."

Their blades clashed again and again, the clink of steel creating rhythmic sounds that reverberated through her training chamber. It was a sound she used to hear often in this room when she trained the young boys of the castle. Those men had grown up over the last twelve years. Some had left to help protect their countrymen, and others she had trained as scouts to gather information about the Four Horsemen.

As her sword cut through the air, a pulse entered her blood, bringing a renewed sense of purpose to her soul. He had not lied. A warrior had come to train.

She allowed the MacKinnon one last pass at her before she turned to advance, putting her newfound invigoration into her attack. One swipe of her sword, a twist of her arm, a nudge with her knee and he lay at her feet.

Conquered.

Ian stared up at the blade of the sword against his chest. Foolishly, he lay like a helpless babe, his back pressed into the cold stone floor. For the second time in his score and seven years he felt like an utter failure. The first being when he had been unable to protect Malcolm from the Four Horsemen.

Barely accepted by his clan, always taunted as the "bastard orphan," he had toughened up early. He'd had to fight his way out of squabbles since he had learned to walk. Throughout his life he'd had to prove himself to his clan by being stronger, faster, smarter than everyone else. He had taken down men three times his size in hand-to-hand battle as well as on horseback. And he had never backed away from a challenge. It wasn't in him to do so.

It wasn't in him now. He glared at the redheaded beauty staring down at him. "I dare you to do that again." He gained his feet. Retrieving his sword, he stepped back into the battle.

Over and over he found himself on that hard cold floor, vowing each time she would never send him there again.

"What is the matter, can you not defend yourself?" she asked, tossing her tightly plaited hair over her shoulder.

His irritation sparked anew. The women of his clan had made him feel as though they needed his protection, his strength to keep them out of harm's way. This woman evoked no such response. Ian gripped the hilt of his sword in his hands. There had to be some way to beat this woman at her own game.

With a triumphant cry, he challenged her again. Pass after pass she bested him, until his muscles screamed at the abuse. No matter what kind of combat he engaged her in, she defeated him, sparing him nothing. Not even his pride.

"I should have trained harder," he muttered, starting up at her from his position on the floor. He searched her face for some small hint of humor. But no mischief or laughter lit her eyes.

Nay, instead there was only sadness and a vibrant energy that seemed to move around her even while she remained still. It was as if someone had stolen her soul and given her body an excess of power to compensate her loss.

He had never met anyone like her. He prayed he never would again as he waved away her sword, then sat up. "I shall succeed, eventually."

The corner of her mouth quirked as though she would smile, then thought better of it. "An appropriate attitude for a warrior." A leather-encased hand reached out to him, offering assistance. He grasped it and allowed her to haul him to his feet. She did so with little effort, then turned away, walking toward the far side of the chamber from where they had met the previous evening. "Come with me."

As he followed her, Ian studied the woman years of legend had created. She was tough. That part of the legend someone had gotten right. Ruthless in battle. Perhaps, if the battles he'd experienced today were any indication. Protector of her people. He frowned. That was where legend and reality parted ways.

Her people suffered terribly at the hands of the Four Horsemen. Why had the rumors of her survival only started recently? It was as if an announcement had gone out, informing the country of her existence once again.

The Warrior Trainer existed. He knew the truth now. So why did she not intervene in the terror the Four Horsemen caused? Ian opened his mouth to ask her, then closed it. He had not come all this way to involve himself in her choices. Nay, he was here to learn her training secrets, nothing more. He could handle the Four Horsemen himself.

She stopped walking, moving aside to reveal a large area roped off from the rest of the room. A Celtic cross had been painted on the floor. Ropes went everywhere, crisscrossing the area of the cross. Posts connected by ropes stood in the center of each crossing, forming what looked like the inner workings of a spider's web.

"What is this?" he asked.

"You will learn the answer quickly enough." She stepped into the center and pulled the stump of a log with her. "Follow me."

He ducked under the ropes to join her, wondering just how the log fit into their training. Perhaps she had grown tired of besting him with her sword and now meant to whack him with a tree trunk instead. He stifled a smile. He would not put it past her.

Ian raked a hand through his hair. Had his father known what awaited him here? If so, why subject him to this humiliation? Had he not endured enough of that growing up in the shadows of his foster brothers, Malcolm and Griffin? Or was the first secret to learn that he was not as good a warrior as he thought?

"Step on the stump and balance on one foot," she said in a stern tone as she patted the wooden center.

With only a slight hesitation he tried it, thankful the log was to stay on the ground this time. Following her directions, he found his balance by holding his arms away from his sides. "Pray tell me why I am doing this? I feel more like a bird perched on a branch than a warrior preparing for battle."

"That is exactly why. Sometimes a warrior must perch and listen to the sounds around him and be comfortable with himself before he charges forth."

Her words nearly felled him. For a moment he wondered if she teased him, then he remembered she was not the teasing sort. Nay, she was more the sort to torture a man just to see him break than to lighten a situation with humor. Ian scowled at her for what must have been the hundredth time that day. She would not break him—now or ever.

She moved outside the ropes and started for the door. "I shall return when the shadows pass to the opposite side of the chamber. You may switch which foot you balance yourself on, but you may not get down from the log."

"What kind of game is this?"

"It is no game, I assure you."

"I am here to train, not—"

She held up her hand, stopping his words, but not the frustration and fury coiling through him. If the need for revenge did not consume him, and the safety of his clan were not so dire, he would leave.

But if he left without her special training, how could he hope to defeat the Four Horsemen and their army? How many others would die? The thought kept his booted foot on the log. But it did not still his tongue. "You have a very strange way of training a warrior."

She looked at him blankly. "This method has worked well over the centuries."

"Your methods are arcane and ridiculous," Ian snapped, his voice hard and flat with frustration. "Perhaps that is why the Four Horsemen have not yet been defeated."

She recoiled as if he had slapped her. Her face paled and pain crept into her wide green eyes. Yet a moment later, she drew a shell of aloofness around her. Without saying a word, she left the room. The click of her bootheels upon the stone floor faded as she went, until only a heavy silence remained.

His words had hurt her, he realized too late. He found no pleasure in the thought.

* * *

Ian studied the shadows of the training chamber, trying to ignore the deep ache that had settled in his shaking legs. He had never realized how difficult it was to remain in one position for so long. As Scotia had said, he had become more aware of the silence that surrounded him, accentuating the beat of his own heart. He'd also had plenty of time to consider his cruel statements. She might have bested him with her sword, but he had annihilated her with his words.

The shadows had reached the opposite side of the chamber a while ago, and still she did not come for him. He would have no one to blame but himself if she left him atop the log forever, proving what he had thought all along. His foster father should have ordered Griffin here instead. His foster brother would have been the better choice to lead their clan and save them from the dangers the Four Horsemen posed.

Just then, the soft echo of footsteps sounded and he straightened, intending to prove he had done as she had asked without revealing the strain it had put on his muscles. Ian looked up in expectation as a figure appeared. Only it was not Scotia, he realized with disappointment. It was the stout old woman he had met upon his arrival. Her crusty expression was enough to make him wish Scotia had come back for him instead. Another battle where he ended up on his back he could survive. A lecture from this woman he was not so certain.

"Ye're free to leave."

"I beg your pardon?" Ian asked, expecting something much worse.

"The mistress sent me to tell ye to go home."

She could not make herself any clearer. He had been dismissed. Ian jumped down from the log, less steady on

36

his feet than he would have liked. "What about the training?"

"'Tis obvious ye find any trainin' a waste of yer time." She gave him a hard look.

Ian met her gaze. He deserved her contempt and more for acting the part of a brutish fool. He did not want to leave, he realized suddenly; not until he had completed what his foster father had set out before him. "I wish to train." He would not give up now, not when he had already suffered through humiliation and defeat.

The older woman's eyes narrowed. "My lady could send ye to yer maker before ye could even begin to defend yerself."

"Aye." He dipped his head in true remorse.

"She would not hesitate to do so if ye insult her thusly again."

"Agreed."

"I'll talk to her on yer account." She relaxed her rigid posture. "Life has been hard for Scotia since her mother's death many years ago. I beg ye not to make things any worse."

"I give you my word, I will cause her no further trouble," Ian pledged in a solemn tone.

The woman nodded. "See that ye doona or ye'll have cause to regret it."

Chapter Five

Scotia sat at the head table in the great hall as the rest of her household gathered around her for their evening meal. The hum of voices usually calmed her. This eve it had no such effect. An empty trencher sat on the table beside her, an unnecessary reminder that her guest had chosen to remain in his chamber alone, despite the fact he had asked Maisie to stay so he could continue his training.

With a nod of her head, Scotia set the meal in motion. Burke shouted orders at the scullery maids. Moments later, the fragrance of roasted chickens and onions permeated the hall as serving trays were brought forth and trenchers were filled.

Scotia stared down at her chicken leg surrounded by turnips and onions and realized she had no stomach for food. No doubt due to the MacKinnon.

Her gaze shifted to the empty chair beside her. *Your methods are arcane and ridiculous.* The words still stung. She should be glad at his absence, and yet she could not argue that what he had said had a spark of truth. The training methods she had shown him earlier *were* arcane, but they were not ridiculous. She ripped off a section of bread from the corner of her trencher, reducing it to a pile of crumbs.

What would he think of the new techniques she had created over the last five years? Dexterity, she had found, was at least as important as strength when battling. For some time now she had wanted to share her newfound knowledge with someone other than the members of her own army, but no one from the clans had come to train.

Until the MacKinnon.

A murmur of noise brought her attention to the back of the room. He had decided to come down for supper after all. He strode toward her table as though her thoughts had summoned him forth. Unbidden pleasure rippled through her. He had changed his clothing to a simple muslin shirt that laced up the front of his broad chest. Fawn-colored trews encased his legs, revealing muscular thighs that had been hidden beneath the pleats of his plaid. Damp tendrils of pale blond hair fell forward across his brow.

"Forgive my tardiness." He greeted her with a slight nod of his head. "A bath seemed appropriate after our battles this day. May I join you?" he asked, his tone sincere.

Unable to reconcile the change in him, she nodded. His manners had been barbaric and gruff before, but no longer. He took his place beside her with the charm and refinement of a lord. Scotia could not wrestle her gaze from his clean-shaven cheeks or the sight of his damp hair as it curled against the nape of his muscular neck. He had bathed before joining her. Most men would not have bothered.

Oblivious to her appraisal, he filled his trencher with a whole chicken, several helpings of vegetables, two apples, à generous slice of cheese and two fruit tarts. He spared her not a glance as he tore off a hunk of chicken and popped it into his mouth. His eyes drifted closed as he chewed. "All that training has left me famished," he managed between bites.

With an effort, Scotia forced herself to gaze out among the occupants of her hall. Why would he not meet her eyes? Did he harbor resentment that she had defeated him?

She bristled at the direction of her thoughts. Did she care if he did? Her responsibility was to train him, not care what he thought of her.

From beneath lowered lashes she studied him. The MacKinnon continued to eat his meal, at the exclusion of all else, appearing more like a man who had gone days without food than a warrior with wounded pride.

Scotia frowned. Never had she met such a complete puzzle of a man.

When only bones remained on his trencher, he gulped two mugs of wine, then pushed back from the table with a contented sigh.

"Are you quite done?" she could not help but ask, feeling somewhat irritated that he had bathed before coming to dine with her, then managed to ignore her entirely while he ate.

"It was delicious. Thank you." He offered her a smile that brought out a tiny dimple on the left side of his cheek.

Somehow that tiny indentation added to his allure and increased her irritation.

His gaze dropped to her food. "Are you not hungry?"

She eyed the demolished bread. "Nay."

His expression grew somber. "If I am the reason for

your lack of appetite, I apologize. I had no right to say what I did."

She dismissed his apology with a gesture of her hand. "You were correct."

"About what?" He leaned toward her and her heart beat a little faster. He smelled of mint and musk, the combination fresh and complex.

Disconcerted, she shifted to the far side of her chair. "I trained you today the way my mother taught me. If you still wish to train, we will approach things differently. I have information about the Four Horsemen, their strengths and weaknesses, that I will teach you. I also know less 'arcane' ways of training that I have yet to reveal."

"Information about the Four Horsemen?" A dark expression crossed his face, then vanished. "That is why I came to you."

Scotia did not know whether his response pleased or worried her.

"Then we shall get started right away." He pushed his chair back, but she stalled him with her hand.

"We have had enough of battles for one day."

He froze, and for a moment she thought he might refuse, but he relaxed. "Agreed. Besides, it seems your people have other plans for this evening's entertainment." He nodded to the musicians who entered the hall just then, sending a sparkling refrain of music through the murmur of voices. A hush settled across the room as a dulcimer, a bagpipe, a lute, and a harp chimed a steady beat. A cheer arose. In an instant, the tables were cleared and pushed back, making room for dancers.

Two lines formed. Men and women joined in pairs. Even Maisie reached for Burke, parading him into the fray. Scotia leaned back in her chair and watched, as she had for years, though she could not still the light tapping of her foot beneath the table. She liked to dance, had often done so as a small girl. But things were different now. She had an image to maintain as a warrior first and a woman last. She sighed at the falsehood. It was not that she should not dance, it was more a fact that she could not dance and still be on guard against those who would challenge her.

"Dance with me, Scotia." The MacKinnon held out his hand.

She shook her head. Such spontaneous adventures were not for her. She must keep her guard up, her defenses sharp.

"Then you cannot dance?"

"I can," she said, crossing her arms over her armored chest. "Armor tends to make things a bit more difficult."

"You could take it off." He offered her a smile that brought his dimple out once more.

Scotia scowled at him. "Never."

"Then you must learn to dance with it on."

Giving her no time to object, he grasped her arm and hauled her from her chair and into the ring of dancers, locking his arm through hers. She knew she should dig in her heels and stop him, but she did not. Instead, she allowed him to pull her forward, sending her into a spin as though she were dressed in gossamer cloth instead of the heavy metal and boiled leather that gave her as much bulk as it did protection.

The men and women of her household stared at her with open grins and their faces lit up with surprise and merriment. Cook nodded her encouragement. Her huntsman clapped his hands and shouted a rousing "For the mistress!" that was soon taken up in a cheer by all.

Scotia's cheeks warmed, but she decided she did not care. For the moment she was dancing like all the other women of her household. She was dancing! And with the most handsome man in the great hall as her partner.

The room spun by in a whirl of colors. She closed her eyes and let joy flood her spirit. She felt the heat of the MacKinnon's presence as he took her arm in a promenade. It had been so long since she had experienced even a moment's pleasure. She let the rhythm of the music move through her swaying body. A swirl of air caused by the dancers brushed against her fevered cheeks. What other delights had she missed by sitting back and merely watching others live? She had spent the whole of her existence concentrating on warring and protecting the Stone.

The thought slowed her steps. She opened her eyes. Guarding the Stone was the reason for her existence. Training warriors came second. Her feet suddenly felt weighted.

It was then that she noticed Maisie hovering nearby, grinning at her with a calm, knowing smile. Scotia froze even as the dancers continued to swirl around her. The MacKinnon stopped dancing as well. A puzzled look crossed his face.

What had she done? She tugged down the edge of her brigandine with an unsteady hand, then winced as the metal cut into her shoulder. How could she have allowed this man to break through the barriers she had so carefully erected since her childhood? He made her think about things she did not want to consider.

She was a trainer of warriors. She had no right to enjoyment, or pleasure, or most of all romance. How could she have allowed her own ridiculous notions about dancing make her lose sight of her purpose? Her life was about fighting and warring, not about finding enjoyment in the arms of a man.

And she *had* enjoyed herself, she realized with a sinking heart—enjoyed this dance with the MacKinnon very much.

"Had your fill of dancing already?" he asked, joining her, somewhat breathless from the dance.

She dipped her head to avoid his gaze. "I must leave this room."

He nodded, and with a hand on her arm led her through the dancers, out of the castle, and into the bailey, where the soft strains of music followed. Silver streaks of moonlight spilled across the pebbled courtyard, providing the privacy Scotia needed to regain her composure. She pulled away from his touch and pressed her hands to her heated cheeks. Longings that she had kept trapped inside her for so long rushed forth as though she had never managed to suppress them at all. Why? Was the man standing before her the reason? Or had Maisie's reminder of her obligations bothered her more than she had thought?

Scotia drew in a measured breath and caught the heady scent of musk from the MacKinnon as it mingled with the night air.

"You dance well." His voice was light.

"Well enough for a trainer of warriors." She stepped away from him, putting some distance between herself and that intoxicating male scent. She must think like a warrior, be a warrior. She gripped the hilt of her sword until the corded metal bit into her flesh. Her sword always reminded her of her purpose.

"You might be a warrior, Scotia, but you are also a woman."

She rounded on him, sword drawn. "I am no woman."

"Nay?" He raised his brow in question. "That is not what I see. You are beautiful." The corner of his mouth drew up in a half smile. His dimple winked at her again.

"That matters not," she said, uncertain how to react. No one had ever told her she was anything other than a warrior. How could he think she was beautiful, dressed as she was in leather and iron? "What matters is your training."

She drew herself up. A new, even more lethal battle had taken hold of her, she realized with a start. The battle with herself against her own attraction to this man. Maisie was right after all. Mother Nature's lure was strong. In order to win this battle, her defenses must be stronger.

Scotia tightened her grasp, once again feeling the metal of her sword press into her palm. With a grunt of disgust at her behavior, she waved the tip of her weapon close to his chest.

He gave a harsh bark of laughter. "I am not afraid of you, Scotia."

"You should be." She glared at him in the darkness. "We will begin again at sunrise," she said before striding away.

Chapter Six

Ian leaned against the cold stone wall in Scotia's training chamber the next morning, hoping the chill would keep his mind on warring, on battle, and not on the beauty before him.

With surprise and alarm he watched Scotia brandish her sword against her imaginary partner. He had spent the better part of the night contemplating the ceiling of his bedchamber, seized by madness. It was the only explanation. Why else would he forget his purpose here at this castle? Because last night he had. He had seen the light tapping of her booted toe as the music started, had noted the look of longing that filled her eyes. And he had done the unthinkable. The moment he folded his hand around hers, all thoughts of revenge against the Four Horsemen had fled from his mind, replaced by the need to see her smile.

She had looked enchanting swirling about the hall. For a moment, the shadows that filled her gaze had disappeared. And although she had not smiled, a joy he felt certain she rarely experienced had radiated from her.

After the previous day's training, he now realized the woman's skills with a sword far exceeded his own. He had no choice but to accept the fact. He had claimed he would not humble himself before her again, but he already had—every time he found himself on his back staring up at her sword. He would do so again today in order to learn how to fight with the same agility she now displayed. He would do anything to gain the knowledge he needed to defeat the Four Horsemen.

Faint morning light forced its way through the windows above, spilling a hazy light about the room. "You are paying me no heed." Scotia scowled at him from inside the weblike network of ropes that made up her training cross.

"Aye, but I am." Ian tried to look away from the trap of her green eyes, tried to look anywhere but at her. Yet he could not. Her movements captivated him and held him in her grip. Like a lithe cat, she wove her body first over, then under the web of ropes arranged at different heights. Her sword rose and fell as she went through the training routine she had set forth for him.

Her movements were tightly controlled, graceful and elegant despite her heavy armor. Movements he had never seen before. Her actions held not only strength, but a power he had not witnessed in any other woman. He saw something else in her features this morning as well—something that had not been present last night. Loneliness.

Ian folded his arms over his chest and studied her closely. How long had she been in charge of this keep and in the role of Warrior Trainer? Maisie had said Scotia's mother had died many years ago. Had her father as well?

Scotia performed the intricate steps moving her way through a timeless dance. He could see the outline of the well-honed muscles in her arms and legs. And though she appeared stronger than any woman he had ever met, a softness, a suppleness, was evident in her body as well.

Feminine strength—an alluring combination. He found himself snagged by the sight before him, drawing in a breath with each lift and extension of her sword, then exhaling as her shoulders dipped, bringing the blade down, protecting her chest from exposure to an enemy sword. His heart pulsed as her blade flashed upward in a fluid, confident stroke better than any he'd seen. Her eyes showed no fear, betrayed no vulnerability. Yet what he glimpsed in their depths gave him pause. Her face looked a score and five but her eyes spoke of twice that age.

"How long have you been in charge here?"

She continued her movements, only a slight hesitation on her upswing proving she had heard his question. "We are here to train, not talk."

Her unwillingness to answer only brought more questions to mind. What in her past had left such a scar that she cut herself off from the people around her? The members of her household cared greatly for her. He had seen proof of that last night. She might have blocked out the encouraging looks others had thrown her way, but he had not. Had she once been free of responsibilities? Did the burdens of her role rest even more heavily upon her because she had once known the lightness of being free? Was that what brought the current shadows to her beautiful green eyes?

What was it about her that made him care? He had to admit he admired her dedication to her craft. But it was more than appreciation that drew his gaze to her lips over and over again. Lips that were generous and full. Kissable. The word formed in his mind before he could stop it, and an answering warmth flared in his loins. He would not mind kissing her at all.

Kissing her?

Ian shook his somewhat cloudy head and tried without success to pull his gaze from her mouth. He was here to train, to focus on his revenge, not to find pleasure.

Besides, the woman would most likely eat him alive before she allowed him the opportunity to kiss her. And yet, such an attempt might be worth the risk. For he was certain if she ever gave herself over to such emotion she would embrace it with the same intensity with which she fought.

At the thought, arousal roared through him. He gave up trying to look away and continued his exploration. The formed metal plates of her brigandine were no doubt meant to conceal the soft flare of her breasts and hips. They only accentuated them, though. Yet no one could say her soft curves lessened her image as a dangerous warrior. Nay, if anything she appeared even more powerful, leaving no doubt that her family carried a warrior's bloodline in its veins.

Leather cross-garters held her cuisses against her legs and peeked out from beneath the hem of a red skirt that skimmed the tops of her shapely thighs. An image of smooth, creamy thighs filled his mind. Underneath all that armor existed a woman who had no idea how enticing she was.

Ian bit back a groan and tore his gaze away. What was he thinking? Perhaps that bash he had taken on the head had rattled his brains more than he had realized.

He could appreciate her looks all he wanted as long as he did so from afar—from the end of a sword, preferably. That would at least remind him of why he was here. The last thing he needed was to complicate his life. It was best if he kept his fantasies to himself, focused on his training, then left to exact his revenge on the Four Horsemen, who had altered his life for the last time.

Scotia felt Ian's gaze upon her. He was supposed to observe her motions, then join her in the training cross. But his gaze was nowhere near her sword, and he had yet to imitate what she had shown him thus far.

"Have you finished watching me practice, or would you care to rest some more before you begin?" She could not hide the touch of irritation that laced her voice. His blatant observation left her off-balance and uncomfortable.

Ian drew his sword. "I could watch you forever."

The husky baritone of his voice warmed her. She knew he meant he could watch her wield a sword forever. "You will do fifteen repetitions through the ropes, advancing, then retreating."

"With no opponent?" He offered her an innocent smile.

"Use your imagination. That is, if you have one."

His smile shifted from innocent to playful. "I assure you I do." He lunged forward against his unseen enemy, but his gaze remained on her, assessing her as he moved.

She turned away from his verbal sparring and those distracting eyes. She drew a slow, shaky breath, trying to still the rapid beat of her heart. What was happening to her? Before Ian had come to Loch Glencarron she had cared not a whit how people looked at her or spoke to her. She rarely exchanged a civil word with her challengers before they attacked. As the Warrior Trainer, she expected nothing more.

Yet when she was around Ian, the sound of his voice did things to her insides, and his gaze made her feel . . .

soft. Nay, that was not it exactly. He made her feel feminine and more aware of her own sexuality than she ever had before.

That realization struck terror in her heart such as no warrior ever had before. Her only purpose as a female was to breed the next descendant in her lineage. And as her mother always told her, it was an act that would give her no pleasure.

Her hand flared across her womb. A moment of longing pulled at her. What would it be like to feel a child growing inside her? To be free to raise that child with no destiny or obligations to fulfill? Her hand fell to her side. That kind of freedom was not to be for her or for any daughter she might produce. Scotia pulled the edge of her brigandine back into place. With a sigh, she turned to face her student, for she must only think of him as such.

Ian stilled, allowing the tip of his sword to dip to the ground. Concern flooded his gaze. He left the training cross and came toward her. "Are you ill?"

His genuine concern caught her off guard. None but Maisie had ever thought she might require care or gentleness. She managed to absorb the odd sensations that knotted her stomach. "It is time to battle. If you can apply the skills I taught you this morn, who knows?" She shrugged, forcing a nonchalance she did not feel. "Perhaps you will best me this day." She could feel his focus intensify.

"And when I do finally best you?" he prompted softly.

"It is highly unlikely." She opened her mouth to continue, but he laid one callused finger against her lips.

"I do love a challenge." He traced the sensitive outline of her lips with his finger, moving slowly across the top, then the bottom.

Her mouth tingled. She fought the urge to press

against his touch. No man had ever touched her thusly. Saints alive, it was a pleasurable feeling indeed. One she was not certain she wanted to stop.

"Shall we begin?" he asked as he drew his finger away.

"Aye," she breathed and brought up her sword, suddenly determined to win this fight at all costs.

"Did ye see the way he touched her lips? Did ye?" Burke whispered from behind the doorway to Scotia's training chamber. "Ye were right, old girl. Our betrayal of Scotia's existence and location seems to have worked. It prompted Abbus MacKinnon to do as Scotia's mother bid him so many years ago."

"Aye." Maisie clutched Burke's shoulder affectionately. "He's sent Scotia a man worthy of fathering her child."

Scotia would give herself over to the man. Of that, Maisie was certain.

What the young couple needed was time, and a little encouragement to set in motion the event neither of them could deny. And Maisie knew just how to accomplish that Herculean task.

"Come, Burke. There's work to be done."

Chapter Seven

The sword came within an inch of separating Ian from his right ear. But Ian shifted his stance just in time. Scotia grinned, pleased that he was doing so well.

Over the last five days, Ian and Scotia had developed a routine. Scotia worked with him individually in the morning hours. After the midday meal and a short rest, she tossed him into the lists with her men to practice what he had learned.

Scotia stood a short distance away from her pupil as he engaged her best warrior in a rigorous session of swordplay. Richard had just returned to the keep that morning with news of the Four Horsemen's latest conquest in the village of Banavie. He reported that he and his troops had interceded in the battle fray, sparing many lives with their efforts.

A small blessing among so much destruction. Yet it was one blessing she was grateful for if it kept her people alive. If only they would come to her to train, as they used to during her mother's reign as the Trainer.

Scotia pulled the edge of her brigandine down with a

sharp tug. That line of thinking would accomplish nothing. With an effort, she turned her thoughts to the two warriors before her.

Richard charged Ian again. A clash of metal reverberated through the air as Ian met the thrust with one of his own, then twisted upwards and sideways, taking his opponent off-balance, then down to the ground. It was a move she had taught him. "Well done," she said.

Ian responded with a smile. Not just any smile. An arresting smile. A disarming smile. One that made her legs feel less than steady. No one had ever smiled at her like that before.

Ian offered Richard a hand up, then strode to Scotia, his smile shifting to something less about mirth and more about . . . what? She had no word for it, but some part of her admitted she was intrigued. She tried to look away, but failed. Saints alive, he unsettled her.

"Who am I to battle next? Or will I be subject to more of *your* abuse instead?" he teased.

"The abuse would be against me, I fear . . . you and your barbaric thrusts."

The look in his eyes shifted from playful to something more intense. "I can be gentle when needed, Scotia. I promise you that."

The intensity of his gaze mixed with the subtlety of his words and brought a slight trembling to her hands. She fumbled for the hilt of her sword, not intending to use it, merely needing the security of the smooth cold metal beneath her palms. Her sword steadied her. "We are done here today."

"With which battle, Scotia?" he asked, his brow rising in question. "The one with swords or the one with words?"

Heat flooded her cheeks. Again, he caught her off

guard. "Maisie has prepared a surprise for us all in celebration of Beltaine Eve," she said, trying to change the subject.

He took a step closer. "We used to call Beltaine Eve the 'fire madness' in our clan."

She forced herself to remain where she stood despite the fact his nearness played havoc with her concentration. She gripped her sword all the harder. She needed to think about warfare, not the taut muscles she could see through his sweat-dampened linen shirt.

She tried to look away, but failed. Aye, it was madness indeed that had her in its grip. Why could she not control herself around him? Things like this had never happened to her before he had arrived. With an effort, she ripped her gaze from his chest. *Distractions could cost you your life,* came her mother's admonishing whisper in her head.

Scotia took two steps back, putting some distance between them. And for the first time, she considered her mother might have been wrong about one thing. It was not her life she was in jeopardy of losing to this man. It was her sanity.

"I shall see you this eve." Then, without another word, she strode for the safety of the keep, knowing as she did that he had won the battle of words between them this day.

As Scotia gazed upon the enormous Beltaine Eve fire that had been set in a pit in the inner bailey, she could not help but agree that this was indeed "fire madness." Darkness mixed with moonlight, bathing the celebration area in a silver glow broken only by the red-gold fingers of flame that danced toward the sky. The wind carried the musical strains of the bagpipes across the night, blending the sound of music with voices.

The kitchen maids and stable hands mingled about the fire alongside the warriors and their squires, the archers and hunters. Nearby tables groaned beneath the abundance of ale, oat cakes, cheese, and creamy custard.

Pennants atop poles draped with long ribbons and garlands of mountain ash transformed the area where she usually trained her warriors into a haven of magic. And Beltaine Eve was magical—a night where all who participated could forget who they were as they welcomed the arrival of summer along with the hope of a good harvest and prosperity for all.

For a moment her spirits dampened. Their prosperity—their very future—depended on her plans to outmaneuver the Four Horsemen, but she forced the somber thought away. Tonight nothing mattered but Beltaine Eve. Their country was in chaos because of the Four Horsemen. Festivities such as Beltaine Eve bonded her people to their heritage and made the struggles of life seem a little more bearable.

Scotia closed her eyes and drew a deep breath of the heavy night air, allowing the music and the magic of the evening to bewitch her, swaying with the rhythm and cadence of the pipers' song. She opened her eyes and gazed upon the the Beltaine Eve fire.

She caught his scent a second before he slid silently next to her with that oddly dizzying aroma of mint and musk. "Welcome to the madness," he said as he placed a wreath of mountain ash atop her head. "Perfect. Now the Queen of the May looks the part."

Scotia steeled herself against her instinct to reach up and pull the flowers down. Having flowers in the place where a helmet should be felt wrong. The soft petals caressed her skin, taunting her own perception as a hard-

ened warrior. Warriors *did not* wreath themselves in flowers. Did they?

Her people seemed to think so, for they gave a raucous
cheer, "Long live Queen Scotia." The pipers took the
cheer as a cue to play a lively tune that set the crowd to
dancing about the fire.

Scotia took a step back, moving out of the way as the
crowd circled the fire, first dancing to the left, then shifting to the right. Ian remained beside her, pulling her into
the intimacy of the shadows.

"Care to join in?" Ian asked.

She shook her head, the flowers shifting, threatening
to slide from their perch. Ian was there, his hand caressing the side of her head as he repositioned the wreath.

His hand trailed along the curve of her cheek down to
her chin, then up, until his fingers caressed her lower lip.

His hand stilled there and the light in his eyes shifted.
To what? Boldness? Desire?

Beneath his scrutiny her mouth went dry—as dry as
the kindling that snapped in the fire before them. Or was
the fire inside *her* now? For she was suddenly too warm beneath her heavy armor.

"I need some cool air." She spun away, using any excuse to escape her own response to his presence. She
could feel Ian's gaze follow her away from the fire.

Scotia watched Maisie dance with Burke, and her
kitchen maid, Mary, swirl flirtatiously around a stable boy
named Jacob. Nearby, Richard and several of the other
warriors drank from mugs of ale as they cheered on the
dancers, laughing at the revelry displayed by the others.

For Scotia, safety existed in the shadows. In the shadows she might somehow hide the unsettling sensations
her new student brought out in her. She drew in a deep

breath of the night air and allowed the skirl of the bagpipes to wrap her in sound, feeling more at ease.

After several songs, the pipers took a break and the dancing subsided. "Time to decide who will jump the Beltaine Eve flames," one of her warriors called. To leap across the fire three times was a custom as old as Beltaine Eve itself.

Maisie moved to the food table and carefully broke the oat cakes into as many portions as there were people to celebrate. She placed the portions in a bonnet.

Burke carried one portion to the fire and set it amongst the coals until it burned black. When the task was complete, he removed it with an iron spoon, then waited for it to cool before placing it in the bonnet with the other pieces.

The revelers surged toward Maisie and Burke, eager to play the game. One by one they plunged their hands into the bonnet. Each unburned cake that came forth drew either a relieved sigh or a groan of disappointment.

Ian stepped forward to draw his lot—the black cake. For a moment he stared down at the black coal in his hand, tension vibrating in his lean figure.

"I will accept the black cake," Scotia said, emerging from the shadows. Last year's celebration had badly burned one of her warrior's legs. Ian did not deserve such a dangerous fate. "As a visitor, Ian should not be subjected to our Beltaine Eve customs."

His expression betrayed a momentary flash of insult. "I am up to the challenge."

Before Scotia could say more, the crowd cheered, "To the King of the May."

They lifted Ian onto their shoulders and paraded him around the fire. A moment later she found herself hoisted aloft as well, joining the parade. "To our king and queen."

The cheer was met with laughter as the wild, spirited strains of the pipers began again.

A warm exhilaration came over Scotia as she and Ian found themselves parted by the merrymakers, then thrust side-by-side. Excitement bubbled up, but not just from the frolicking. Nay, it was the way Ian looked at her. The way the stiffness slipped from his gaze to be replaced by something darker, more sensual. And a responding honey-eyed heat flared within her. And for the second time in two days, Scotia wanted to participate, to indulge the urge to relax, to be free to experience this moment as fully as others might.

Ian reached for her hand, and before she could consider what she did, his fingers wrapped around hers. The warmth of his palm burned through the leather of her gauntlet as though she wore no protection at all.

She and Ian were twirled about by the crowd, hands joined. The flames of the bonfire blurred before her eyes and the sounds of the pipers echoed not only in her ears but also in her heart and body until the sound of the crowd and the music died away as her senses focused only on Ian.

They were lowered to the ground, standing before the fire. For one long second he looked down at her, the moonlight outlining the planes of his face, of his lean muscular body, before he took a step closer, creating a startling intimacy.

He was so close, too close, and yet not close enough. What was it about this man that captivated her so? Was it the liberties he took with her that no one else did? He had placed the flowers on her head when no one else would have dared. He had touched her lips. He had taken her hand, not in battle, but with a gentleness she had not experienced before.

With his large hand wrapped around her smaller one, she felt no loss of strength, but there was a shift, a shift she could not quite name.

As if reading her thoughts, his gaze moved to her hand and his fingers folded around the leather encasing her palm. "Your hands are warm."

Not just warm, for suddenly they felt as though they were melting at his touch. She could only watch as he lifted her hand, turning it palm up. He stroked his thumb across the well-worn leather. She inhaled sharply.

He stopped, his gaze searching her face. "May I take it off?"

"I never . . . ," she said quickly, seizing wildly at the excuse she had always given before, but the words died in her throat at the return of his sensuous smile.

"Never?" His fingers unbuckled her gauntlet, then let it fall to the ground. Calloused flesh covered her palm and scars of abuse lined the back of her hand from all her years of training. They were the hands of a warrior, proving she was no real Queen of the May. She tensed as the thought. "So strong yet so feminine," Ian said with a touch of awe, as if not seeing what was truly there.

Scotia swallowed against the sudden tightness in her throat. Feminine. There was nothing feminine about her. But the way Ian smoothed his fingers over the roughened texture of her palm, as though her skin were as smooth and unmarred as other women's flesh, made her feel soft. *Soft?*

She tried to pull away, but he held tight. "It was not an insult, only an observation."

An observation she had never allowed herself to pursue. Ian's fingers stroked her palm, her wrist, her forearm. She watched, fascinated by the strangely seductive exploration of her flesh.

His touch brought excitement, heat, hunger.

A chant of "jump, jump, jump," mirrored the beating of her heartbeat. And in that moment the crowd pulled him away, turning him toward the ravenous flames. "Show us how it's done, mighty King of the May."

Ian shooed the crowd away, gaining himself some space as he took several steps back. His body coiled, but before he ran toward the flames he spared one last glance for her—a glance that said he did this for her and her alone.

Scotia held her breath as he leapt over the enormous fire, high above the flames. A second jump, then a third, and a cheer broke out from the crowd. "The king is triumphant!"

A mug of ale was pressed into his hands by Richard as he and the other warriors drew him away from the fire, away from her, to celebrate his victory.

And suddenly the night seemed hollow as she stood there among the merrymakers, alone. It was how she had celebrated Beltaine Eve over the last many years. Why did she expect it to be so different now that the MacKinnon had arrived?

Scotia turned away from the celebration, suddenly tired, and headed back to the keep. Damn Beltaine Eve for momentarily making her long for more.

Chapter Eight

At dawn the morning following the Beltaine Eve celebrations, Ian had given up trying to sleep. Now he sat between one of the carved stones that formed the crenellations of the tower and gazed out at the land before him. On one side of him, a bank of chilled mist sat over the shoreline and soared up to kiss the morn. On the other side, high, wild, and lonely cliffs dropped to meet the green tide as it curled against the rocks below.

No one could deny that Scotia's land was beautiful, breathtaking even. It was land a man, or a woman in Scotia's case, would be proud to possess. Her ancestors had owned this castle for hundreds of years. In her veins flowed the blood of the warrior woman who had sailed to the Isle of Destiny promised to them by Moses. Ian envied her lineage, her connection to a family whose very beginnings were the source of all the Scottish people.

With a history like that, he, a lowly bastard, had no right to think about kissing her. Yet after their encounter last night, the idea had filled his mind to the point of obsession. Just the touch of his finger against her flesh made him long for further exploration of her perfectly sculpted lips. Lips so desirable. Lips meant to be kissed. Groaning, he tore his thoughts away from the image. Scotia was a vehicle for his training, nothing more. The sooner he accepted that fact, the better. There were other things of greater importance to consider, such as when he would leave to find the Four Horsemen and take his revenge.

The Four Horsemen could be anywhere in Scotland, wreaking further destruction and death. He had to stop them, even at the risk of his own life. Anger forced his hands into tense fists as he thought of the pain the Four Horsemen caused, all for the Stone of Destiny. An artifact so important to the people of this country they would be willing to give their lives in order to keep it safe.

The only way to protect his clan from further assault was to learn what he could from Scotia about the Horsemen. With her help he would defeat the enemy and end the terror.

But he still had more to learn. He needed time to build on the things she had taught him—how to channel his anger, move with dexterity, be more in tune with his body. All would help him when the ultimate battle took place.

Ian swung his feet around, then jumped down onto the wall walk below. If he could keep his thoughts off Scotia and on her training, he could leave to find the Four Horsemen and avenge his brother. And to do that he would have to leave this castle and Scotia behind. The sooner the better if he were to help his clan survive a second attack.

"MacKinnon." At the sound of her voice, his spirit lightened.

He turned toward the open doorway where she stood framed by the gray sandstone. Her shoulders looked tense, her hair pulled back in a tight plait, her sword pointed down toward the ground before her. She looked so fierce and yet so fragile.

He steeled himself against the pull of desire that rippled through him. He knew what he had to do to save his clan, to strike the Horsemen down before they destroyed all he held dear.

"Are you avoiding your training today?" No accusation hung in her voice, only slight disappointment.

"I could not sleep, so I wandered up here. Time must have passed without my realizing." He took three steps toward her, then stopped. Before they continued training, he had questions to ask her.

She nodded, and her face brightened a little, as though she were pleased that he had not meant to avoid her. "I have something new to show you this day."

"How much longer before I have completed my training?"

Shadows descended into her eyes. "You are so eager to leave?"

"Aye," he replied honestly. "I fear for the safety of my clan."

"The Four Horsemen."

"Have you encountered them?" he asked, knowing even as he asked the question that he should not. The more he learned about her and her life, the harder it was to keep himself closed off to her.

"Only once, twelve years ago, on the day they killed my mother." The color bled from her face, and her chest rose and fell with the sudden force of her breathing. Not the slow steady breath of the controlled Scotia he had seen up until now, but the ragged breath of a woman torn apart by a haunting memory.

Ian went motionless. In her gaze he recognized the

same overburdened soul that drove his own actions. He saw her pain, her fear, her exhaustion.

He moved toward her. She did not back away even as he removed one hand from the hilt of her sword to weave her icy fingers with his.

Her fresh heather scent filled his nostrils, his mind, clouding his thoughts of anything but her. "I am sorry," he said in a voice so hushed the words were nothing more than a whisper. Yet the flare of her eyes told him she'd heard.

"I had not come into my strength back then." Guilt laced her words.

Without thinking, only reacting as he would to another human in need, he drew her closer against his chest. Like a creature unused to human contact, her eyes filled with a mixture of fear and wonder. The woman in his arms might be a warrior, a legend even, but she was as vulnerable as anyone else, he realized with a start. "What did you do?"

"I could do nothing but flee with Maisie and Burke to safety." Her body remained stiff, unyielding in his arms, but she did not try to pull away. He prayed she would. He needed her to break the contact, because he found he could not. Instead, he pulled her closer, molding his body against hers, dominating her smaller frame. A surge of protectiveness erupted within him, the need to shield her from all she had suffered.

"Ian . . ." Her armor-covered body relaxed against his chest, and he was lost. He angled his head and lowered his mouth until he could feel her breath on his lips. Her eyelids fluttered closed. And he took what he so desperately wanted.

With his lips, he demanded her to respond, challenging her to acknowledge the tension that had been building between them since his arrival.

She tasted of innocence and hunger, as though he had opened a tap that had been left closed off for too long. Her lips parted in an invitation he openly accepted, not quite believing it was Scotia he held, yielding her body for him to explore. Yet she was here, granting him liberties only a lover should take.

A lover? He was not here to woo her. And yet he could not deny the appeal the thought held.

He had no right to pursue such things. He let her go.

Dazed and disoriented, she stared at him, then stepped back into the shadows of the doorway, acting as if the darkness could hide the pleasure they had shared. But even the hazy light could not conceal her lips, still moist from his kiss.

She turned, closing herself to him, hiding the last sign of their mindless exchange. "We must train." She clutched her sword firmly as she strode down the stairs.

Ian started after her, his hands knotted in fists at his sides, fighting the stirring desire she had awakened. His urge to leave Glencarron Castle to seek revenge faltered. Yet how could he consider any other option with so many lives at stake?

It was yet another twist of fate, a fate he could not turn away from. He knew his duty, and he would see it through.

At the soft tinkle of a bell near her bedside, Scotia jerked awake. A warning she had constructed. An intruder had entered the keep through the secret tunnel hidden among the cliffs.

Clasping her sword, she rolled from her bed—alert, aware, and ready to defend herself. With her heart pounding, but in full control of her emotions, she slipped from her chamber, moving down the stairs and out into the night. Using the darkness as a shield, she headed toward the passageway that led to the walled garden. Inside the garden, she sensed the intruder's presence. If she remained still, eventually her enemy would reveal himself. Her senses sharpened.

It did not take long. A soft creak sounded to her right. She turned, searching the moonlit darkness for a sign of his presence. There, near the tall stalks of rosemary, she could make out the faintest glimmer of his eyes. "Who are you?"

A flash of metal flickered in the ghostly moonlight—a blade. "Who I am is not as important as my purpose here," a harsh, unfamiliar male voice said from the shadows.

Scotia drew herself up, widening her stance, preparing for the battle to come. How many times had she heard those words before? "How did you know about the tunnel?"

"That is my secret. But if I made it in, so will others. Does that scare you?" the intruder asked, stepping toward her.

"Nay." The moonlight revealed a tall, muscular figure dressed in the plaid of her countrymen. A Scot had come to challenge her this time. A momentary pang of disappointment gripped her. Even her own countrymen came to challenge her now. "I find very little use for fear."

The challenger laughed as he strode toward her, his sword raised, his body tense. "Then you are a fool."

"Perhaps." Scotia kept her body loose, preparing to absorb the blow she could see coming. Her injured shoulder could take some battering if only she kept the muscles relaxed. "Better foolish than dead. Which is what you will be in no time at all."

His blade came down. A thunderous clang echoed in the night. Scotia easily blocked his assault. Before she could strike back the light of a torch flooded the garden, illuminating the intruder's face.

"Griffin," Ian called out from behind her. She yearned to turn to him, but her instincts warned otherwise. Keep your eye on the enemy at all times, her mother had instructed over and over again.

The intruder's eyes narrowed, then moved to Ian as he came to stand beside her, the torch in one hand, his sword in the other. From the corner of her eye she could see Ian's feet were bare, as was his chest. He wore only his trews and a scowl that looked both fierce and intimidating. She could not hold back the ripple of pleasure that having him by her side, as though ready to defend her, brought forth.

The man he had called Griffin scowled. "Glad to see you, too, brother."

Scotia froze. Regardless of her training to stay focused on her foe, she allowed her gaze to slide between the two men. These two were brothers? They could not have been more different than night from day. Where Ian was blond and fair, Griffin was dark and swarthy. Clearly they bore no love for each other. It was not what she had expected from two brothers.

Ian planted the torch in the soft earth, then clasped his sword with both hands. "If you are here, where are Father and our clansmen?"

"Back home where they belong."

Ian's gaze grew dark. "With you gone there are only a few warriors left to protect the entire clan."

Griffin's expression became dark and foreboding. "The Four Horsemen were sighted heading north. Our village is safe for now." He turned back to Scotia, his sword poised to strike.

She braced herself to fight the intruder, be he Ian's brother or not. The violence in his gaze told her one thing—he meant to kill her. Fear crept past her guard, but she caught it, cutting the emotion off. After so many years, she knew herself well enough to recognize her own weaknesses. And family ties were her biggest failing of all. This man might be Ian's brother, but if she softened her resolve toward him, it could mean her death. She latched on to her sword, fighting the humanity that threatened to swamp her.

Griffin swung his sword. She feinted to the right, easily avoiding the blow.

"Griffin, what are you doing?" Ian asked, his voice both savage and controlled.

"Claiming a birthright that is rightfully mine. Stand away, Ian," Griffin demanded, his hand tightening on his hilt. "I challenge the woman."

"I doubt you could do so and live," Ian said dryly. "Go home, Griffin. You do not belong here."

The force of Griffin's wrath shifted from Ian to Scotia. "Not until I succeed in my challenge."

"I hope you are used to disappointment," Scotia said, fully prepared to battle.

Griffin slashed at her once more. Scotia caught the blade with her own, trapped it and threw it back, knocking her opponent off balance. He had skill, but she had more.

"Scotia, nay." Ian stepped in front of her sword, concern written into the very texture of his face. "He knows naught what he does."

With the tip of her weapon, she waved Ian back. "Then my task will be that much easier."

Griffin regained his balance, and prepared to attack once again. "Stand down, Ian. I know exactly what I am doing."

"You shall not harm her." Ian's face hardened.

The warmth of Ian's words curled inside her, bringing an unfamiliar sense of security. "Do as your brother says," she said to Ian. "It will be but a moment's work to dispatch the man."

Griffin charged forward with an angry cry, knocking Ian out of his way. "I'll show you."

Scotia stood her ground and once again blocked Griffin's assault. She cleared her mind of all but the battle, keeping her steps precise, calculated for the most efficient use of her speed and strength. She wished to disarm Griffin, not send him to his grave. Perhaps when the first thrill of battle wore off he would be more reasonable.

Griffin lashed out at her with his sword, their blades clashing. When she failed to yield, Griffin spun away, his face hard, his jaw squared, his eyes catching the glow of the torch and smoldering like embers in a fire. He lunged at her with a slash of his weapon.

Without much effort, she blocked his attack. Griffin bared his teeth in a snarl and launched himself at her again. A stinging whip of metal on metal, then Scotia's blade sliced the flesh on his temple just above his ear. A dark ribbon of blood spilled from the wound, running down the side of his smooth-shaven jaw in rivulets that disappeared into the plaid at his shoulder.

Griffin flinched and retreated, but Scotia followed, pressing her advantage. She had him now. He was hers. "Do you yield?" she asked.

"Never to a woman." Griffin sidestepped and advanced again.

Scotia shook her head. "The multitude of grave markers beyond the castle lay testament to how many times men have said those very words to me." Scotia met Griffin's blade with a forceful blow that locked with his sword at the hilt. She schooled her features to remain expressionless as she turned her sword to the left once, then twice, causing Griffin to gasp with pain. His wrist rolled, forcing the sword from his grasp. The weapon landed with a thud against the dirt.

Griffin stared at her and the predatory light faded from his eyes. "We . . . are not done here," he said between ragged breaths.

"Aye, but we are." Scotia bent down to retrieve Griffin's sword before facing him. "If you ever challenge me in such a way again, I will kill you. Because you are Ian's brother, I will let this indiscretion pass. But if you remain at my castle, you will never again approach me like a coward or a lowly thief in the night, but as a man." She turned away. "You may bed down in the stable tonight."

Griffin pressed his lips into a thin white line and nodded.

Scotia headed toward the doorway that led back to the castle. "Come, Ian, your brother has suffered enough humiliation this eve."

Ian stared at his brother. Hard. Only the squared ridge of his jaw betrayed the control it took to keep his anger in check. "Go home."

With the tips of his fingers Griffin dabbed at his wounded temple. "I want her secrets."

"Killing her would truly have accomplished that task," Ian said through gritted teeth.

Griffin shrugged. "Seemed like the shortest means to my goal. If I had bested her this night, I would have held the title as the best fighter in the land. Father would have had no choice but to recognize me as leader of our clan."

Scotia paused in the doorway as the truth of Griffin's visit slipped out. She spun toward him. "So you think your father will make you leader of your clan if you kill me?"

Griffin's silence was answer enough.

She looked into his face, his eyes, his actions, searching for a small sign of regret or remorse. She saw only undisciplined, boyish pride. Scotia stifled her disappointment. The young man still had much to learn. "Leaders are made, not born. Remember that the next time you challenge me."

Before Griffin could reply, Ian stepped forward, towering over his brother, his expression more somber than anything she had witnessed yet. "You are lucky she did not kill you. Try that again, and it will be my sword, not hers, that sends you to your end."

Chapter Nine

Darkness covered her way as Scotia headed back inside the castle and into the great hall. Each step put the newcomer and the anger she felt toward him further from her mind. Ian's brother had dared challenge her in her own castle as she slept. Had the codes of noble behavior and honor disappeared along with the desire of her countrymen for training?

Still angered by the exchange, she entered the great hall and wove her way through the rows of straw pallets strewn across the floor, where members of her household lay sleeping. Soft snores punctuated the silence of the night. A fire in the hearth cast a gold-red light throughout the room, making it easy to locate what she sought. A tankard of ale would help calm her nerves, though the footsteps behind her warned that Ian followed. When he was around, her nerves were anything but calm.

Scotia grabbed an earthenware jug filled with ale and a wooden tankard from a nearby table, then wove her way back through the hall to the door. Outside once more, the cool night caressed her skin as she took a seat on the wooden stairs near the door. Ian sat next to her, his hip brushing hers. An overwhelming urge to lean into him seized her, but she scooted away, refusing to acknowledge the melting effect this brief contact had upon her.

"Are you well?" Ian asked, his tone solemn, his body tense beside her.

She did not want to speak about Griffin. Not until her anger lessened. She feared she would say something she might later regret. Instead, she filled the tankard with ale, then drank. When she had finished, she refilled the cup and handed it to him.

"I wonder which is worse," she asked, breaking the silence between them, "having family that acts without honor, or having no family at all?" The topic seemed safe enough.

She felt him relax as he returned the tankard, obviously finding relief in her avoidance. "The worst day with a family is better than the best day without."

Scotia poured herself another cup as she pondered his words. She had to agree, but thought his statement odd coming from a man who had grown up in the thick of his clan. "What would you know of such things?"

"I have been with family longer than I have been without. Even so, the memories of being alone still remain."

Scotia nodded more to herself than to him. She knew the feeling of loneliness well. Even in a castle surrounded by people, she often felt an emptiness that, when stirred, bordered on panic. She risked a glance sideways. He looked not at her, but at the night sky.

"I am sorry about my brother." The statement implied so much more than he said.

She returned her gaze to the stars above. "You do not control his actions."

74

"Regardless, he had no right to challenge you in that way."

She shrugged into the darkness. "I am used to challenges, Ian. Your brother has much to learn before he would become a threat to me."

"Then you really mean to train him?"

"If that is what he chooses, aye. It is my obligation."

"Is the security of your castle your obligation as well?" Ian asked.

"Aye." Everything within the castle fell under her care. It was a huge burden, but she would not tell him that.

"Then there is a breech somewhere for Griffin to enter unnoticed." There was no censure in his voice, only honesty.

"He did not enter without my notice," she admitted. "There is only one other way inside these walls besides the front gate. How he knew to enter there I do not yet know."

Ian shifted beside her. "I will look into the situation with Griffin if you agree that I might."

She felt Ian's gaze upon her and resisted the impulse to look at him, even though she longed to see what she might be able to read there. Did he think she had failed in her duty to the people of her household? Or was he earnest in his desire to help her?

Help her. What an unusual notion. And yet, she could not deny her relief at the idea.

"By your silence I take it you do not approve," he said.

"Nay," she replied. "I would welcome your help in this one area."

"Agreed." She could almost hear the smile in that single word.

They sat in silence, sharing ale as two companions

might after a day of battle. Even though they were not comrades in arms and the battle in the garden had been against his own kin, Ian's presence was welcome—even comforting if she were honest. How little time she'd had in her life for friendship.

Scotia startled at the thought. Was that what she felt when he was near? Feelings shared between friends? She turned toward him in an effort to read his emotions, but his face was wrapped in a veil of moonlight and shadow. His presence at Glencarron Castle had changed so many things. She had been on the verge of giving up when he had arrived. Now, she could honestly say she felt renewed. Scotia bit down on her lip. It was the closest thing to happiness she had experienced in a long while, despite the night's events.

He shifted beside her, and for a moment she tensed, fearing he would leave. Not wanting him to slip away into the darkness, she tried to think of something to say, anything to keep him by her side until the ale settled her nerves and she could face what remained of the night.

When no words came to her, she turned her gaze to the sky. A thousand stars glittered in the cloudless expanse, stretching across Scotland like a banner of serenity. If only that falsehood were so. Scotia leaned back and let her head rest on the stair behind her. To her surprise, Ian did the same.

"What are you looking at?" His voice was calm, soothing.

She relaxed against the wood riser. "I was wondering which star to wish upon this night."

He chuckled, the sound deep and rich. "Forgive me, but you do not seem the type to wish upon a star. Or the kind of female who engages in wishes or fantasy."

She bristled at his words. "Do you find me so rigid that you think there is no room in my heart for wishes?"

He turned toward her. Only fragments of his features were clear to her in the silver moonlight. "I meant no offense. I thought you would never allow yourself to become distracted by fanciful things."

"I am not distracted," she retorted despite the fact his words were partial truth. The stars paled in comparison to her preoccupation with him. Never in her life had she experienced such difficulty remaining disciplined and focused as she did when he drew near. She returned her attention to the stars. "Do you want to quibble or choose a star?"

"Hmm," he mused. She could hear a touch of amusement in his voice. "Sparring with you does hold an appeal, there is no denying that. But until I master your fighting techniques, it would be safer to play with the stars."

"You will never best me." She kept her voice light despite the sudden heaviness that settled in her chest.

"An intriguing challenge. There is no doubt about that."

She let silence fall between them. No one had ever bested her. No one ever could unless she allowed it. As Trainer, she controlled how much she taught him, and how much she held back. If she taught him everything, would he one day use it against her? She had never considered that possibility before. There was always a chance that the student's abilities would surpass the master's.

She and Ian had weeks of practice ahead of them before he reached that level of proficiency. In an effort to hide the tension that suddenly gripped her at the thought of Ian besting her, Scotia smoothed her fingers across the tops of her leather-clad thighs. Her mother had never prepared her for that eventuality.

She forced her hands to still. Now was not the time to worry about such things. When Ian's abilities neared her own, she would consider what to do. Until then, she did not need to borrow trouble. But perhaps, just to make certain, one wish on a star would not hurt. Scanning the heavens, she found a star far off from the rest, bright and steady, that appealed to her. She closed her eyes, and—

"What did you wish for?" he asked, breaking into her thoughts.

"I cannot tell you that." She did not bother to disguise her annoyance at the interruption. After all, she had been about to send out a perfectly good wish for strength. Continuing to study the sky, she asked, "Which star did you choose?"

"The one over there, off to the left." His voice grew soft, and if she was not mistaken carried a touch of sorrow in its depth.

He pointed to her star. Scotia frowned. "Why did you pick that one?" she asked, curious as to why he had picked the same star as she in a sky filled with so many other more worthy choices.

"It reminded me of my position in my clan. Alone, yet surrounded by many."

Her frown deepened. "It is how I always feel—alone, yet surrounded by all of Scotland. But how is it the same for you? How can you be alone within the bosom of your clan?"

"It is easy when you are not truly one of them. I am a MacKinnon in name only." His voice was flat, devoid of all feeling as he spoke, sparking the compassion she tried to hold in check.

"And yet you came here to learn, to help protect your clan."

"I am to lead them after my foster father is gone."

"He must care for you greatly and trust you to ask such a thing."

"He does. It is Griffin and the rest of the clan who question my leadership."

Scotia frowned. "Will the others follow you when the time comes?"

"Aye. All except Griffin, who will challenge me always." Ian groaned. "I think I finally understand why my foster father sent me here to you—to gain the skills necessary to keep the others, especially Griffin, in line."

Their fingers rested on the wooden plank, mere inches apart. An overwhelming urge to reach out to him, to place her fingers atop his swamped her, but she forced herself to remain still.

Instead, she studied the way Ian reclined against the stairs, his pose casual, yet ready to spring forward should there be a need. A true warrior.

Scotia wished for a glimmer of moonlight to reveal his face. No one had ever confided so much of himself to her before. She could not help but wonder why he did so now. Did he feel the same companionship she felt this eve? If she could just look into his eyes, she would know his feelings, but the darkness made that impossible. "Why did your foster father choose you to lead your clan over Griffin?"

He gave a short laugh that held no humor. "Because I am a better warrior. In these uncertain times, the protection of my clan is vital." He turned his face toward her, though it still remained shadowed. "It is not only the Four Horsemen who stir trouble in our land. Their fellow Englishmen threaten our freedom with their efforts to constrain Robert the Bruce and those who support him."

"My men are out there now, fighting for those very

causes. I only regret that our people do not come to me to train. I could help them if they would. . . ."

"By training me, you are helping your people, Scotia."

"I had not considered that." How did he always manage to take her by surprise? In battle she was prepared for any eventuality. But in this new game with Ian, she never knew what to expect. His sympathy, his humility, his humanity could strike her to her knees before she knew what hit her.

Like now, she could only watch, hardly daring to breathe, as he captured one of the tendrils of her hair that had escaped her tight plait during her battle with Griffin. He twined it about his finger. "Scotland might have forgotten how lucky she is to have you, but I have not." His voice deepened to a husky whisper.

Before she could react, he leaned down and placed his lips against hers. His kiss was swift, even chaste, but it set off a wistful yearning deep inside her. When he drew back she was tempted to grab his shirt and pull him close again. But she could not lose herself to her desire, no matter how desperately she might want to. Instead she curled her hands at her sides.

Twice tonight he had caught her off guard. A dangerous state that could get her killed.

Scotia jumped to her feet. "I had best return to my chamber."

"What about Griffin?"

"He would not dare to challenge me again this night."

Ian stood beside her. "He will not, I will make certain of that. I intend to stand guard over him all night if I must."

A warm glow moved through her at his words. She did not need his protection, but the sentiment was comforting all the same. "Until the morrow then."

She picked up the now empty jug of ale and the tankard they had shared, then headed back into the castle. With each step her resolve to end their intimacy faltered. Only reason and logic kept her moving forward. She dared not look behind her. She could not bear the thought of seeing him standing in the doorway, looking as forlorn and confused as she now felt.

It was best to hurry away and not think about anything at all.

The next morning, Scotia entered the inner courtyard of the castle and watched Griffin fill a flask with water from the well. His expression was solemn as he concentrated on his task. In the light of day, he appeared much younger and far more vulnerable than he had seemed the previous night. Where Ian's features reflected a toughness brought on no doubt by years of living as an outsider in his clan, Griffin's face held the first flush of youth and inexperience. Perhaps that accounted for his erratic and sometimes childish behavior. He still had not discovered the man inside himself.

He finished at the well, then secured the bladder to the saddle of his horse. "You decided to leave?" she asked as he moved to mount the animal.

He swung around. For a moment a glimmer of surprise crossed his face before he schooled his features into the petulant look he bore. "I did not think I was welcome to remain."

"That depends." Scotia stopped a sword's length from him.

"Upon what, may I ask?" His hand moved to cover the hilt of his sword.

"Your reasons for coming here." Her gaze remained steadily on his face, yet she was aware of the tension of his fingers on his weapon, of the way he widened his stance to support a strike with his sword. "You should not be so hasty to draw that weapon, or I will cut off your fingers before you free it of its scabbard."

He grasped his weapon, testing her.

Scotia drew her sword. The weapon sliced through the air and halted a hair's breath above his exposed knuckles.

His eyes widened, filled with disbelief, as he jerked his hand away. He winced at the sliver of a cut across three of his fingers. Tiny droplets of blood trickled toward his fingertips. "Must you always wound me?"

"Must you always challenge me?" Scotia sheathed her sword.

His disillusioned gaze swept over her. "Because you're a—"

"Woman?" Scotia finished for him.

"Aye." He leaned back against his horse, his bravado spent. "It is unnatural for a female to fight as you do."

She had to agree. What she did was unusual for most women, but her mother had trained her to be more than her sex usually allowed. "That may be so, Griffin, but this is what I am." She resisted the urge to tug down the edge of her brigandine under his scrutiny. She would not apologize for what she was. "You may use it to your benefit to help strengthen your clan, or you may turn away from me and remain as you are."

He frowned. "What do you mean?"

Scotia watched his eyes. She could always tell how a person would react by watching their gaze. "You claim you want to lead your people."

"Aye." He pushed away from his horse. His gaze sharpened, but with interest, not ill intent. "I want what should be mine."

"No man, or no woman, can live another's fate. But

you can prepare for your fate by sacrificing your hostility toward Ian for the good of your people."

His eyes darkened and she tensed, waiting for him to react. "What do you mean?"

"Train with me. Let go of the anger you feel for your brother."

"Ian's not my brother, not by blood."

"We are all brothers and sisters, Griffin." Memories of her conversation last night with Ian sprang to mind. He had admitted to being an outsider even among his own people. "We are all Scots, regardless of rank or bloodlines."

Griffin narrowed his gaze on her as though assessing her words for the truth. "You would train me after my behavior last eve?"

"As Warrior Trainer, it is my duty to do so." Scotia stepped back and waved a hand toward the arched doorway leading back into the heart of the keep. "Will you join me?"

He nodded. "I accept."

Scotia called to the young boy cleaning out the stables, "Jacob, please see to this horse." The stable boy bobbed his head, then led the horse toward the timber and straw shelter.

"We will break our fast, then train. You, me, and Ian." As she spoke, an idea formed in her mind. She would train them both, that much she knew. But perhaps during her training she could also try to find some common ground between the two brothers, reconcile the differences that separated them and kept Ian from feeling he belonged. With a renewed sense of purpose, she hurried into the keep.

With her back turned, Scotia did not see the smile of satisfaction that crossed Griffin's face as he followed her dutifully back into the tigress's den. Nor did she see the satisfied gleam that entered his eyes while he rubbed the hilt of his sword.

Chapter Ten

With Griffin by her side, Scotia strode into her hall with as much enthusiasm as reserve. A different type of training would take place here this morning, with two very different sorts of warriors.

Griffin's arrogant stride faltered at the doorway when his gaze lit upon Ian. "I should have known where the lady led you would not be far away."

Before she could continue into the chamber, Ian's sword flashed as light caught the polished edge. He did not strike Griffin, his action merely a warning. "You decided to stay, Griffin?"

"Aye."

"I cannot like that your presence here leaves the clan vulnerable. But perhaps there is advantage to you training with Scotia, then returning to the clan to train the others."

"And what of you, brother?" Griffin asked, his gaze sharpening.

Scotia waited for Ian's answer with an interest she was incapable of explaining. What *did* Ian plan to do once he left here? He had alluded to training his clan with the skills she taught him, yet some instinct told her that was not the truth. So what did he mean to do with his knowledge?

Ian broke his gaze from hers. "I say we return to the training." His hand tightened around the leather-wrapped hilt of his sword. His grip was personal, deadly, and dangerous.

"Weapons are not part of our training this morning." Tamping down her irritation, Scotia stalked past Ian to take her usual seat at the head table. She would not be party to a feud between these two. They were here to learn. "May we begin?"

"As you wish." Griffin reluctantly moved to join them at the table.

"Warring is about more than wielding a sword. Strategy is a warrior's most effective weapon." She'd spent hours compiling information from her warriors about the Four Horsemen, interspersing it with the strategies her ancestors had used to defeat their enemies since their arrival in Scotland centuries ago.

Scotia reached for one of the scrolls she had removed from her vault earlier. She untied the leather cord and stretched the scroll across the table.

She watched as both men's faces filled with bewilderment at the sweeping lines, mathematical equations, and notes etched across the parchment. On the page lay details about the military strength and weakness of her army, the surrounding territory's effect on movement, and the detailed strengths and weaknesses of the enemy.

"I have never thought of battles or fighting in this manner." An intensity filled Ian's expression she had never seen before.

He approved. The thought brought an odd jumble of pleasure and warmth to her chest.

Griffin leaned forward, his interest now fully engaged. "So how do we best the Four Horsemen?"

Encouraged by Griffin's reaction, she reached for a second scroll and unrolled it over the first. "Science, mathematics, and history."

She watched Ian's reaction as he studied the parchment. What did he think of the details she had added to the notes her mother had made from her experience with these men? The lists were long since they were constantly updated, detailing each warrior's strengths and weaknesses.

"The Green Horseman has great strength at the onset of a battle," Griffin read, "but he tires easily and then favors his left side over his right." His gaze came up to meet hers. If she was not mistaken, satisfaction shone in his eyes before he dipped his head, studying the parchment once more.

"The White Horseman's list is the shortest," Ian said with a frown.

"Aye. The man has very few weaknesses." A chill crept over her at the thought before she could steel herself against it. She would not give in to her fear of that man. The day would soon come when she would confront him. There could be no vulnerability in her when that time came.

"The best way to defeat these men is to separate them. In isolation, they are not as strong."

Griffin leaned back. "Impossible. They always travel together."

"My own warriors are among Scotland's clans, working to do what you say cannot be done." She pulled out a third scroll and unveiled the reports her men had sent to her of their progress.

"I dispatched half my best warriors to fight with the

Bruce in the lowlands. The others are grouped into scouting parties and feed me information about the Four Horsemen."

Understanding filled Ian's face. "That is why the warriors who remain at your castle are either very young or very old." He frowned. "They are not adequate protection for you."

Why did he care so much about her household? "I can protect myself."

"Perhaps. But what about everyone else in your castle?"

His question hit its mark. She knew the castle was no longer as well guarded as it once had been, just as she knew her current army was comprised of young men filled with more enthusiasm than skill, despite her efforts to accelerate their training. "I will find a way to protect them." She turned her attention back to the scroll.

Ian's gaze lingered on her; she could feel it as though it were tangible. She ignored him, continuing with their previous conversation. "My warriors are trying to create doubt and insecurity among the Four Horsemen, trying to get them to break themselves into smaller fighting parties."

"Nay. I need them together if I am to find the White—" He broke off his words, and that same moment intense determination filled his eyes.

"Why do you need them to stay together?" Scotia asked, with growing unease. "You cannot fight all of them alone, at least not fight them and survive." Is that what he planned to do? Was that the destiny he spoke of? How did he expect to do what no one had done before, even with her training?

"A pattern is emerging as to how the Horsemen strike. My men are out there, anticipating the Horsemen's moves with the intent of evacuating the villages before the villains strike. Their frustration and lack of success will force the Horsemen to separate."

"If the Four Horsemen separate, how will the clans know where they will strike next?"

"We will not know for certain. But the risk of not knowing their exact locations is the only way to defeat them once and for all."

"It is too dangerous for the clans," Ian said, his voice hard.

"All battles have risks," Scotia said, hiding the hurt his dismissal caused. She snapped up the top scroll, rolled it with overly precise movements, then returned it to the basket. "Some will die before we finally succeed. It is the inevitable price of war." She reached for the second scroll.

Ian covered her hand with his own. "I did not mean to sound so critical," he said, his voice softer now. "It is just that our people have already suffered so much at the hands of these men."

Irritated by his move to pacify her, she pulled her fingers away. "I feel the same, but that does not change what must be done."

"Enough of this talk." Griffin stood. "If we are to defeat the Horsemen, we must do it with swords. When do we battle?"

Scotia was glad of Griffin's impatience this time. She, too, felt the sudden need to wield her sword. Ian once again did not agree with her methods. The first time, when he attacked her training techniques, he had been right about how arcane her methods were. But this time he was wrong. Dead wrong. Strategy was her strength. And she refused to back down.

Scotia secured the last scroll, then stood. "We battle now." Without waiting for her students to follow, she headed out of the great hall and down the long corridor to her training chamber.

"You first, Griffin." Inside the empty room, she waited for Griffin to ready himself before she drew her sword. "Let us see if you can defend yourself."

Ian wanted to protest. He would welcome the physical challenge of a battle with her right now. But the dark look that suddenly shadowed Scotia's features changed his mind. Anger burned her cheeks. If the two of them battled now, she would likely spear him through the heart. But would Griffin fare any better?

Yet after Griffin's challenge to Scotia last night, perhaps a bit of her anger would put his brother in his place. Ian knew from experience where Griffin would end up— at the base of Scotia's feet.

Ian stood off to the side, studying the two warriors. His brother clutched his heavy claymore, a feral gleam in his eyes. It was a look Ian was familiar with, a look that had often brought nothing but trouble between the two of them.

In preparation for the sparring, Scotia held her lighter broadsword in one hand before her. Her other hand stretched behind her as a counterbalance. She appeared composed now, no longer allowing their previous disagreement to affect her. It was almost inhuman the way she shielded her emotions from others. But he knew her to be all too human, indeed.

The battle began as Griffin lunged forward. His movements were hard, short, aggressive. Scotia avoided his blows with quick and fluid movements. She made fighting appear so simple. Like a mere dance, but with a lethal partner.

High color filled her cheeks as she wove her way about her enemy. Griffin did not stand a chance against her.

Four passes later, Griffin lay on the floor. With one booted foot on his chest, Scotia held him captive, as did her sword at his neck. Ian tried to suppress a smile at the memory of his and Scotia's first battle. It had taken her six passes to bring him down.

"You cheated," Griffin exclaimed, his face contorted in rage. A growl came from deep within his throat as he hooked Scotia's calf with his hand and sent her flying backward.

"Nay," Ian objected, but before he could make a move to defend her, Scotia absorbed the blow, springing to her feet, her sword in hand.

Griffin tried to stand, but she caught his leg with her heel and sent him to the floor once more.

"A reckless maneuver when my weapon was against your throat." Scotia allowed her blade to rest against his skin.

Griffin's eyes hardened and Ian thought about intervening, but somehow he knew she would do nothing to seriously injure his brother despite his ill behavior.

"Let us try that again, shall we?" She drew her sword away from Griffin's neck, then resumed her fighting stance. "This time you will follow the rules of engagement."

Griffin roared like an enraged bull as he gained his feet, launching himself at Scotia, his sword clutched in his outstretched hands.

With an almost effortless grace, she captured his right wrist with the hilt of her sword and snapped his weapon free.

Griffin bellowed in pain and thrust his left fist toward her face. Again, she intercepted the punch with her sword hand and delivered a forceful blow to his jaw with the other. Griffin hung there a moment, his eyes rolling, his body shuddering with the stunning effect of the blow until he crumpled slowly into a dazed heap on the floor.

Chapter Eleven

Ian moved to his brother's side, relieved for Griffin's sake that the lesson had been short. Scotia had been kind to him, whereas she could have been harsh in return for his dishonorable behavior. Ian had seen Griffin in many battles, and never before had he fought with such vehemence.

When Griffin opened his eyes, Ian helped him sit up. "There are things Scotia can teach you about fighting if you would give her a chance."

Griffin batted his dark hair out of his eyes, revealing a gaze that reflected both humiliation and frustration. "Leave me alone. That woman has nothing to teach me." The lack of violence in his expression lessened Ian's own anger. His brother might be hotheaded, but at least he was not foolhardy. Perhaps now Griffin would go home and resume his obligations to the clan.

Scotia moved to Griffin's side and handed him his sword. Her face was blank, devoid of anger or the disappointment Ian had expected to see. "You are right. I do not have anything to teach you if you cannot learn to channel your anger. You have skill, Griffin, if you would only learn to use it as an asset and not turn it as a weapon against yourself." A slight catch in her voice told Ian she was not as impervious to Griffin's behavior as she appeared.

On unsteady legs, Griffin stood. "My anger has served me well in the past."

"It did not help save Malcolm," Ian interrupted, unable to still his irritation. Griffin froze, but Ian continued. "I, like you, did not truly believe in Scotia's ability to teach me when I arrived, but I soon learned I was wrong. She is the best warrior I have ever seen."

From the corner of his eyes Ian glanced at Scotia. Her expression was that of faint surprise, as though she had not expected him to pay her the compliment. That he had done something she had not expected pleased him.

A blaze of defiance burned in Griffin's eyes. "Less than a week in her presence and she has tamed you into a kitten. How shameful you are to your Highland heritage, brother. That is, if you are a Highlander at all."

Ian held a flare of anger in check. "You dare to challenge my heritage when you have abandoned your own?"

"What?" A dark scowl shadowed Griffin's features.

"You left our clan alone, exposed to attack, to follow me here. Make that dereliction of your duty worthwhile. Open yourself to what Scotia can teach you."

Ian stole a glance at Scotia, where she stood behind Griffin. Her expression remained shuttered. He could only assume it was her anger she hid.

Scotia sheathed her weapon. "It is your choice to train or not, Griffin. I shall never force a person to accept what I freely offer to all my countrymen. If you wish to leave, do so with my blessing. If you chose to stay, it will be on my terms. Until you accept those terms, you are not welcome in this chamber, for it is only a place where I train true warriors." Her face darkened as she moved in front of Griffin. "Now leave so Ian and I may continue his training."

Griffin said nothing, but Ian saw the tightening around his lips, the slight clenching of his hands at his sides. From years of watching and measuring Griffin's reactions, Ian knew his brother was not ready to concede. If anything, Scotia's dismissal would only make him more determined. The question was what it would make him more determined to do—train as he should or see that Scotia was defeated?

"I shall leave this room, but not the castle," Griffin said. "You will not be rid of me that easily."

Nay, nothing had ever been easy where Griffin was concerned. Ian just hoped the hot-tempered fool would come to his senses before he got himself killed.

Silence hovered between them until Griffin left. When they were alone, Scotia crossed the room until she stood before the training cross. "You and I will continue our training here." Her voice was soft and her actions determined as she climbed between the ropes to the center of the cross.

Ian frowned at her response as he followed her inside. She wanted to pretend nothing had just happened. "I will talk to Griffin."

"No need," she said without looking up.

"He does have manners sometimes," he said in his brother's defense.

Her shoulders dipped ever so slightly when she paused in the center of the cross. She placed her sword on the ground below the ropes. "Griffin's opinion of me will either shift or it won't. But the change must come from within him. You cannot do the work for him." She brought her gaze to his, and he saw something different in

93

her eyes this time. Instead of the usual stoic determination, he saw hurt.

"Scotia," he said, not really knowing how to make things right between them. He set his sword down beside hers, then reached for her hands.

A shudder passed through her as he laced their fingers together, but she did not pull away. Beneath her gauntlets, he could feel the warmth and strength of her hands. "We must continue your training," she said.

"Scotia—"

"Nay, Ian. No more talk." She swallowed hard, and he could see a battle of emotions cross her face—tenderness, fear, desire, pride.

"All right," Ian conceded, yet he did not release her fingers when she tried to tug them out of his grip.

After a moment's hesitation, she said, "Move with me." She would train him even now. Scotia swayed first left, then right, winding her body through the different levels of ropes. Ian followed, focusing more on the feel of her hands tightening and relaxing around his own than on her movements. They stepped over a low rope, then ducked beneath a higher rope, synchronizing their movements through the web.

A flush of pink stained her cheeks, and her breath came in ragged gasps much like his own. Her steps grew stronger, and the turmoil in her eyes shifted to satisfaction with a hint of something more.

As her confidence grew, so did her gaze. Beneath the veil of her lashes she studied his chest, his arms, his thighs, and now, his lips. When they dipped beneath another rope the outside of his thigh brushed against the leather encasing hers. Despite the protection, she gasped at the contact.

His body tightened, thickened at the brief touch. The next thing he knew, they were falling. She had tripped over the rope. He shifted his weight, taking the impact of the fall on his back and shoulders as he rolled her on top of him. Despite her armor, she felt light and pliant against his chest.

Her green eyes widened, first filled with surprise, then horror. "That has never happened to me before," she breathed.

"Nay." He smiled at her. "Most warriors find staying on their feet leads to better combat."

"My apologies." She tried to pull away.

Ian held her tight, not wanting to break the moment.

At the contact, warmth flooded him. Then heat, fiery heat. She was soft and hard all at the same time. A heady combination. Her armor thrust against his chest, but he could imagine the soft rise of her breasts beneath. Her weight straddled his leg. Her well-toned thighs brushed against the most male part of him.

She shifted her body, no doubt meaning to pull away. Instead she only brought herself into full contact with his growing arousal. Heat shimmered between them, causing his muscles to clench and flex. This woman stirred his senses, regardless of his efforts to keep his distance. Her touch, her scent, her words, all had the power to make him forget his own goals and think of nothing but holding her in his arms.

"We should continue." Her voice was raw and as jagged as his own breathing.

Ian drew her up against his chest. "Continue what?" The rapid beat of her heart matched his own. He breathed in the scent of soft spring heather and nearly groaned. Why did she have to smell so good? Was it not

GERRI RUSSELL

enough that every other aspect of her person intrigued him? Could she not have some flaw, some fault that would turn him away from what he wanted now?

"The training," she whispered, her gaze once again on his lips.

"Is progressing well," he said, even though his thoughts turned toward other things. Pleasure . . . possession . . . passion. He slid his hands up her leather-covered arms, the coolness strangely seductive against the heated flesh of his palms.

Scotia shivered, but did not pull away as his mouth met hers.

He kissed her, and this time his kiss was far from chaste. Nay, he kissed her deeply, thoroughly, as though searching for the answers of his unexplainable attraction. But instead of answers he only found more questions. Why now? Why did he have to meet this woman right now, when his life was filled with nothing but revenge and necessity? Knowing he should stop, but unable to wrench himself away, he parted her lips, gently persuading her to open herself to him.

Her response was as desperate as his own. She reached up to grasp his shoulders. Slowly, hesitantly, she caressed his shoulders, then his back, her touch explorative as her lips softened beneath his. He deepened the kiss, demanding more from her in a world that had suddenly become both dark and sensual.

Ian pulled her tight against him, until her body fit into the hardness of his thighs, thighs she meant to make stronger, more flexible with her training exercises. Saints! He would train with her every day if these reckless sensations were the way to improvement.

What was he thinking? He could not stay and train with her forever. Ian dragged his mouth from hers and shifted her head down against the frantic hammering of his heart. "I did not mean to do that," he breathed against the softness of her hair.

She twisted out of his embrace, then stood. "Neither did I." She touched her lips with the back of her gauntlet-covered hand.

"Sometimes the forces of nature are stronger than even we are ourselves." He got to his feet and stepped over a low rope, placing a physical barrier between them.

"Forces of nature?" She wrapped her hands around her middle and stared at him with a mixture of confusion and hurt. "Did Maisie put you up to this?" she asked in a shaky, breathless voice.

Ian frowned, confused by her reaction. "What does Maisie have to do with it?"

She closed her eyes, as if doing so would help her gather her senses. When she opened them again, her vision was clear and steady. "Since I would not agree to her plans of bearing a child as I am supposed to, has she asked you to seduce me into it instead?"

"A child?"

"A daughter. I must have a daughter." She dropped her gaze to the floor. "Damn her," Scotia whispered, her voice raw. "It is my choice to make."

Ian stepped over the rope and took her icy hands in his. This time she shook off his touch.

"Look at me," Ian demanded. He waited until she brought her gaze to his. "Maisie has said nothing to me about your need for a child. I kissed you because I wanted to. There was no other reason."

The uncertainty in her eyes cleared. "Truly?"

He brought his gaze back to her lips and a familiar hunger crept over him. "Even though I know I should not, I want to kiss you again."

"Nay." She moved further away. "That would not be wise."

"Neither is playing with fire," Ian admitted. "But I am finding it harder and harder to resist the flames of temptation."

She gasped, but did not answer him with words. Her actions said it all when she turned and ran from the room.

The warrior had fled the battle.

The question was, did he want to pursue?

Chapter Twelve

Scotia sank to her knees in front of the unadorned iron cross that stood at the far end of the castle's chapel. In this room she felt safe. For only a fool or the most determined of warriors would seek her out in the sanctity of a holy place.

She drew in a breath of the cool, incense laden air, allowing it to seep inside her and calm the turmoil that one kiss from Ian had stirred inside her. Alone in her sanctuary, she let her hand slide from the hilt of her sword and pressed her tingling lips together, trying to blot out the memory of his kiss.

When the action failed to bring the calm she longed for, she focused on the peaceful atmosphere of the chamber instead. The chapel seemed overly quiet without Father Colin's melodic humming. She missed him, as she had for the last five years when she had sent the old priest off to aid the oppressed and ailing among her people. Their need for his counsel far outweighed her own. Although at times like today, when her soul felt heavy and confused, she longed for his steadfast advice.

Even in his absence, she knew Father Colin would warn her to tread cautiously around Ian, to avoid the unsettling longings he brought out in her. Her attention, her duty remained on the Stone—the reason for her existence.

And the reason to bear a child, Maisie's voice echoed.

Heat flooded Scotia's cheeks. She put her chilled hands against her face, dampening the uncharacteristic response of her body. This reasoning was getting her nowhere. She knew her obligation to bear a child just as intimately as she knew her reservations. How would she ever reconcile such a division within herself? Was it even possible?

At least until Ian's training was complete, he would stay at Glencarron Castle. That would give her the time she needed to decide what she should do. She had time to weigh her duty against her own resistance.

Scotia drew a heavy breath and studied the fading twilight as it spilled through the chapel's only window. It mixed with the candlelight to send shadows flickering along the handworked stone of the floor. In the peace of the moment, she rolled her injured shoulder forward and back. If only the slow, burning ache would ease, she could accelerate Ian's training.

Weariness invaded her limbs. Is that what she truly wanted, to assist him in leaving her sooner? She sighed, the sound as torn as it felt. And behind that sound came another, yet not from herself. The shadows of the room shifted. Movement. There to her right. Scotia tensed and reached for her weapon. Sword drawn, she turned in a fluid motion that fractured the tranquility of the room.

"Hold," came Ian's voice from the shadows. He took a step forward and she saw him then, standing in the aisle of the chapel. "Forgive the intrusion, but I could not leave things as they were between us."

The memory of his mouth pressed against her own played across her mind. "There is nothing between us." In a brisk motion, she sheathed her weapon. "What do you want?"

He smiled. "Straight to the point." His voice was warm and low. "That's fair. I will try to be as accommodating." In the openness of the room, his voice seemed to reverberate all around her, playful, but with a purpose.

"I am tired, Ian. I beg thee, make your intentions known."

His humor vanished and raw impatience flared in his cool, dark eyes. "Release me from my training."

The air around her became heavy and still. "You wish to go?" There was no reason to ask the question. She could see the answer in his eyes.

"This day."

Numbness shimmered across her flesh. She braced herself against the emptiness that followed. "I hold no power over you, Ian. You may leave if you wish."

"It is not as simple as that." As he came forward, his jaw tightened. "I request your release from this obligation."

"So it is still an obligation to you." She tried to hide the hurt in her voice, but failed.

He brought his hand to her cheek. She held her breath, willing him to stop. He did not. He brushed his thumb along her jaw in a slow, gentle caress. "One of your scouting parties has just returned. They carry information that the Four Horsemen attacked another village. Their violence is growing, and I must stop them." With exquisite tenderness he trailed his thumb down the line of her neck. "I take no pleasure in abandoning my duty. But I must go. Now. Before I forget what purpose drives the course of my life."

"I am prepared to send more of my warriors to fight the battles. It is what they've trained for."

"Which will leave you with few men to guard your own walls."

"I know what I am doing, Ian." Scotia pulled away from his touch, angry now, and grateful to feel something other than the confusion his nearness brought. "And you are avoiding the real issue here. Why do you want to leave? What is so important that it outweighs adequate training and preparation?"

"What more could you teach me?" He towered over her, his large body blocking the light from the window beyond. Twilight dappled his broad shoulders and sent flickers of light dancing through the blond streaks of his hair. In the odd light she could barely make out his expression, but his eyes searched hers clearly enough. Determination stared back at her.

She understood his need for escape. No warrior enjoyed being kept from battle, including herself. She vanquished the thought as quickly as it came upon her. Her duty to protect the Stone kept her behind the castle walls. For her, there was no other option.

"Ian, do you trust me?" The words tumbled out of their own volition.

"Aye." His gaze softened, became sincere. His admission filled her with gratification. A warrior did not take trust lightly; its presence in battle could mean the difference between life and death.

Her throat tightened. For an instant she considered granting his request. But the fact remained—he was not ready. Sending him off now could do more harm to him and others than good. "Then trust me when I say you are not ready to leave. There is more to learn." She was tempted to stop there, not to hit him where she knew it would hurt. Yet she continued in spite of herself. "You gave me your word that you would stay until your training was complete. Do not go back on your duty, your honor, now."

A low growl came from his throat. "You challenge my honor?" Seconds clicked by and silence hovered between them. "I know my duty," he said finally. The intensity in his eyes darkened. "I will stay."

He had spoken the words she wanted to hear, but his eyes had lost their warmth. For honor he would stay until she released him, though he had no desire to do so. The realization stung.

She tried to find her voice, to frame the words she needed to say. But how could words express what she had just this moment discovered?

She needed him there.

Without him, she would once again be alone. The sudden understanding made her throat tighten further. She had never regretted isolating herself in the castle, making warriors who wanted training come to her as her mother and grandmother had before her.

Somehow, over the years, she had forgotten what it felt like to have companionship. It was out of necessity that the memory had slipped away, she was sure now; the twist in her gut told her so.

Scotia drew herself up, biting back the emptiness that threatened to consume her. She had to release him. She had to let him go.

"Ian, I . . . I . . ." She tried to force the words.

"I shall see you at supper." He cut her off with his brusque tone. Something in his expression shifted, and for a moment she thought she saw a flare of understanding in his eyes, but before she could be certain, he turned and left the room.

Scotia swallowed hard, forcing back the sudden heaviness in her throat. He must have known what she tried so desperately to say. Yet he had given her a reprieve. She should be happy.

A pang of remorse stirred within her. If this was what happiness felt like, she would be better off without it.

If she could not find the words a while ago, she would find them now. Scotia cast a wary glance at the man beside her at the head table in the great hall. Voices hummed around her, but she heard not a word. All her thoughts centered on Ian.

She had made a terrible mistake. Never had she put her own needs before others. Now was not the time to start. If Ian wanted to leave, she would release him. *I need no one,* she reminded herself. *Relying on others makes a person weak and vulnerable. Weakness can get a warrior killed.* The words of her mother's training played over and over in her mind, but they did nothing to ease the emptiness that had invaded her soul.

Scotia looked down at her untouched trencher. She had no stomach for food. She pushed her meal away and turned to the man beside her, feeling uncharacteristic nervousness creep upon her. "Ian." Scotia knotted her hands, then pressed them flat against the table instead. The time had come to say good-bye. Her gaze locked with his. "I . . . made a mistake."

A glimmer of hope sparked in the depths of his dark eyes. "About what?"

"I release y—"

"Mistress!" The doors of the great hall flew open, hitting the walls with a bang that echoed throughout the chamber, stilling the voices inside.

As she had been born and trained to do, Scotia reached for her sword, then checked her movements. The interruption came from one of her guards, not a challenger. She wished the guard had chosen a better moment to interrupt, but realized he would not have burst in unless the matter was urgent.

The guard halted before her, his breathing ragged, his youthful cheeks flushed. "There is something you must see at the front gate."

Scotia released the hilt of her sword and pushed away from the table. "What is it, Keddy?"

The young man shook his head. "You need to see this for yourself," he gasped.

A flicker of apprehension coursed through her. Scotia stood, but she was not alone. Ian's chair scraped against the floor as he abandoned his own meal. "I shall come with you." He drew his sword as he tossed a look at his brother in the chair next to him. "Are you coming?"

Scotia waited while Griffin sank his teeth into a mouthful of kippers. "Nay," he said around the food in his mouth. "You and the goddess of warriors can handle things on your own."

"Suit yourself," Ian said, his displeasure obvious in the clipped tone of his voice.

Scotia was hurrying out of the hall when Ian unexpectedly took her hand. She tried to keep her mind fixed on whatever trouble awaited her at the gates and not on the comforting sensations of Ian's hand wrapped around her own. His nearness, his awareness of her should have made her feel weak, perhaps even vulnerable. Instead she felt strangely safe.

It had been so long since she had felt at ease in the presence of another warrior that it was all she could do to let him lead her out of the hall and into the courtyard beyond. Outside, the evening torches had been lit, casting a pale yellow glow across the outer bailey as they approached the gate.

Her guard's eyes widened when his gaze lit upon their joined hands. Flustered by the reaction, Scotia pulled out of Ian's grip.

"Keddy, what did you wish me to see . . . ?" Her words trailed off as the young man held his torch toward the gate.

Chapter Thirteen

In the pale torchlight Scotia could just make out the image of a person—a small person—standing in front of the iron portcullis. A child. "Open the gate."

The portcullis had never opened so slowly. Clenching her fists at her side, she waited. Finally the barrier lifted enough to reveal a forlorn looking girl with a half-burned yellow skirt, a dirty face, and hair streaked with blood. She stood deathly still as the sound of grinding chains and creaking wood filled the night air. Scotia turned to the young guard. "Where did she come from?"

Keddy shrugged. "After the sun set, she was just there."

Ian ducked beneath the half risen gate. Holding a torch aloft, he scanned the approach to the gate. "No one came near the castle this eve?"

"Nay," Keddy replied, clearly baffled by the child's appearance. "We have men on each watch, and no one saw a thing."

The grinding of the gate finally stopped, but the little girl remained where she was, saying nothing. A mournful look darkened her eyes, made old before their time.

How could a child end up here? At her gate? Had her own men been so distracted that they had missed the young girl's approach? Or was she the one to blame? Had she shifted so much of her attention to Ian that she'd neglected the safety of her own household?

Regardless of how the child had slipped past her guards, they needed information. Scotia took a hesitant step forward, approaching the little girl, stopping a sword's length from her. "Where did you come from?" Scotia asked, feeling more like she was interrogating a prisoner than speaking to a frightened child.

The girl remained silent, and tears pooled in her eyes.

"What is your name?"

No answer.

Frustrated by the lack of response, Scotia turned to Ian. "Why will she not talk?"

He merely raised a brow as he brushed past Scotia to kneel before the child. "Much has happened to you lately." Ian reached up to brush a ringlet coated in dried blood from the side of the child's face, tucking it behind her ear.

The child flinched from his touch. Ian continued despite her reaction, caressing the side of her face with a gentle touch until her tears stopped and the girl nodded. An odd tenderness filled Scotia's chest at Ian's treatment of the little girl.

"What is your name, sweeting?" Ian offered her an encouraging smile, making Scotia cringe at how forcefully she had spoken. She had demanded where Ian coaxed.

"Lizbet," the girl whispered, and tears once again filled her eyes.

"Lizbet, I am pleased to meet you. I am Ian." He urged her forward, toward his chest with a gentle hand on her back.

108

Icy fingers gripped Scotia's soul as her half formed suspicions coalesced. She lacked even the most basic of talents when it came to compassion and sympathy. She would never make a decent mother—especially since those traits did not come to her naturally. And there was nothing natural about her reaction to children.

Ian continued to stroke the girl's hair and coo to her softly, until she all but melted in his arms in a puddle of tears and body-wracking sobs.

Scotia flinched at the sound, not from fear but from the wrenching sadness the child now expressed. Many times she had felt like crying in her youth, only to be silenced by her mother. What would it be like to let go like that, to give oneself over to the turmoil inside? Scotia looked away from the girl's tear-stained cheeks, unsettled by her emotional release. With a trembling hand, Scotia tugged at the edge of her armor. She could never be so free with her pain. Her mother had hammered that sentiment into her head during her youth. "What has happened to her?" Scotia asked through a sudden thickness that invaded her throat.

Ian did not answer. But as he gazed up, sympathy and understanding shone in his eyes. "*Shh* now, sweeting. Nothing can harm you while Ian is here."

He continued to talk, his voice low and soothing. When her crying slowed, he lifted her in his arms. "Let us take her inside. She has been through enough tonight. She will tell us what has happened when she's ready. For now, she needs a meal and a warm bed near the fire."

A grating sound filled the air once again as the gate came down. Scotia looked at Ian with the child in his arms, and a strange feeling fluttered in her stomach. Lizbet looked so at ease curled against Ian's body. It was how Scotia had felt the morning he had kissed her on the

GERRI RUSSELL

parapets. Welcomed, cherished, comfortable. Oh, but to be that child.

It looked as though little Lizbet had been in some sort of battle. Or was her presence here a ploy orchestrated by a challenger to catch her off guard? A worse thought occurred to Scotia: Did the man she feared most have a hand in the girl's sudden appearance?

"Keddy," Scotia called to the guard. "Gather a scouting patrol of at least ten men. I want information. Where did the girl come from? Are her parents nearby?"

Keddy straightened and a solemn yet proud expression crossed his youthful features. "We shall find the answers ye seek, mistress." He offered her a terse bow, then raced toward the guard tower, no doubt eager to perform his first adult duty within her charge.

Scotia turned back to Ian and the child. "Bring her in, and then we will press her for answers. We must know if the Four . . ."

She broke off, not wanting to speak out loud the worst of her fears. Ian nodded, his eyes reflecting the dread she could not utter as they headed inside. Only one other group could render this type of trauma to the Scots besides the armies led by Edward II.

With trembling fingers, Scotia grabbed a straw pallet from a stack near the wall, then arranged it before the hearth. The warmth of the flames cast out a gentle greeting. Ian laid the child down with her feet closest to the flames, then wrapped a blanket about her small, beaten body. He cradled her head in his lap. He looked so natural, like he had done this same sort of thing a hundred times before.

As if reading her thoughts, Ian looked up and offered her a half smile. "My foster mother was the medicine woman in the clan. I used to visit the sick with her. It was always my job to comfort the patient while she mixed her remedies. The clan did not judge me at those times." His smile slipped, and he averted his gaze, but not before Scotia saw shadows enter his eyes.

She wanted to say something, anything to wipe the shadows away, but Maisie appeared, clutching a wooden bowl that usually held one of her curatives. She offered the bowl to Scotia. "You will need this to treat her."

"Nay." Scotia waved the bowl away. "I shall not let you drug her. We need answers before she can sleep."

A gentle smile came to Maisie's lips. "This is merely water for cleanin' the child, Scotia."

"Oh." Scotia sat back on her heels, chagrined by her reaction to something any mother would want to provide a child, especially one in distress. It was a blatant reminder of what a poor mother she would make.

Maisie offered Scotia the bowl and linen again.

Scotia shook her head, keeping her hands well away from the objects. "You had best cleanse her. I do not wish to harm her further."

"Children are far more durable than you think," Maisie chided as she set about gently removing the blood and dirt from the child's face. Maisie wiped the deep cut, and the girl winced.

"There now, sweeting. You are safe with us," Ian soothed while Maisie worked.

Lizbet's gaze moved from Maisie and Ian to Scotia. "Make the bad men go away," she said in a voice thick with fear. "Mama tried, but she was not strong like you."

Ian and Scotia shared a wary glance across the child's makeshift bed. "What kind of bad men?" Ian asked.

Lizbet closed her eyes and started to tremble. "A big man on a white horse."

The king and his armies Scotia did not fear. The current English king had yet to prove himself as powerful a leader as his father before him. Nay, there was another force of destruction she feared above all others: the Four Horsemen. Her blood ran cold at the thought.

"Was he alone?" Scotia prompted as she stroked the rounded pink cheek closest to her. When tears spilled from Lizbet's eyes, Scotia snatched her hand back, fearing she had hurt the child.

"I only saw . . . the big man and the fire," she whispered. "He killed Mama . . . with an arrow."

A cry of sorrow echoed deep within Scotia as she remembered that image from her own past. Her heartbeat thundered in her ears, mimicking the sound of horses approaching the castle.

She had been older than Lizbet during her own encounter with the Four Horsemen, but the fear had been the same. A gust of wind had swirled through the great hall as the door slammed against the wall, one more sound in a monotonous litany heard since the siege on the castle began that morning. The cry of war tore through the open space, raising the gooseflesh on Scotia's arms. A formless shape emerged through the doorway, a crossbow raised to strike. It was then that she realized this sound had stood apart from the rest. So near, so threatening.

Her body began to quake as the shape took the form of a man, his white cape billowing around his shoulders. He flashed her an eerie smile, one that made him look almost familiar. He moved closer.

Scotia knew she should run, yet her feet would not obey. He moved closer, then closer still. Recognition flared in her memory. She had not seen him before, but she knew who he was, a specter of death who had come to kill.

The air in the room seemed to press in around her, warning her to flee. With his free hand, the man reached out to grab her. Her feet shuffled backward and, thankfully, he grabbed only air. She continued backward, out of his grasp.

His smile dissolved as his face twisted in rage. A roar that seemed to come from the depths of hell itself filled the chamber. The sound went on and on, sending the other occupants in the hall fleeing for their lives.

He lifted his bow again and took aim at her. Only in the face of death did her feet find flight. She spun around just in time to feel the bite of an arrow in her back as she ran toward Maisie and Burke. They stood at the edge of the shadows, but she could see them clearly. As her heartbeat drowned out all else, they coaxed her to them, anxiety and fear written on their usually serene faces. Scotia thrust herself into the protection of Maisie's bosom before she drew a rasping breath around the pain exploding in her back and dared to look behind her.

Her tormentor had turned away, toward more worthy prey. Scotia tightened her grip on Maisie's arm, and cried out, screaming in sharp pain like a child who has just put her hand on a kettle from the fire.

"Mother!" she screamed as an arrow pierced her mother's armor. "Mother!" she shrieked, struggling within the arms that held her like a vise. Before she could break free Maisie pulled her away, into the depths of the castle.

Mother. The word echoed through her head as the memory faded. Scotia stared at the young child before her, trembling with the same terror that had changed her life so many years ago.

The Four Horsemen.

The thought of the mounted warriors sent icy fear to her core. Scotia shot to her feet and bolted from the hall, the ghosts of the past chasing at her heels. Only one thing would keep the memories and her growing panic at bay.

As she ran blindly from the hall, down the long corridor, her footsteps echoed the question burning in her mind. Could she, one woman alone, be enough to right the wrongs the Four Horsemen had inflicted on her and her country since her mother's death? When she was younger, she had thought so. But that was when her life, her beliefs, her experiences were all black and white, like the fairy stories where good always prevailed over evil. But in the last few years doubts had replaced her confidence, tarnishing her hopes and dreams.

And without hope, without dreams, what else was there to provide strength to her spirit?

Training, discipline, hard work, her thoughts answered back. Those actions had always brought her comfort when she had foundered. They would help her now.

At the doorway of her training chamber, Scotia paused to bow her head, waiting for silence to fill her mind as it always did when she entered this room. It was how her mother trained her to approach her fighting—with a clear mind.

This evening, that sense of solitude eluded her. The unsettling memories of her mother's death whirled through her thoughts. Scotia raised her eyes and looked at the wall of weapons before her, her gaze coming to rest on her mother's sword. The weapon was all that remained of the once great warrior, except for the memories held in the recesses of her daughter's mind.

With great difficulty, Scotia grasped her trembling hands together and struggled to clear her thoughts. Her mother would disapprove of any sort of emotion while in the training chamber. Scotia drew in a slow, deep breath until she felt the tension in her shoulders ease and her inner turmoil fade.

Once more in control of herself, she entered the room, making an effort to leave the outside world and all her uncertainty behind.

Silver shafts of moonlight spilled across the open floor. She wrapped herself in the warmth as she unfastened her belt and placed her sword at her feet, within reach if she had need of it. For now, her training would be only for her—a reminder of her beginnings and of her connection to her past.

She closed her eyes and allowed the silence of the chamber to flow around her. Cool evening air bathed her skin as she began to stretch, muscle by muscle, isolating each one, from her feet to her neck, preparing for the rite she would push herself to endure.

As her body began to relax and her breathing focused her mind, she started to move, sending her body through a ritual of precise movements until all thoughts disappeared and only her body and breathing remained.

Forget your fears. The mantra began, matching the beat of her heart. Over and over the words played through her mind until the shadows receded and light took its place. The future stretched before her, new, unwritten, a void filled with hope once again.

As the light of the moon shifted to overhead, Scotia finally sank to her knees before her sword, her body bathed in sweat, too exhausted to push herself further. Her muscles burned, and she welcomed the pain. It gave her focus and silenced her fears.

In this chamber, she had no doubts about who she was. Her purpose seemed clear. Here, she felt the presence of all the Scotias who had come before her. Their strength and wisdom would protect her, help her remember her purpose.

"I defend Scotland by training other warriors," she whispered, reminding herself of her goal. "I must defend the Stone." She pulled her shoulders back. "I must have a successor." The last words escaped her before she could stop them. Those were the words she had learned, but they were words she could not embrace for herself. Not until her battle with the Four Horsemen was through. The image of Ian crept inside her mind. He held her close, his arms warm and sheltering. With him she felt safe, cared for, even . . .

She refused to let the sentiment form. She and Ian had no future together, temporary or otherwise. The sooner she accepted that, the better off she would be. When she finished here, she would find Ian and continue the conversation her guard had interrupted earlier.

By tomorrow he would be gone. With the resolution came a bittersweet ache that opened the deepest, darkest wounds inside her. Whether she liked it or not, Ian's presence in her life, however short, would forever leave a footprint across her soul.

But even wounded warriors went on, and somehow she would find a way to do just that. Scotia forced her breathing into a slow, even rhythm. She had to think about her challengers, her duty, the battle ahead. When the Four Horsemen came for her, she would be ready. She placed the palms of her hands on the flat blade of her sword, finding further comfort in the coolness of the metal.

Her mother's past mistakes would not be her own. She would make certain of it.

Chapter Fourteen

Outside the training chamber, Ian leaned against the open doorway, unwilling and unable to intrude as Scotia wove her lean and muscular body through the steps of a primal dance. There was no doubt she was a woman of action, a warrior, who had lived by the strength of her body, her wit, and her sword.

She was a woman who had admitted to making a mistake.

A woman. Not a mythic being. Not some supernatural entity. A woman of flesh who could live *and die* by the sword.

Suddenly uneasy, Ian pushed away from the door. He had always courted death, taunted it even, wishing to find some sort of release from his failings within its grasp. No one but Abbus would miss him if he were gone.

But if Scotia died, an entire country would mourn her loss.

He narrowed his gaze upon her as she continued her punishing routine. How could he have possibly thought the Warrior Trainer was only a legend? While growing up in the clan he had heard stories of her, just as he'd heard stories of other Scots throughout history. But he had assumed she had died, along with all the other historical figures. At least that's what the storytellers had wanted him to believe.

How had she, a living legend, faded from the memory of her people for the last twelve years? And more importantly, why?

Ian studied the legend before him. Her concentration focused on her movements, on the inhuman physical endurance she forced herself to attain. With all her efforts elsewhere, her guard had dropped, revealing a haunted desperation in her eyes. He also noted the determined set of her chin and the violence in her swordless thrusts.

The violence of her thrusts. The need for revenge.

The realization shocked him. It was revenge that drove her to this room. Revenge against the Four Horsemen? Her behavior had certainly changed abruptly after Lizbet's revelation.

Along with the heated emotion, he also saw vulnerability, hurt, and betrayal. He recognized the emotions, understood them, because he walked the same nightmare, shared the same double-edged sword of fear and fearlessness.

Ian closed his eyes, bracing himself against the onslaught of compassion that swept over him. He did not want to care about this woman. He did not want any kind of connection to her at all. He had followed her to this room to finish the conversation they had begun earlier. Freedom from his training and her castle was all he sought.

Ian opened his eyes, regarding Scotia with new insight. He wanted to leave, needed to forward his own goals. So why did he suddenly long to stay?

"MacKinnon."

His gaze moved to hers. Green eyes filled first with uncertainty that faded to a soft, pleased glow.

"I did not mean to disturb you." Ian attempted a smile, but failed. "I shall leave you alone."

"Nay." She picked up her sword, then stood, the movement exuding strength and vibrancy despite the fatigue she must feel. "I am done here."

"Battling demons?" He remained at the doorway, the distance between them a sudden buffer of safety.

The pleasure on her face slipped as she refastened her belt and sword. She hesitated only a moment before bringing her gaze back to his. Her open vulnerability brought mauve smudges to the smooth skin beneath her eyes. "How did you know?"

She had not tried to lie or cover up her feelings. Instead, she had confessed her inner thoughts to him. This brave, strong, independent female had dropped her armor, however temporarily, exposing herself. He knew he should turn and walk away. Instead he stepped into the room, drawn to the vulnerability she laid bare before him, unable to resist its lure.

"Experience." Ian approached her cautiously, not wanting to trigger her defenses. "From experience I also know nothing will shed those demons until the Horsemen are dead."

A lost, almost tortured expression passed through her eyes. "I shall challenge them when the time is right."

"You will challenge them alone?"

She hesitated, a slight check no longer than a heartbeat, before she drew herself up, pulling that wall of reserve about herself once more. "With my army."

"Of inexperienced fighters," he added. "How will you fight all four of the Horsemen, plus their army, without other strong warriors to aid you?"

Her gaze moved beyond him to the weapons that lined the walls of her chamber and he could only assume the direction of her thoughts.

"You only have two hands, Scotia. Even with all those weapons, you can only fight with one or two of them at a time."

"What would you have me do, turn and run? I did that once when I was a child. I shall not do it again." Pain darkened her eyes. "But if my plan to separate the Horsemen succeeds, I shall take them on one at a time."

"You are not a one-woman army. Aye, you are a great fighter. But even great fighters can die."

The force of his own words hit him. She would fight the Horsemen exactly as he always fought his battles, not caring about his own life, only the outcome of the battle.

"I do not wish to kill all of them." Emotion clotted her throat. "Only one."

"Which one?" He knew the answer even as he asked the question. Scotia's reaction to Lizbet's terror told him all he needed to know. "If you are fortunate enough to meet only one Horseman, then what? You will sacrifice yourself to the other three?" He ignored the stab of familiarity her plan had to his own course of action. "I cannot allow you to do such a thing. It is not your deed." *It is mine*, he finished silently.

She touched his arm and he could feel the slight tremble of her fingers through the linen of his shirt.

He pulled his gaze away, feeling suddenly too exposed to her assessment.

"Why are you so concerned for my safety?" She paused. "Unless it is not my safety you are worried about at all."

Her fingers slipped from his arm, leaving a chill in their absence. "The shadows on your face tell me what your words do not." She moved about him now, in a slow, methodic circle. "I finally understand. It is not your foster father's wish that you train with me that brought you here. Nay, your whole motive was revenge."

"My plans do not matter." He turned away, but she caught him by the arm. Instead of angry and hard, her fingers were soft, comforting.

"They matter to me. *You* matter to me."

He swallowed hard, blindsided by her admission. No one had ever said such a thing to him before. No one had accepted him for who he was, expecting nothing more.

He swallowed again, breathing too hard, overwhelmed and uncomfortable. He did not want her to care. He had other plans for what remained of his life.

With difficulty, Ian pulled away from her touch. "I am honor-bound to avenge the murder of my brother, Malcolm. And I am not afraid of that destiny, Scotia. By my sword, I will see that revenge is mine."

Scotia watched him with gentle understanding. "I do not intend to fight the Four Horsemen alone. Not unless I have to. My warriors will separate the Horsemen, in time. And when they do, I shall be ready."

She made it sound so easy, so effortless. But it wasn't. To fight the Four Horsemen brought only death and destruction. It would bring death and destruction to her unless he did something to intervene.

"We are so alike, you and I," she said as a look of tender sadness crossed her face. "Do you ever wonder why we were given the gift to fight like we do?"

He tensed, disarmed by the quick change in tactic. What was she up to? "Your meaning?"

"Do you wonder why we were given such a wonderful and yet horrible gift? We kill people, Ian. One swipe of our swords and our opponent can lay dead before us."

"We fight against the evils of this world."

"That may be so. But do you ever think beyond the revenge? What is to come of you after the battle, after your revenge is spent?"

After the battle . . . He had never allowed himself to consider such a possibility before. Fighting injustice wherever he found it had always been enough for him.

Until coming to this castle. Until meeting this woman. Until now.

He clenched his fists at his side, willing his old ways to rush back to him, to fill the spaces inside him with the burning need for revenge. Nothing came. His old ways had incinerated at his feet the moment he agreed to train with Scotia.

She had opened his eyes to another way to fight. She had changed him. Damn the woman! In less than a fortnight, she had changed the very nature of what drove his actions.

He should walk away from this place now while he still could, and seek his revenge without hesitation. She had been about to release him earlier. If he pushed, she might do so again. "Release me from my promise."

Was it his imagination, or did he detect the lightest sheen of tears in her eyes? Before he could be certain she looked away. "Will you stand alone against the fury of the Four Horsemen and their army?"

"I will."

She looked at him then, her gaze shuttered once more. "If you face the Four Horsemen alone, you might be able to take down one before the others kill you. But there are no guarantees. You could die for nothing."

"I must try—for my family, for Scotland. Whatever happens, I will accept my fate."

She straightened, tugged down the edge of her armor. "Then go. I release you from your training and your duty."

122

She stepped past him on her way to the door. Halfway there, she turned back. "May you find whatever it is you seek, Ian. But remember this: The course of our lives is not written in the stars. *You* make your own destiny, just as *I* make mine. The choice is ours." She vanished a moment later, leaving him alone.

Her footstep faded until all he could hear was the painful thundering of his heart. His destiny could have no other course.

For him, there was no other choice.

Chapter Fifteen

Two days ago she had released him, and still Ian did not leave. Scotia paced the length of her great hall in long, irritated strides, gathering worried glances from the members of her household who worked near the hearth along the far wall.

Each moment he delayed only tormented her further with memories of feeling safe in his arms, protected in his presence, and an awakening of passion in his kiss.

Scotia scowled as she launched into yet another trek across the rushes strewn about the floor. She needed something to take her mind off him. She needed a distraction. Yet training held no appeal for her this day.

"Wearing a trench in the floor, I see." Scotia turned to find Maisie and Lizbet regarding her with curiosity.

Scotia returned a distracted frown, then knelt before the young girl. "Lizbet. It is good to see you." Scotia glanced up at Maisie. "Is she well enough to question?"

"'Twas why I brought her to ye." Maisie scooted Lizbet forward with her hands. "Go with Scotia. I'll be at the hearth if ye have need of me."

The girl nodded and Maisie disappeared before Scotia could demand she stay. Scotia hesitated before the child, feeling the old fears and uncertainties creep over her. Lizbet must have read something in her expression because she held out her hand.

Scotia stood, then felt for the small hand. Confidently, Lizbet placed her hand in Scotia's larger one. "Let us be seated."

Shortening her stride to accommodate the girl's smaller legs, Scotia led Lizbet to the head table. For two days now the child had only had enough strength to eat and sleep. Yet today, a rosy pink brightened her cheeks.

When they reached the table, Scotia lifted the girl up onto the bench, then sat down beside her. "Lizbet, do you know how you got here?"

The little girl shuddered, as if remembering a bit of what she had endured. "I ran from the big man on the white horse. He killed my ma, and that's when I ran into the woods and kept running until I ended up here. I don't know why, but this is where my legs told me to go."

A surge of protectiveness welled up in Scotia. She curled her hands into fists at her side, fighting the urge to reach up and stroke a wisp of the child's blond hair away from her wide, frightened eyes.

Scotia pressed her lips together. If Ian were here, he would not hesitate to comfort the child. But any attempt on her part to provide a similar kindness would probably just frighten the girl more. Scotia knew she was awkward when showing affection to others, had always been so. Why would that change now? Yet, as tears welled up in Lizbet's brown eyes and spilled down her cheeks, Scotia lost the battle with her reserve and reached a hand out toward the girl.

It was all the invitation Lizbet needed. She thrust herself against Scotia's armor-clad chest and nestled into her body as though she were dressed in soft feather down. Her arms hung at her sides, open and useless. But the girl did not seem to mind as she wept silently and snuggled ever closer. Feeling helpless and uncertain herself, Scotia wrapped her arms around the girl in an embrace, such as Maisie had offered when Scotia was a child. She rocked back and forth, not knowing what else to do. The motion seemed to calm Lizbet, because she stopped crying.

A slow warmth curled in Scotia's stomach, and the hollowness that always existed there seemed to vanish. She stared down at the little blond head against her chest. Her heart wrenched at the sight. Lizbet had needed comfort, yet it was Scotia who felt her muscles relax and her mood soften. Who would have thought she, a hardened trainer of warriors, was capable of giving comfort and feeling content in return? Was this what motherhood would feel like?

Images of Ian's lean, muscular body and his dark, soulful eyes filled Scotia's thoughts. Heroic yet kind, forceful yet compassionate, he would make the perfect mate. . . .

Scotia stilled. She had no right to think such thoughts of Ian or any man. It was madness to want things she could never have, things she could never pursue.

Lizbet sniffled, then sat back, staring up at Scotia, her gaze filled with innocence. Scotia patted the child's head, because she had seen Ian do something similar. "Do you want to play for a while with the other children in the castle, or Mistress Maisie and Master Burke?"

"I want to play with you." The girl's small hands moved to the hilt of Scotia's sword. "Can we play with this?"

Scotia twisted in her seat, moving the sword out of reach. "Nay. You must be much older to learn to use a real sword. But I could teach you to fight with a wooden prop."

Lizbet smiled and leapt down from Scotia's lap, seeming to have forgotten her pain. Scotia marveled at the change in her emotions. The child stood before her with her arms stiff against her sides, her chin up, her spine straight. "I want to be brave and strong like you."

Scotia did not know what to say. No one had ever said such a thing to her before. She knelt before the child. "If you still feel that way when you are older, I would be honored to train you with a real weapon, Lizbet."

The child's lip came out in a pout and her eyes pooled with tears. "That will take forever."

"Not as long as you think." Scotia ruffled the young girl's hair, then jerked her hand away, surprised that she could do something so spontaneous.

Lizbet did not seem to mind. In fact, the tears vanished from her eyes.

"Would you like to go out into the lists with me to find a wooden sword?"

With a nod of the little girl's head, doubts assailed Scotia. What had possessed her to offer such a thing? She had never played with a child before, not even when she was a child. She did not have the faintest clue of what to do. Scotia frowned. Swordplay suddenly seemed an inappropriate activity for a young child, but it was all she knew.

Two days had slipped past with agonizing slowness while Ian stalled, trying to reconcile his compassion for Scotia with what he had to do. Another one of Scotia's scouting parties had returned that morning with the news the Four Horsemen had attacked the village of Glenfinnon a second time.

127

They were turning south. Back toward his village. If he were to help his clan, he had to leave now.

The Four Horsemen. He had to keep his mind on his goal. Destroy the Four Horsemen before they destroyed anyone else he cared about. Thoughts of Scotia assailed him—her strong body pressed intimately against his own, her cheeks flushed, her lips pursed and ready for his kiss, the heady scent of heather coiling around his resolve, drawing him nearer to that place of no return.

He forced his concentration back to the task before him as he wove his way through the castle, methodically searching each room. He had to find her. He had to say good-bye.

Ian hastened his pace through the empty great hall, heading outside. With any luck, by this eve he would meet his destiny head on.

Instead of finding Scotia in the outer bailey, Ian found Griffin. His brother sat with his back against the castle wall, staring mindlessly into the courtyard, twisting a single blade of bright green grass between his fingers. It would not have surprised Ian if the grass turned brown beneath the intensity of his brother's scowl. Clearly something was on his mind.

"Care to share such dark thoughts?" Ian asked as he settled himself on the ground next to Griffin.

"I am merely out to enjoy the fine scenery," Griffin replied.

Ian gazed toward the castle gate. Nothing grew, nothing stirred, nothing existed but rocks and dirt in this section of the outer bailey. "Cease the pretense. I can tell when something is wrong."

"Why should you care?" Griffin asked.

"I could name several reasons, none of which you

would believe. So spare us both." Ian reached out and stopped the blade of grass from spinning. "Talk. Now."

Griffin pulled the grass out of Ian's hand and tossed it to the ground. "Why do you always fit in with others no matter where you go?" He kept his gaze averted.

Ian stilled at the falsehood behind Griffin's words, but at least they were getting closer to the truth. "Fit in? I have been an outcast all my life."

"You were both father and mother's favorite child." Griffin's gaze snapped to Ian's. "You were always so confident in your actions."

"Mother and father tried to make amends for the way the rest of the clan treated me. They loved you and Malcolm just as much. Perhaps our parents were harder on you and Malcolm because they expected more from their true sons." Ian braced himself for the usual hurt that followed the thought that he mattered so little. It did not come this time. Why?

You matter to me. Scotia's words played across his mind. One statement from her had helped heal a lifetime of hurt. A movement to his left drew Ian's gaze. Scotia and Lizbet emerged from the lists. A smile beamed across Lizbet's young face as she poked and slashed the air with a wooden sword.

Scotia cared what happened to him. If he were honest with himself and with her, he would tell her that sentiment was exactly the reason he must now leave her castle and her behind. He did not want her to meet the same end as Malcolm. Not when he could do something to stop it.

Griffin looked at Ian expectantly. "So where do we go from here?"

Ian allowed his gaze to trail Scotia and Lizbet as they walked across the outer bailey to the large iron gate that separated the castle from the rest of the world beyond. "Will you promise me something?"

Griffin frowned. "Depends."

"I leave today. If you remain, will you cease your challenges to Scotia? Protect her instead?"

His brother's gaze sharpened. "I have never been good at keeping promises, not even the promise I made to Father when he told me about the—" Griffin grinned. "There I go again."

Something to do with Scotia, no doubt, judging by the look of satisfaction that shone in Griffin's eyes. "About what?"

Griffin's gaze suddenly became smug. "Her tunnel. There. That is the big secret Father revealed to me. Scotia might be a mighty trainer, but she is not very bright to leave a tunnel along the shoreline at the base of her castle unguarded."

"Why would Father tell you of such a place?"

Griffin smiled. "He begrudgingly revealed its presence to me when I told him I would follow you here. He feared you would slay me where I stood for abandoning the clan. He wanted me to have a chance to explain my presence before you sliced me down."

"So instead of using the tunnel for that purpose, you chose to attack Scotia instead?" Ian kept his words light and teasing, putting aside the anger the memory brought to him. Bashing his brother over the head with his misdeeds had never solved problems between them.

Griffin's smile slipped. "I was angry. Father had chosen you over me once again. I wanted to hurt you, not her. I figured the fastest way to do that was to take away your 'trainer' and gain what I could from her title and lands."

"Scotia is not the problem here."

"I know." Griffin looked away, his expression solemn.

Ian knew that his thoughts also turned to the real reason they were both at Glencarron Castle.

"The Four Horsemen are a real and deadly threat against Scotland," Ian said, fighting the turbulence their very names stirred in his blood. "If I cannot stop them, then it will be your duty to stop them, Griffin."

"You mean to go after them alone? Why not take Scotia's army with you?"

"As soon as her seasoned warriors return with information, she sends them back out to aid the fighting. What few warriors remain at the castle are needed here. Promise me you will complete your training, then take what you learn back to the clan. Teach the others. If you wanted more responsibility when you came here, little brother, you have it now. Scotia will help you strike these raiders and murderers down once and for all if you work with her instead of against her."

Griffin brought his gaze back to Ian's. "You really believe she has that much power? A woman?"

"Her sex matters not. She is a skilled and knowledgeable warrior. The best I have ever seen. Listen to what she can teach you."

Griffin narrowed his gaze. "If that is true, then why are you leaving?"

"Because I must," Ian replied flatly, hoping his brother would let the matter drop. For him, there could be no other outcome.

Griffin's eyes clouded and his expression became sad. "It is guilt that drives you. You want revenge because of Malcolm's death."

"Someone must see justice served."

Griffin shook his head. "I blamed you unfairly for his death. I was just as much to blame."

Ian got to his feet, uncomfortable with the direction

their conversation had taken. As next eldest son, it was his responsibility to right those wrongs. Nothing more remained to be said. "Promise me you will stay with Scotia. Learn from her." *Keep her safe*.

A frown pulled down Griffin's brow. "You are certain you want to leave here?"

"Positive." Ian held out his right hand to his brother.

Griffin released a sigh. He joined his hand with Ian's and for the first time Ian noted an awakening of maturity in his brother's gaze. "You have my word."

Chapter Sixteen

From the mock tournament field she had created just inside the front gate, Scotia glanced away from her opponent. Ian strode toward her. Their gazes met and locked. For a timeless moment she stared into the depths of his dark and unreadable eyes and felt a rush of warmth tease her cheeks. Whenever he drew near, she could not look anywhere but at him.

"I must speak to you. In private," he said, his voice thick and rich.

She knew then what his features did not betray. He had come to say good-bye. The thought brought with it a stab of loss, and for a brief moment Scotia allowed the emotion to linger. When he walked out her gate, he would never return. She would gladly suffer that reality if it guaranteed his survival. Because suddenly, a world without Ian in it seemed a much lonelier place.

With an effort, Scotia returned her attention to Lizbet.

"Lizbet, I will teach you more swordplay in a while. For now, please go to Maisie and Burke over there near the mews. They will take you inside the castle for a rest."

When the child's lip turned down in a pout, she added, "All great warriors need times of rest after their training."

"Then I shall rest," Lizbet agreed, and reluctantly turned and headed to the mews.

Alone in Ian's presence, Scotia stood on unsteady legs. "Scotia—"

"Will anything I say dissuade you?"

"Nay," he said. "I must avenge my brother's death."

"Then you are a fool."

"Aye, a fool who wants to keep the people he cares about safe from further harm." He reached up to smooth a finger against the curve of her cheek.

Scotia tried to still the rioting sensations he created on her cheek with his featherlight touch. "I have spoken to Griffin. He will remain with you to complete his training. If he challenges you, you have my permission to sever his arms or skewer him through the heart." He offered her a wry grin. "Whichever you prefer."

"How kind of you. I can take care of Griffin should the need arise."

"I believe you can."

At the clatter of hoofbeats on the packed earth, Scotia turned toward the stables. A stable boy lead Ian's horse toward them, saddled and ready for travel. She stepped back, away from Ian's touch. "This is good-bye, then."

"Aye." He did not elaborate on his plans, likely so she could not do something so foolish as to follow him.

"If you are ready, then go." She kept her gaze averted, not wanting him to see the sudden racing of her pulse or the emptiness that must surely show on her face. "Be quick about it."

She motioned to Poppie, the gatekeeper, to open the portcullis. The grinding of the heavy chains cut through the silence of the nearly empty outer bailey. Scotia tensed, waiting for Ian to step away, to swing up on his horse and ride out of her castle and her life.

A sound rose from his throat. Instead of moving away, he pulled her into his arms. With a gasp, she brought her gaze to his.

His eyes were nearly black. "Until we meet again."

He pulled her close and pressed his lips to hers in a bruising kiss. Scotia meant to resist, but found herself leaning into his arms. Her hand slid up the softness of his linen shirt, feeling the tautness of his muscles beneath.

Scotia's heart lurched in her chest. How could he melt her resolve with a mere kiss? She had always thought she was stronger than that.

When his tongue flicked against her lips, teasing, inviting, Scotia knew she was lost and retaliated in the only way she could. Sliding her hands around his shoulders, she kissed him back, letting him part her lips and, when his tongue probed, she welcomed the invasion.

She felt his sharp intake of breath a moment before he pulled away, releasing her as suddenly as he had claimed her. "I must go."

He strode to his horse and swung up into the saddle. Without looking back he headed through the gate.

Her vision clouded as she stared after him, but she tilted up her chin and kept her back straight, refusing to give in to her tears. The Warrior Trainer did not cry.

It took only a moment for her vision to clear. When it did, she saw not only Ian upon his horse at the brink of the gate, but another warrior as well.

The man stood statue-still, his hand resting on the hilt of his sword as the early afternoon sun washed the air in gold and gray.

Scotia drew her sword. A challenger. The telltale glint of victory in his eyes revealed all she needed to know.

"Are you the mighty Warrior Trainer?" the man asked with a definite French accent.

"Aye."

The challenger strode forward onto the castle grounds.

The whisper of Ian's sword as he released it from the scabbard drew Scotia's gaze. "Halt, Ian. You will not interfere."

"I will not allow this challenge to continue."

"You were leaving last I remember." Scotia brought her gaze back to the foreigner. Beneath the rugged animal pelts he wore as a cloak and laced up over his lower legs she could see he was tall and well-muscled. Strength would give him an advantage, but she still had speed and agility on her side.

Scotia raised her broadsword in salute. The challenger smiled a gruesome smile and did the same.

"Are you ready to die so that I may be known as the man who brought the woman warrior down?"

"Scotia, please." Ian's raw tone cut through the silence.

Her gaze shifted from her challenger to Ian. His normal reserve had vanished. His eyes pleaded to allow him to help.

Anger washed over her. He had no right to interfere, not when he had made the decision go. She wished he would turn away and leave the fragile pieces of her resolve intact. "Go, MacKinnon." She let anger fill her voice. She welcomed it; it was a safer emotion than grief.

"I will not leave you like this." He nudged his horse forward.

"You cannot decide my fate any more than I can decide yours." With a nod of her head she signaled for the gatekeeper to lower the portcullis, closing Ian out.

The rattling of chains broke through the heavy silence.

Scotia did not have time to watch Ian's reaction as her challenger lunged toward her.

Maisie held on to one of the little girl's hands and signaled Burke to take the other as they entered the great hall. "Our Scotia may bluster and blow about not needin' a man in her life, but there be no denyin' that nature be takin' its course twixt those two," she said smugly.

Burke's smiled, but it soon faltered. "Aye. I am glad we were able to keep Scotia safe, but I wish our people didna have to pay the price for that deception."

"We needed time to allow Scotia to grow up. The clan council understood that. They willingly accepted the devastation the Horsemen would bring to the country in order to keep the Stone of Destiny and Scotia safe."

Burke's shoulders sagged with weariness. "She would not be pleased with us if she knew."

"She can never know," Maisie said as a chill raced across her arms. "Deceptions lie down that path that need never be revealed."

"To be sure. And with Ian here now, all will be well," Burke agreed.

"Ian is leaving," Lizbet broke in abruptly.

Burke bent at the waist to address her. "What makes ye say that?"

Lizbet's lower lip began to tremble. "His eyes have the same look my da's did when he left me and ma."

Maisie shot Burke a startled look. "Leavin'? He canna go." Maisie turned them all around, their hands still clasped together, and pulled them back toward the outside. "We must do somethin'."

Burke dug in his heels, pulling her back. "Maisie, gather yer wits. Ye know we canna just walk out there and tell him to stay. Besides, Lizbet could be wrong. We must trust those looks we saw a few moments ago to bring them back together if he does leave. A man does not look at a woman like that without a reason." Burke's brow came up, and he offered Maisie an engaging smile.

Maisie felt her cheeks heat at the reminder of the passions that had drawn her and Burke together. Still she hesitated before releasing a heavy sigh. "Yer right," she conceded. "'Tis just that we've waited so long for this man to come."

"'Tis true. But the destiny we've waited for is theirs, not ours. We can help them find each other, but they must make the commitment alone."

"Ye always were the practical one." She sent Burke an affectionate smile.

"'Bout time ye admitted that, old girl." He grinned back, and for a moment she could see a trace of the younger man with whom she had fallen in love so many years ago.

"Best we be off to ask Cook for an apple pastie or two for our young friend here," Maisie said.

Lizbet frowned. "No pastie. Scotia promised to play with me again after I rested."

"Are ye certain ye would not rather have a pastie?" Burke worked his lips as though tasting a bittersweet pie already. "Cook's pies are ever so delicious."

The young girl shook her head. "I want to learn more." Her voice held firm.

Maisie smiled to herself. "Scotia would've made the same choice at yer age. Let us get ye settled near the hearth for a bit of a nap then."

But as they went, Maisie's thoughts turned from swordplay to sword fights. A sense of foreboding erased any joy she had felt by seeing Ian and Scotia together. Burke was right. Ian would return for Scotia. Then she and Burke could make certain Scotia continued the Warrior Trainer line before the White Horseman discovered that she and the Stone had never left the safety of Glencarron Castle at all, as he had been led to believe.

A stab of guilt settled in Maisie's breast. There was nothing to be done about what had to happen, guilt or no. She and Burke had to protect Scotia and any future Warrior Trainer, even if that meant forcing her to go into hiding or letting the entire country assume she had died. 'Twas the only way the Stone would be safe and Scotia's destiny preserved.

And what of Ian? her guilty conscience asked. Maisie stumbled at the thought, then caught herself, forcing her steps into a slow, steady pattern. 'Twas the destiny Scotia's mother had set up with Abbus MacKinnon. Abbus would send a man who would father Scotia's child by her twenty-fifth year, a man who would willingly sacrifice himself for the protection of his family.

Maisie's steps grew heavy as she continued on to the hearth, wishing for a sigh, a whisper, a laugh to break the silence that moved all around her and in her heart. How many years had they waited for Ian to come? She pushed away the thought that he had arrived too late. She and Burke had to succeed in their goal, despite the obstacles of the Four Horsemen, Scotia's reluctance to accept her birthright, or Ian's own acceptance of his fate.

They had to succeed. Or die trying.

Chapter Seventeen

The challenging warrior's pompous laugh echoed around Ian as he watched through the iron portcullis, Scotia battle yet another male for her title and her land.

The scene unfolded before him like a surreal drama. The man had appeared out of nowhere and strode into Scotia's castle as if he had every right to do so. With a wave of his sword, he set a stage where Scotia fought for what was hers by birth.

Ian's heart thudded as the iron bars clanged into place. Separate and alone, he could only stand by and watch the battle progress. To defend her honor, Scotia would insist on fighting without aid.

The warrior advanced, dropping his shoulder in an attempt to trick Scotia. The action worked. His sword flicked the top of her wrist above her gauntlets as she parried. A crimson stain spread across her ivory skin.

Fearing for her safety, Ian kept his gaze riveted on Scotia as he slid off his horse and ran to the gate, clasping the bars between his hands. "Let me in!" He rattled the iron barrier, not bothering to hide the desperation he could feel eating away at his resolve to leave this woman behind him.

The warrior's sword flashed toward Scotia once more with deadly force. This time she easily parried the move, then spun to the right.

The warrior countered with a sideways sweep. Again, Scotia anticipated the move. Her broadsword arched up and back, blocking the deadly slice.

"Haldane was right to send me here. You are a worthy opponent if ever there was one." The warrior grinned.

Scotia did not respond. She kept her stance low, appraising the warrior's movements. Ian knew from his own training that she searched for subtle signs of weakness.

The warrior struck. His shoulder dropped once more. She countered the move even before it registered in Ian's thoughts. She parried and spun away, but this time her sword cut deeply into the upper portion of the warrior's sword arm.

He gasped in pain, and the smile slipped from his lips. "I will have your lands and your title." The warrior reacted, his pain and humiliation driving him on. His blade arched toward Scotia in a disemboweling sweep, the thin metal blade whistling a deadly melody.

Scotia rolled and came to her feet instantly. After three quarters of an hour of intense swordplay, a sheen of perspiration had broken out on her forehead and cheeks. She was tiring. It did not help that she had expended so much energy on the training field that morning.

Ian noted the slight tipping of her sword with each successive parry. The fight went on endlessly, each warrior looking for an opening, each blocking the other's advance. It was only a matter of time before one of them made a mistake. The blows were mere breaths apart. Metal to metal, life to death.

Ian had barely finished the thought when the warrior's blade swung wide. Scotia moved inside the opening. With an upward cut she drew her sword across the warrior's lower arm, chest, and cheek.

The warrior's sword dropped to the ground with a sickening thud. He staggered, then fell in a crumpled heap near his blade.

Scotia swayed on her feet, but remained standing. The battle was finished. An unreasonable rush of relief shot through Ian. "Scotia," he said through the iron bars that separated them. "You fought well."

Her gaze lifted to his. Sorrow etched itself across her features and tears pooled in her eyes. "Go away, Ian." She clutched her shoulder as she visibly struggled to keep her composure.

The sight of her, tired, worn, battered, and miserable, brought an ache to his chest. She hated these challenges, hated them as much as he hated to leave her. "Open the gate, Scotia."

Ignoring him, she knelt beside her challenger, placing her bloody fingers alongside the man's neck. Poppie shuffled to her side. "He lives," Scotia proclaimed, then stood.

"What do ye want me to do with the lad?" Poppie asked.

Scotia turned away from the gate. "Toss him out of my castle along with anyone else who refuses to respect me." She kept her head high, her body tense and erect as she walked away. "I need to rest now, before the next challenger arrives."

The next challenger. There would be others. He had blinded himself to Scotia's problems in his quest for revenge.

With a frown, Ian stared after her retreating back. Could he stay and protect her? Did he want to?

She had made her wishes perfectly clear. Her stiff posture only reinforced what he already knew.

It was time for him to go.

Ian spent the rest of the afternoon hoping the distance he put between himself and Scotia would help him forget the naked vulnerability he had seen in her eyes.

Somehow, it only made him feel worse.

She was only one woman. Even with her extraordinary talents, how long could she hold off the countless challengers who would come to face her?

The sense of foreboding he had tried to deny gripped him with full force. He tensed, every nerve raw and exposed. He had allowed his own feelings of unworthiness to color his actions. He had deserted Scotia before she could see into the true nature of his heart—the part of him so many others had found lacking and unlovable.

Ian reined in his horse at the top of a ridge. He stared unseeing into the distance. If he had been honest with himself, he would have seen before now that the more vulnerable she appeared to him, the more desperate he became to seek his own goals. Ian closed his eyes. Perhaps Griffin had been right during their youth to call Ian a selfish, unfeeling bastard. Because only a heartless man would leave Scotia alone when he knew her life was in as much of a crisis as his own.

Her confidence had faltered. He had witnessed that painful truth in her eyes when he had found her in her training chamber the day Lizbet had arrived. He had seen the look again later in the chapel. And today, there was no mistaking Scotia's vulnerability after her battle with the foreigner.

But how could he help? How could he get her to once again embrace the destiny she had been born to? Give her what she needed—men outside her own household to train. Provide her with faithful warriors, and her confidence would reemerge of its own volition.

Ian looked around. Before him stretched two trails. The southeastern route led to Glenfinnan and the Four Horsemen. The other path led to the western shoreline. From the top of the ridge he could see the small Isle of Rum. His father had always told him if he ever needed help, the Ranald clan of Rum would assist the MacKinnons with their very lives if necessary.

Ian touched his heels to his horse's side and loped off in the direction of the shoreline. The time had come to put his father's claims to the test.

For only when he was freed from the pull of Scotia's destiny could he leave her once again to follow his own.

The late afternoon sun hung low in the sky, lengthening the shadows and casting a warm, spring freshness over the shore and the hills beyond. Ian grasped the edge of the boat he had borrowed to cross the Cullin Sound, then pulled the vessel to rest upon the shore. After tucking the oars inside the boat, he hoisted a boiled leather pouch filled with provisions over his shoulder and set out on foot for the trail leading away from the beach.

He had no time to waste; the sun would set within the hour. Now that he had made the decision to go back to Scotia, it seemed he had already been gone too long. Not knowing how she fared, or if she remained safe during his absence, stretched each moment into an eternity. Ian wondered whether he would be able to leave her for good after he returned with warriors. For he must. His own goals could wait no longer.

The men he sought now would provide her sufficient protection, see she remained unharmed regardless of the

Four Horsemen's presence in their land. As the sun started to fade into early evening, Ian had almost convinced himself of that.

He paused to survey his surroundings. He had walked through a sparsely forested area for a time now and had yet to see any signs of a village. A chill rushed through the trees, teasing the exposed skin of his hands and neck and knees. A sure sign that when the sun went down the night would turn cold. Regardless, he would continue on until he found the Ranalds.

He set off through the trees for a slight rise in the terrain to his left. As evening descended, the noises around him stilled until only the whisper of his footsteps sounded on the soft earth beneath his feet. It was only a brief pause between day and night.

A branch snapped. Ian froze. The sound came again. He searched the hazy dusk with a growing sense of unease. Something was not quite right. He reached for his sword.

Looming figures came out of the shadows of the trees to surround him. There were eighteen men to his one. Ian tensed, but did not draw his sword.

"Are you so eager to die that you refuse to draw your weapon?" the biggest of the men taunted as he swung his sword easily, round and round.

"I come in peace in search of Douglas Ranald."

The man's weapon stilled, and a frown came to his face.

"Who wants to speak to the Ranald?" a gray-haired man asked from behind the others. The men blocking him stepped back, revealing an older man dressed in a mantle of green. His bright blue eyes searched Ian's face with interest.

"Ian MacKinnon. Son of Abbus MacKinnon. Friend of the Ranalds."

145

"How do I know ye speak the truth?" The old man's brows came up as he regarded Ian with a mixture of intrigue and suspicion. "How do we know ye aren't one of the Four Horsemen who's got the mainland up in a fury?"

"For one thing," Ian said, "I have no horse." He'd left his horse on the mainland, at the shore.

"Aye," the older man admitted with a bit of a smile.

"I am here to find men to help fight the Four Horsemen alongside the Warrior Trainer if they should attack her castle."

"The Warrior Trainer? She is dead."

"Nay, she is very much alive. I have seen her and trained with her myself."

"Praise the saints." Relief filled the old man's face for a brief moment before the look shifted, appraising Ian critically. "So yer a MacKinnon." He shook his head. "Ye doona look like a MacKinnon."

The barb pierced his skin, but Ian clamped his jaw against the slight. He had been treated that way all his life. "Perhaps not, but I am just the same."

"And ye have proof of yer claim, have ye?"

Ian's restraint snapped. He needed to get to the Ranald and he would get there through all of these men if he must. He drew his sword, the sound sharp and lethal.

Instead of fear, amusement reflected in the old man's eyes. "Aye, yer a MacKinnon all right." With a wave of his hand he signaled for the others to drop their swords. "I am the Ranald. Happy I am to greet ye after years of waiting for yer arrival."

Ian frowned. "What do you mean? How could you know of my purpose here?"

The man stepped forward to clap Ian on the shoulder. "Yer father warned me years ago there might come a day when ye would need my help."

Ian narrowed his gaze on the man. "I did not know I would come here myself until a short while ago."

The Ranald's smile deepened to a grin. " 'Twas foretold by a prophet years past that a MacKinnon would help bring the Warrior Trainer's importance back to Scotland. 'Tis ye who was sent to fulfill that destiny."

Ian did not understand. "But I am not a MacKinnon by blood."

"Ye will be what ye want to be, laddie. Yer blood matters little. All men have their calls to duty, just as my clan does now. 'Twould be to our honor and glory to serve the Warrior Trainer with ye." He turned to his men. "And since there'll be no warring this eve, come back to the village with us. We would gladly share all we have with ye this night, then send ye off with men and supplies in the morn."

"Thank you," Ian said humbly.

The Ranald turned back to Ian. "Doona thank me yet. Not till we scour our country of these vandals who invade us. Agreed?" The old man held out his hand.

Ian clasped his hand with his own. "Agreed."

Chapter Eighteen

Scotia stood in the lists surrounded by her students. Half the young warriors of the castle began their daily exercises, while the other half had left earlier on patrol. Two new students joined them today—one eager for her knowledge, the other resentful. Lizbet and Griffin trained a distance from the others, practicing basic defense.

A slight afternoon breeze sent wisps of hair to tease her cheeks, reminding her of the featherlight caress Ian had placed there before he left. Two days had passed and still she could not put Ian from her mind. She missed him. She missed his presence in her castle. She missed the easy banter when they talked. But most of all she missed his sensual smile—the one that brought out that irresistible dimple at the corner of his lips.

But Ian was gone, quite possibly forever. Her sanity and her concentration would improve if she accepted that fact. And despite all the logic that told her to let go, she still held out hope that something would draw him back to her.

And then what? What would she do if he did return? The thought brought an ache to the center of her chest.

Scotia straightened, then tugged down the bottom of her brigandine, as if doing so would force away the emptiness Ian's absence created. Duty called for her to live in the moment, not the recesses of her mind.

Griffin's lips curled up in an arrogant smile as he glared at his sparring partner. He lifted his weapon high over his head and swung at Lizbet. The girl saw the blow coming and did nothing to counter the move. Instead she stepped back, allowing Griffin to swing at only air. He stumbled sideways with the force of his movements.

"You must strike your blows with less force and more control," Scotia said, grateful for the much needed redirection of her thoughts.

He lowered his sword and gave her a long measuring look. "This is no sword, but a stick. And I am no warrior to fight with an infant."

"It matters not whether you hold a sword, a stick, or use only your hands. Skillful manipulation is the key to mastery."

Griffin tossed his weapon on the ground. "A stick is a stick."

Lizbet charged forward, stick in hand, and whacked him across the knees, garnering a yelp of pain from her opponent.

"I won," Lizbet shouted, waving her stick in the air. "My sword and I won."

Griffin dropped into a sitting position and hugged his stinging knees to his chest. "I am going to kill that child if she does not stop hitting me," he grumbled as he cast a dark glare at Lizbet.

"Then do not drop your weapon, and she will have no

149

chance. As you said, she is only a child." *A child with much talent and promise*, Scotia mused as she picked up the stick and handed it back to Griffin. "Let us try that again, shall we?"

Lizbet immediately sobered and assumed the fighting stance Scotia had taught her. The child's blond curls bobbed about her face as she tried to contain her excitement at this new challenge.

The image reminded Scotia of herself at that age—how she hungered for her mother's knowledge, and how she would have done anything to gain the approval that her mother never gave to her. "You did well, Lizbet," Scotia said.

A smile reflected in Lizbet's eyes at the compliment, but she did not take her gaze from her opponent.

Griffin shook his head. "Nay. I have had enough child's play this day. Until a more worthy partner can be found, count me out of the training."

"I would be willing to step into that role," a familiar male voice said from the far side of the lists.

Ian.

A rush of joy made Scotia's knees weak. She turned toward him, her gaze filled with both relief and joy. He was safe. His face was shadowed with both fatigue and a day's growth of beard, but the smile on his lips told her what she wanted to know. He had returned and he was glad to see her.

Scotia swallowed against the sudden thickness in her throat. "You came back."

"I did." The words were simple, but the look in his eyes spoke of something more complex. His emotions mirrored her own—the depths of her fear and the richness of her joy. A shiver of sensation sent her heartbeat into an erratic flutter. She clamped her hands together to try to tame her reaction to his return.

Slowly, he moved toward her, as though giving her time to adjust to his presence. Scotia drew a steadying breath, feeling more in control of herself. It was then that she noticed the others. A crowd of rugged men gathered behind Ian. They stopped before her, a dozen men, clothed in plaids of blue, green, and brown, worn over shirts of saffron yellow, with legs bare from the knee to the top of their boots. The dress of her countrymen.

"These men have come to train with you, Scotia, and protect you if the need should arise." Ian stepped aside to introduce the men, one by one. Keith, Angus, William, Donald . . . their names blended together as each man came forward, offering a bow and expressing his desire to serve her and learn from her.

By the time the last man had made his introductions, Scotia was numb with joy and disbelief. She stared at the men assembled before her. "I am honored that you would come." She paused as she tried to gather strength in her voice. They expected a commanding trainer, and that they would have. She drew herself up. "Training will begin on the morrow. Today, you will rest, feast, and familiarize yourself with the castle."

A rumble of excited masculine voices filled the lists— a sound not often heard in this place of training. The noise echoed through the gray rock of the castle, making the old tired stones seem a little bit brighter as her people, too, embraced their purpose with a renewed vigor. Even Griffin's usual stormy gaze had taken on a softer note as he chatted with the men. He would have plenty of worthy sparring partners among this bunch.

Scotia's gaze caught Lizbet's as the girl skipped in circles around the group of men. The tender smile on her face reflected the same pride Scotia held in her heart. These men had come to train with her, the Warrior Trainer, to learn how best to fight for their people. The Four Horsemen would not win once she finished training these men. For they would leave here to train their own clan, and others, in the ways of the ancients.

With a sense of wonderment, Scotia turned back to Ian. The very breath in her chest stilled at the look of hunger in his eyes. "Thank you for your aid," she said in a breathless tone.

"I missed you," he breathed.

The words assailed her as no weapon ever had. She felt weak, her body drugged, and her pulse fluttered irrationally.

He leaned toward her. "I want to show you something." His husky voice sent a wave of heat coursing through her. He held out his hand. "Please?"

The man knew just what to say to break through her defenses—defenses that were growing ever weaker as he held her gaze. "But the men?" she offered halfheartedly.

"Will wait."

"And your challenge to Griffin?"

"It too can wait." Ian beckoned her forward. "Please, Scotia, I want you to remember why it is you train warriors at all." He clasped her gauntlet-covered hand in his and led her out of the lists toward the front gate.

She found any desire to protest had abandoned her. All that mattered now was the feel of his hand in hers. He had come back to her. The knowledge was as heady as it was freeing.

"Poppie, raise the portcullis," Ian called. As soon as the gate lifted, he pulled her through, outside the castle.

How many years had it been since she had stepped beyond the gates of her own castle? She could not remember. Her duty to protect the Stone had kept her from leaving the castle.

Thirsty for a drink of what she had not realized she missed, Scotia's gaze moved beyond the bluff where her castle sat, to the landscape that surrounded her—rugged, snow-topped mountains, lush rolling hills, and a sea that glittered in the late afternoon sun. This was the Scotland she loved and protected. The land her ancestors had protected before her.

Again, she turned to face Ian, feeling more at peace with her purpose than she had in years. "Thank you for this reminder."

"You are welcome." He drew her up against his chest. She did not move away from the intimate embrace despite the fact she knew she should. She did not have the will any longer; all that mattered was his touch.

She looked at his mouth the way he had once looked at hers. A spiral of warmth coiled in her stomach. Now she understood the fascination. Her fingers traced the fullness of his lower lip, delighting in the warmth and the softness.

Ian groaned and turned into her caress, nuzzling her hand with his lips, which sent tingles of sensation up her arm. "You are impossible to resist," he said with a grin that brought out the dimple that intrigued her so much. Her fingers left his lips to explore the indentation. He tightened his arms around her, and his smile deepened. "I tried to stay away from you, to control my need for you, but I find I cannot."

As unsteady on her feet as she had ever been, Scotia laid her hand on his chest for the support her knees refused to give her. She could feel the thunderous beat of his heart beneath her palm. She watched him, suddenly wanting more, but not quite knowing what that more entailed.

Helplessly, she stared at his lips, hungry for his kiss. Her senses spun, dipped, whirled. She melded herself to his strength, to the feel of his hard body.

He brought his lips to hers, soft and quick at first, merely a brush of his lips against hers. When she relaxed into his arms, he kissed her again. This time his lips were far from teasing. His mouth closed over hers with a sweetness, a tenderness, that was devastating. Scotia gasped at the sharp explosion of longing in her womb. Ian caught the sound in his mouth, muffling it with a groan of his own.

When their lips finally parted, they were both breathing as though they had been battling with heavy swords instead of sharing such a pleasurable kiss. Warmth crept up Scotia's throat and across her breasts as something inside her began to tighten and ache.

"We must not continue this." She tried to pull away, but could not find the strength. "I am sworn to my duty. I must always remember that."

"As I am sworn to my revenge," Ian replied as he caught her lips with his. His hand slid into her hair, loosening its tight plait as he cradled her head.

She sighed with pleasure and closed her eyes, relishing in the feel of such delicious and unknown sensations. "We cannot do this."

"Nay," he breathed against her ear, capturing her earlobe between his teeth, teasing the sensitive lobe, igniting a fresh spark of sensation so hot it threatened to incinerate her where she stood. "There will be naught between us."

"Nothing," Scotia breathed, and she knew the words to be a lie, but did not care. At this moment she cared about nothing except feeding the hunger growing deep inside her. Was this the force of nature Maisie had spoken of? If so, she finally understood what Maisie had meant. This desire, these sensations, there was no controlling them when they had you in their grasp.

Scotia held on to Ian's shoulders as the sweet torture continued. He rained kisses down her throat, then across her neck just above her brigandine. And for the first time since she had vowed never to remove her armor, she wanted it off. Its weight suddenly became too heavy, its heat too intense.

"Help me take off my armor," she whispered, not trusting her voice. She reached for the ties at the sides that bound the two pieces together.

With gentle fingers, Ian pulled the ties, loosing the grip the brigandine held on her chest. Air coursed between the padding that lay atop her skin and the metal plates of her armor. She drew in a startled breath at the feel of the breeze as it moved across her in a way it had not for many years, not even as she bathed. But even more startling was the feel of Ian's hands as they slipped beneath the padding as well as the short, sleeveless chemise that protected her flesh.

She clutched at his shoulders, totally unprepared for the intense pleasure of his touch. His fingers flared across her ribs and teased the fullness of her breasts. A shiver of yearning rocked her when his hands stroked the sides of her torso, then moved to stroke the sleek line of her back. Never had anything felt so enticing and unnerving all at the same time.

Ian's eyes remained steady on her face as he took the brigandine in his hands and slowly lifted it over her head. A slight afternoon breeze washed over her, cooling the heated flesh beneath her padding and chemise. Ian set the brigandine at their feet, then flared his hands about her waist. She made an incoherent sound of panic. The feeling of exposure, of vulnerability, was too sharp to bear. He stilled his movements and she knew he was allowing her to set the pace. Continue or retreat, the choice was hers.

"So you are human after all," came a male voice from behind her.

Scotia's hand moved to her sword as she pivoted toward the gate to face the challenger she had known would someday return. "Brodie Haldane."

Haldane offered her a mock bow. "At your service."

Scotia's gaze dropped to her brigandine. If she reached for the armor, Haldane could strike. She cursed herself for a fool. One fleeting moment of pleasure could never be worth the danger she found herself in now. She pulled out of Ian's grasp, mourning the loss of his warmth and protection.

Ian appraised Haldane. His hand moved to his sword, but before he could draw the weapon from its sheath, Scotia nudged him aside.

Without the aid of her armor, she drew her weapon and began her advance, feeling naked, exposed. "So you did not get your fill the first time around?"

"Aye," Haldane said, his voice dripping venom. "I came back to finish what I started since none of the foreigners I sent seemed up to the task." He offered her a cocky grin. "It seems fitting that I finish you off here, at the gate of your castle where your new warrior protectors cannot help you."

Ian moved around her, forcing her behind him. "She has me," Ian growled. "I shall take care of him, Scotia."

Scotia stared at Ian's back, torn between anger and mirth and fear. No one could fight her battles for her. "I am quite capable, I assure you."

"Who are you?" Haldane spat out, lunging at Ian.

Ian easily avoided the blow, but Scotia took advantage of his backward motion and jabbed Ian in the ribs with her elbow as he moved beside her. He gasped at the impact but remained standing. "Scotia, nay," he choked out.

She ignored him, facing Haldane once again.

His lips twisted into a knowing smile. "I have learned a thing or two since our last encounter."

Scotia assumed her fighting stance, trying to cast off the remnants of sensation that lingered from Ian's touch. She focused on her enemy. She had learned a thing or two about *him* during their last battle, like how he moved and where his weaknesses lay. She would use all that knowledge against him now. She cut to his left, remembering he favored his right. Her tactic worked. His cuts became less accurate, the weight of the sword became unbalanced, and his movements grew weak.

"Are you prepared to sacrifice your title to me, along with the Stone of Destiny?" he asked, his eyes locked with hers as he slashed violently at her chest.

Scotia slammed her sword into his, blocking the attack, yet feeling the impact in the depths of her previously injured shoulder. "Never," she replied around the pain radiating through her arm.

"I finally put the two things together. The Four Horsemen are back, ravaging your country, looking for the Stone that presumably they already have."

His brow shot up in question as he circled her, casing her for an opening. "If you are still alive and it is your duty to guard the Stone, then the Stone must be here with you."

Scotia tensed, not from Haldane's assumption, but from the tension she could suddenly sense in Ian's posture.

"Will you neither deny nor confirm the truth of my logic?" Haldane taunted.

Scotia remained silent. She protected the Stone with her strength, not with lies.

"I take it from your lack of words that I am correct." He spat at her feet. "You are a woman. You do not merit such a valuable prize as that Stone. It shall be mine." He lunged forward.

She stumbled back, catching herself before she fell. She twisted to the right, evading a blow that could have easily taken her leg. "I mourn for the women in your life," she taunted. He forced her backward, and she let him. Better that he should wear himself out before she pressed her own assault.

"You are the only female of interest to me." He furrowed his brow, and the long red slash that ran from his cheek to his chin puckered as a result. A wound from their last meeting. A visual reminder of their last conflict.

"Lucky me."

"No." Haldane bared his teeth in savage delight. "Lucky me to be the one to take you down."

Chapter Nineteen

Metal to metal, their swords rang a peal of power and violence. A quick attack, then withdrawal. Scotia and Haldane studied each other as they circled like wolves, two warriors engaged in a life-and-death struggle.

Ian clenched his fists at his sides as a mindless panic set in. Haldane had mentioned the Stone. Whether Scotia possessed it or not did not disturb him as much as the fact that she would not allow him to fight for her. How could he just stand back and watch? As a warrior, the battle was everything to him. Yet this was a battle he could not fight.

Cursing the rules of honor that forbade him from interfering once the first strike had been made, Ian kept his sword poised. The sound of the clashing swords rose above all else until even the slight breeze that had crept down from the north abated, as though it too held its breath.

Ian clenched his teeth. His gaze clung to Scotia. He had seen men like Haldane before. Loathsome adventurers who would rather steal others' success than earn it themselves. Men who would kill without remorse. A sickening fear tightened Ian's gut. He would never allow that to happen. Not to Scotia.

No one could keep him from interfering in her battle if the fight turned against her. He would do anything, even break a code of honor, if it kept Scotia safe. He clutched his sword in his right hand and drew his dagger with the left. He tensed, balancing on the balls of his feet as she had taught him, waiting, watching.

Several of the castle's inhabitants suddenly appeared at the gate; no doubt the sounds of battle had pulled them away from their daily tasks. Each time Scotia's sword caught her opponent unaware, a cheer rose from the crowd. Tension mounted as Griffin and the new warriors gathered among the growing crowd, forming a semicircle around Scotia and Haldane.

"They are boxing her in," Keith Ranald said as he tried to push the crowd back with his strong arms, giving Scotia more room to maneuver. His attempts were unsuccessful, but Scotia did not seem to notice the lack of space. Her broadsword slashed right, then left, and back again, as she pressed her attack.

Ian drew an easier breath when he detected a slight shift in Haldane's stride. Scotia's opponent was beginning to tire. She must be every bit as tired, yet she showed no sign. Instead, she stood tall and proud, moving on full attack. Haldane spun away. Scotia feinted to the left and drew her sword across Haldane's thigh, drawing blood through the boiled leather cuisses that covered the tops of his legs.

Haldane did not cry out in pain, but his eyes flared with outrage. He slashed a wide, furious circle around Scotia. His attack no longer held any kind of predictability as he savagely cut at anyone and anything in his way. The crowd scattered like leaves in a strong wind.

Ian remained where he stood, unable to move away despite the danger. Haldane had turned from dangerous to lethal. A wounded animal willing to sacrifice all for the sake of triumph. And if Scotia were not careful, Haldane would kill both himself and her before this battle was through.

Ian stepped forward, unable to stay uninvolved. "Hold." A hand on his arm restrained him. The old gate-keeper, Poppie, stood beside him, his gaze gentle with understanding. "She made her wishes known. Let her continue."

"Nay, I must—"

"Interfere now, and Haldane will only come back again. Let this battle be the end. I beg ye."

Ian knew the gatekeeper was right. He forced his feet to remain still despite an almost desperate desire to go to her. He had no one to blame but himself for this situation. He had been so eager to see Scotia again, had wanted to bring a smile to her lips, that he had dropped his usual guard, charging forward without a second thought, until only the need to kiss her had dominated over reason.

And now, Scotia would pay for his indiscretion. He kept his gaze upon her, fearing to look away for the slightest of moments. Her sword dipped slightly, growing heavy in her arms, a sign of the strain the battle put on her. Despite that weakness, her reflexes were still strong, but they could not hold out forever. With the next clash of sound, his thoughts proved him right. Both swords struck flesh and came away red. A dark, red ribbon of blood spilled from her padded shoulder.

Ian tightened his grip on his sword. He shifted forward, ready to rescue her. Scotia's gaze left Haldane and blazed into Ian's. She voiced nothing aloud, but her gaze said *This is my battle.* He forced himself to remain still against an overwhelming tide of anger and frustration. He answered her with a look he hoped conveyed his faith in her abilities.

Bolstered by his gaze, she attacked with a renewed vigor. Haldane's eyes widened in surprise. Their blades came together with such force that sparks flared off the metal. The two swords locked together at the hilt. Scotia wrenched the sword from Haldane's grasp, sending it arching wildly across the hard-packed dirt of the outer bailey.

Her opponent fell backward to the ground as he stared after his sword in shocked disbelief.

She used his distraction to finish the deed. She poised her sword at the soft flesh of Haldane's neck. If he moved, the lethal blade would end his life. "Do you yield?"

Haldane remained still except for the harsh rise and fall of his chest. "Aye."

"Do you swear that you will never return to challenge me again? Or send other men to do the task for you?"

His gaze turned mutinous. "I have been defeated twice. My pride cannot take much more."

Scotia pressed the blade more firmly against his throat, drawing blood. "Your word, Haldane. I need your word."

"I promise never to return," he spat out.

"And?"

Haldane's gaze hardened. "I will cease sending mercenaries to challenge you as well." Her sword lifted and the challenger twisted away. He staggered to his feet, gathered his sword, then limped away.

Ian sheathed his sword and his dagger before he raced

to Scotia's side. The Ranald warriors walked behind Haldane, making certain he caused no further trouble.

The battle was over.

Ian had never been so glad of anything in his life.

As quickly as he could, he ripped off a length of linen from the bottom of his shirt and bound it across the top of Scotia's shoulder, then under her arm. "Let us get you inside."

Scotia stumbled, then regained her balance as she walked back to where her brigandine lay against the dirt. With stiff movements, she pulled the armor back over her head.

"Your shoulder," Ian said, trying to remain in control of the overwhelming guilt that flooded him. If only he had been more careful.

"Maisie will tend me later." She began to fasten the ties when Ian stilled her hands.

"Nay. I will see to it now."

She began to protest, but Ian ignored her, sliding his arm about her waist. She gave in, and leaned heavily upon him as he led her back to the keep amid the stares of her people. If their curious gazes bothered her, she did not show it.

Ian scattered the observers with a piercing gaze. Did they take Scotia's challenges and her winnings so much for granted that they regarded these occasions as moments of casual interest?

He gritted his teeth against a sudden rush of anger. Scotia might be the Warrior Trainer, but she was also mortal. Over the years of caring for the sick with his foster mother, he had seen many great warriors die from wounds like this. He shut himself off to the memories. Such a fate did not await Scotia, not while he was near.

With a renewed sense of urgency, he whisked her off

her feet. She made a small sound of protest, but did not fight him. A sign of the seriousness of the wound. Like a man possessed, he hurried into the keep and up the stairs to her chamber.

He deposited her in a chair by the hearth. "Thank you," she murmured.

"Do not thank me." He knelt down beside her. "I am the reason you left the protection of your castle." He could not keep the guilt from his voice.

Scotia took up his hand. He stared down at their fingers, hers encased in gauntlets, his roughened by years of hard work, and felt his guilt and anger fade into surprise. It was the first time she had reached for him. For hands so small, there was great strength in her grasp.

She caught and held his gaze. There was no blame in her expression—only forgiveness. "Haldane would have come back sooner or later. At least now the suspense of waiting for him is over."

At her acceptance of her fate, a kind of peace settled inside Ian. "Do you believe Haldane will keep his word not to challenge you again?"

Scotia released his hand. She leaned her head back against the chair. "He will stay away for a while. But with men like him, the lure of success often outweighs the honor of their word, especially now that he's guessed about the Stone." A weariness invaded her voice. She closed her eyes.

She had the Stone. The *real* Stone. A part of him rejoiced that the English had failed to steal the artifact from them at the Abbey of Scone. But what price had Scotia paid for that deception? He stared down at her tired, beaten body.

She might accept her destiny as protector of the Stone and a warrior who could count on no one but herself, but he intended to prove her wrong. "I must check your wound." Gently, Ian lifted her armor from her shoulders, then pulled the heavy protection over her head.

The armor had barely left her skin when her eyelids fluttered open. Uncertainty shone in her eyes. Her hands came up to shield her padded chest from his view. A rush of color flooded her pale cheeks. "I will be well once I rest." Her voice was weak, hesitant. "And I am certain Maisie is mixing up some sort of remedy."

"I want to see the wound for myself." Ian set her armor aside, then turned back to her shoulder. After removing the blood-soaked linen bandage he had tied around her shoulder, he pushed the padding and her thin chemise aside to examine the wound. He breathed a silent sigh. The gash in her flesh was deep, but none of the sinew beneath the muscle had been disturbed.

"How is it?" she asked. Her face paled, but her eyes held an underlying strength that he doubted would ever fail her, no matter how grim the circumstances.

He thought about telling her a falsehood, then decided against it. He had learned from his many hours spent in his foster mother's company as she healed the sick of their clan it was best to tell people the truth. "The wound is serious, but the arm is not damaged."

"That is a relief," she said with a tinge of nervousness in her voice. "It would be difficult to be the Warrior Trainer with only one functioning arm."

"Scotia." The word was more a plea than a warning. "The arm is fine, but the wound is deep. I must stanch the bleeding. I can either seal it with a heated sword, or knit it together with thread. Which will it be?"

"The sword." She stiffened her back and sat up straight in the chair. She put on a brave front, but Ian could hear fear in the slight quaver of her voice. "Make it quick."

Ian paused to consider her decision. Her words spoke one thing, but her actions suggested something else. "It will leave a scar," he explained, loath to inflict that kind of pain or lasting disfiguration on her flesh.

"I care not what it looks like. All warriors have scars."

"You are far more than a warrior, Scotia." He drew his dagger and carefully cut away the padding from first the back, then the front of her shoulder. He pulled the thick fabric away, exposing her creamy flesh. When he saw a second red gash lower on her shoulder, his heart seemed to freeze. Though not a fresh wound, the purple and brown gash was recent and had never healed as it should have. "What is this?"

"A memento from my last encounter with Haldane." Scotia kept her gaze trained on Ian as though waiting for something.

His anger built, matched only by the fierce wave of protectiveness that washed over him at the thought that Haldane had not injured Scotia once, but twice. Violent thoughts of how he could repay Haldane over-took him until he realized Scotia's gaze had not changed.

Did she expect him to think less of her because of this additional sign of weakness? Did she equate wounds to failure? If so, she needed his reassurance, not his anger. "As you said. All warriors have scars. You are no different from the rest." He sheathed his dagger. "Now," he said in a matter-of-fact tone, "I will take care of this wound."

"Are you certain you know what to do?" she asked, but a look of relief passed across her features.

"Aye, but you might want a bit of ale to dull the pain before I begin." Ian was about to continue with his in-structions when the door of the chamber burst open with a resounding whack against the opposite wall. Two cries of anguish sounded from the doorway—one a wail, the other a screech—followed by two bodies as they hurried across the room, staggering to a halt at Scotia's feet. Ian stepped back, giving Maisie and Lizbet access to Scotia.

"Scotia," Lizbet wailed, thrusting her head into Scotia's lap.

Scotia stroked Lizbet's golden hair as the little girl sobbed. "I am all right. Look at me. I am well, and will be ready to battle you again on the morrow."

The little girl's head came up and the tears stopped. "Truly?" she asked with a sniffle.

"I promise," Scotia said in a soothing voice that made Ian pause. Much had changed between these two since he had been gone. He could see the slight tightening of Scotia's lips, no doubt from the pain, despite the fact she tried to appear calm and at ease. It was something a mother might do to protect her child from fear.

"My dear sweet child," Maisie said from near Scotia's side, "this is not exactly the homecomin' I had envisioned for the two of ye." The older woman glanced up at Ian. She managed to keep her face composed despite the lines of worry etched around her eyes and mouth.

"I will be fine, Maisie," Scotia said, ignoring the woman's comment. "It is just a cut."

Maisie's gaze shifted from the red linen on the floor to Scotia's shoulder. "It appears to be more than a cut." She held two bowls in her hands, one filled with a soft yellow paste, the other filled with dark-colored leeches. "I brought a poultice of clary seeds and yarrow. It will ease the pain until I can bleed her. Move aside young man. I shall see to her needs."

Ian stared at the bowl of leeches and remained where he stood. "Nay," he said in a stronger voice than he had intended.

Maisie took a step back, and the bowls in her hands trembled ever so slightly.

"We shall have no need of those here. My foster mother never used them. Besides, Scotia has lost enough blood already."

Maisie drew back her shoulders. "What know you of healin', Ian?"

"Enough to heal Scotia, not make her worse. Her last wound has never healed. See for yourself," Ian gestured toward Scotia's exposed shoulder. "If this is what your leeches do for her, I say it is my turn to try my hand without delay." Ian found it difficult to keep the anger from his voice.

Ian knew the moment Maisie's gaze lit on the wound. Her face turned a pasty white before settling into an ashen shade of gray. "Mercy be. I had no idea." She held out both bowls to him. "All right. Ye can proceed. What might I do?"

With a sense of relief, Ian accepted the poultice, then turned back to Scotia. "I shall need a jug of strong ale, a bucket of boiling water, strips of fresh linen, thread, and a very sharp needle."

"Aye," Maisie agreed. "Lizbet, if ye wish to help Scotia, come with me." The girl hesitated until Scotia nodded her head, then stood and followed Maisie. The swish of their skirts and the closing of the chamber door told Ian they had left to do his bidding.

"I did not ask you to sew me up." Concern danced across Scotia's features. "Sealing the wound will be faster. I cannot remain here for long. I have men to train."

When she made to stand, Ian held up his hand, keeping her in her chair. "You need to heal before you will be any good to anyone."

She shook her head. "There is no time to waste on

such trivial things. The Four Horsemen could be headed this way. I need to protect my people for once, Ian. Lizbet has shown me how much my people suffer. I will stand for it no longer." When he remained silent she added, "If you will not use a sword to stop the bleeding, then bind the wound. It will heal eventually."

Ian crossed his arms over his chest. Did she not realize how ill she truly was? Or was this stubbornness a shield for some other emotion? "In every other battle we have, I am willing to accept defeat because your skill and talents far outweigh my own. But in this battle with your wound, I will not concede. You will leave this chamber and return to your training when I say you may."

She gave him a thunderous look.

He returned the look with one of his own. She would not win. Not this time. "Do we understand each other?"

Scotia was saved from a response by Maisie's return. "I left Lizbet with Cook. It took some talkin' to keep the child from yer side, Scotia. She finally agreed to remain behind after I fed her an apple pastie and promised her she could visit when the wound was closed." As she spoke, Maisie set the items Ian had requested near the hearth. "Tell me what to do now."

Ian picked up the jug of ale and held it out to the older woman. "She must drink this before I begin."

"I shall not—"

Ian shot Scotia a glance that dared her to argue.

"Give me a tankard," she muttered.

While Maisie handed Scotia the ale, Ian moved to the fire to run the needle through the flames as he had seen his foster mother do many times before. His hand was steady above the flame, but not his heart. He had watched his foster mother knit wounds together a thousand times. She made it look so easy, although he was certain it was not.

He stared into the red and gold flames, waiting for his nerves to steady. He had to do this if he wanted the new wound on Scotia's shoulder to heal properly and not become putrid, as her last injury had. The tip of the needle grew red, and the metal warmed against his fingers. A needle. The tool of a woman looked small and insignificant in his large, masculine hand—a hand made for wielding a sword. He stared at the flames in the hearth pondering the irony of his situation. And with that tool he would mend a delicately molded feminine shoulder for a woman wielding a sword.

A twist of fate.

Ian removed the needle and dipped it in a pitcher of water to cool while he waited for the ale to take Scotia in its grip. When her gaze grew less focused and her objections tapered off, he knew it was time to begin.

When he washed out the wound, Scotia flinched but said nothing. Instead, she held her gaze steady on something behind him, most likely using one of her training techniques to focus her thoughts.

Each time the needle bit into her flesh, he tensed, longing for just a pinch of her composure. With painstaking care he pulled the edges of her skin together, binding them slowly despite his great desire to hurry. The thick needle tugged at her flesh as he worked it from one side of the wound to the next. By the time he reached the end, his hands were shaking. Beads of sweat dotted his temples and the back of his neck, yet she remained as calm and peaceful as if they were sharing a cup of tea—until he unsheathed his dagger.

"You will torture me with first a needle and now your knife?" A tremor of fear flickered across her features when he reached back and ran the blade through the flames as he had the needle.

"I must reopen the other wound and drain the putrefaction away." Could she hear the agony in his voice? The thought of his dagger slicing open her flesh twisted his gut. "If I do not, you will become ill, and perhaps die." He had seen it happen far too often during his foster mother's time as a healer.

Scotia nodded grimly. "Be quick."

After cooling the blade, he pressed the point against the ugly purple flesh. Slight pressure would open her flesh, yet he hesitated. He had never willingly drawn blood from another person outside of battle.

His gaze moved from the wound to her face—a face covered with streaks of dirt and sweat as well as blood. Hair from her once neat plait framed her face in long, wet tendrils. Her cheeks were flushed, her color high from the trauma he had imposed on her. Her gaze came up to meet his. She had never looked more beautiful or more frightened. But beneath the fear there was also trust.

"Why do you pause?" she asked in a tight voice.

"It is difficult to be the one to inflict pain on someone you care about." Yet in order to heal her he must hurt her first.

"You truly care for me?" The shadows that usually haunted her eyes slipped away and radiance filled her. The first true moment of happiness he had seen in her face.

Her fingers crept up the back of his hand, until she wrapped them around the hilt of his dagger. Her touch was both comforting and reassuring. She understood how difficult this was for him. He could see it in her eyes.

She thrust against the dagger.

Ian drew a startled breath at the unexpected motion.

The knife went in. Blood spilled across the tip of the knife, down the blade, until it mingled with their joined fingertips. A surge of gratitude erupted inside him. She had done what he could not. "Thank you," he said with a catch in his voice.

Her hands left his to settle at her sides once more. "Make it quick, Ian." Her voice was barely a whisper. "If I must lose this battle . . . at least allow me to keep my wits about me. I feel them . . . slipping away."

She closed her eyes and her head lolled against the back of the chair. "Must stay . . . in control of my destiny."

Chapter Twenty

Ian sat in a chair near Scotia's bedside in the overly warm room. He had stoked the fire into an intense blaze to keep away the chill that usually hung about the castle. The light of the fire illuminated the woman and small child who slept within a tangle of bed linens. After he had finished sewing Scotia's wounds, she had fallen into a fitful slumber. It was not until Lizbet came to snuggle beside her that Scotia grew calm and relaxed.

Like mother and daughter, they appeared so at ease together. For that one miracle, Ian was grateful. Because Scotia seemed happier now that she had allowed someone other than Maisie and Burke into her heart. Would she allow him the same access? Ian frowned at the thought. He had never been worthy of anyone's love before. What made him think he deserved such a precious gift now, especially from Scotia?

Ian tore his gaze away from her, shifting his attention to the length of cloth in his lap—a gift from the weaver in his village. A plaid of red and green and blue and white. The colors of the MacKinnon, designed by the

GERRI RUSSELL

weaver herself. Almost against his better judgment, his
gaze drifted back to Scotia. He should have given the gift
to her upon his first arrival, but her dismissal of him had
held him back. Why it suddenly seemed urgent he give
the gift to her now, he did not know. But it did.

Most likely it was his own guilt over her injuries that
made the effort seem vital. At least that was what he told
himself as he moved to the bed and spread the cloth
across her, tucking the top ends near her face. He
brushed his hand against her cheek and allowed his fingers to linger there. Within moments, his tenderness
slipped into unease. He pressed his hand closer against
her skin. Saints! She burned, and not from the warmth
of the room.

"Maisie," he yelled as he reached for a cool wet cloth
near the bedside. He kicked off his boots and sat above
her in the bed, cradling her head in his lap. Methodically,
he sponged her face and neck with his other hand to
draw away the heat, leaving a trail of coolness behind.

The door burst open. Maisie panted to a halt at the
bedside, her face contorted with worry. "A fever?"

"Aye," he replied without a break in his duty. With
gentle fingers, he smoothed the hair back from Scotia's
brow. "Please take Lizbet from the room. Then I need you
to make me a mixture of peppermint, chamomile, and
elder flowers to cool her. It was one of my foster mother's
most successful remedies."

Without hesitation Maisie nodded, scooped up the
sleeping girl, then hurried out.

Ian returned his gaze to Scotia. As he did, an odd pang
flashed through him with such force that he was not even
certain what it was.

She appeared so pale and weak wrapped in the cocoon
of his plaid. He could see the outline of her slim body be-

174

neath the woolen fabric. Soft curves barely hidden from view were so at odds with the well-defined muscles of her legs, arms, and shoulders. This mighty warrior had a fragility not obvious beneath her armor. The thought might have made him smile had it not been for his next observation. Her usually creamy skin was the ashen gray of the dying.

Ian pushed aside his fear. He had no time for such emotions. Not until he knew whether she would live or die. "I shall not lose you, Scotia. I cannot."

The words were spoken with such force that she flinched, as though hearing his plea.

"You will not die," he informed her as desperation gripped him with more brutal force than Scotia's fiercest attack. "Stay with me. Scotland needs you. *I* need you."

Scotia thrashed against the coverlet. She thrust her arms out, as if holding her sword, fending off the silent attacker she had conjured in her fevered mind.

Ian took her hands in his and brought them to rest on her chest, holding them gently with one hand while he wiped her forehead with the other. "You are safe with me, Scotia. I will protect you," he crooned near her ear. A brush of his lips grazed the side of her cheek, her forehead, while he continued to whisper soft words and bathe her fever away.

Barely aware of where she was or how she came to be there, Scotia shoved the feather coverlet down to her feet. Her body was on fire. "Water," she moaned through parched lips. The sound was no more than a whisper. She tried again, but no sound came forth, only the heat that left her bathed in sweat. She pushed at the damp ends of her hair, trying to find some coolness anywhere on her overheated flesh.

GERRI RUSSELL

This is what it must feel like to not make it over the Beltaine Eve fire when leaping the flames—to burn alive. Trapped among the blankets, overwhelming heat coursed from her ankles, over her torso, to her brow in a wave of intensity. Flames licked their way across her injured shoulder, consuming her as they went.

"Water," she tried to speak. When nothing came out, she thrashed against the soft heather tick beneath her, hoping and praying someone would hear her.

A cool, wet cloth pressed against her lips. She sucked at it greedily, relishing the sweetness that bathed her dry throat. The cloth left her lips. She tried to cry out at the loss, but was soon rewarded by its return to her brow as it stroked her fevered skin in a wash of blessed coolness.

The heat lessened, and she found herself relaxing against the damp sheets. The scent of mint pervaded her senses, as did the soft brogue whispering at her ear, gentle words, calming words, words spoken by Ian to quiet her turmoil.

"Hush, sweet warrior. All will be well." He stroked her brow with the cool cloth.

At the tender sound of Ian's voice, a rush of gratitude swept through her. She struggled to open her eyes against the heaviness that invaded her. He brought his head down and kissed her cheeks, first one, then the other. In her whole life no one had ever cared for her with such exquisite tenderness, not even Maisie.

Scotia's eyes drifted shut, seeking respite from her own emotions. But instead of release, memories filled her mind—images of being held by Ian, wrapped in arms of protection and comfort. His voice calling to her over and over, commanding her to stay with him, to fight. Whispering words of encouragement and . . . what? What else had he said? She tried to remember, but could not.

176

She relaxed against the bed. Perhaps if she slept she might remember. And then she wondered why. Why were the words he had spoken important?

If only she could remember.

The purple-black haze of dusk shadowed the land as the White Horseman gave the signal to attack. The Four Horsemen led the charge on their horses while their army followed on foot, spears raised with a fervor that left the very air around them trembling. Over the ridge, they advanced on the unsuspecting village of Inverlochy.

The White Horseman lit his torch. A familiar surge of power raced through his body as he set fire to the first small house, then another, and watched the thatch go up in flames almost instantly. Smoke began to fill the air, and the thunder of footsteps surrounded the village. The cries of terror and rage that sent a thrill through his blood would come any time now.

He raised his bow, ready to strike at anything that scrambled from within the burning structures, but no one came forth. In fact, no cries of torment sounded from the village at all.

"My lord." One of the foot soldiers ran up to his horse and stopped, pausing to gather his breath before he spoke. "There be no one here."

Anger flared and anticipation faded. "What do you mean?"

The ragged and dirty soldier he had promoted to lieutenant mere days before dropped his gaze to the ground, refusing to meet his superior's eyes. "They are gone, my lord. Abandoned the village."

The White Horseman lowered his crossbow and frowned as night crept across the village now rimmed in a fiery glow. *So they think to outsmart us?* "Check the buildings again," the Horseman growled, disgusted he had been so easily duped by the heathens he sought to destroy. "They must be hiding somewhere."

The lieutenant scurried away to do his bidding. The Horseman pulled back on the reins, sending his horse's front hooves into the air, using the added height to inspect the surroundings for the wretched betrayers.

Nothing.

His horse came back down before prancing in a circle, releasing its agitation at being sorely used. The villagers' absence could mean only one thing: they had known the Four Horsemen were coming. They'd had time to prepare, and instead of fighting, they had chosen to flee.

"Burn the entire village to the ground," the White Horseman bellowed, sending the soldiers near him running to do as he bade.

From the other side of the village, three horsemen appeared from amongst the ash and smoke that drifted heavily about the village.

"This is the third village we have found empty." The Red Horseman halted his horse and sheathed his sword before his battle companions.

"There is nothing here to plunder," the Black Horseman interrupted as he joined the group.

The Green Horseman reined in and turned an accusing eye upon their self-appointed leader. "You are wasting our time. For what purpose? Saving the plum pickings for yourself?"

"Quiet," the White Horseman snarled. "I had nothing to do with these events."

"Why should we believe you?" the Green Horseman countered, his face contorting with anger.

An answering rage flared within the White Horseman as he raised his loaded crossbow, fixing each of his fellow warriors with a gaze that left no doubt about how he would handle such insolence again.

Instead of fear, boredom shone in their faces at the unspoken threat.

"I have had my fill of your threats." The Green Horseman narrowed his gaze. "I have had my fill of your empty promises as well. I do not need you."

"You think you'll succeed in finding the Stone without me?" The White Horseman lowered his bow to rest atop his thigh, reigning in his anger in the face of his men's mutiny.

"Aye." The Green Horseman turned his gaze to the Red and Black Horsemen. "Either of you wish to come with me and head south in search of a village to loot?"

"I'm with you," the Black Horseman replied as he reined his horse alongside the Green Horseman, creating a divide between the four of them. Two stood on the left, two on the right.

The White Horseman shifted his attention to the Red Horseman. "Where does your allegiance fall, with them or with me?"

His gaze darted between the two groups before it came to rest on the White Horseman once more. "With you, as always."

"We shall head north then," the White Horseman replied, barely managing to contain his fury. He clenched his bow in his hand, feeling the wood itch against his palm as he fought the urge to lift and shoot. How dare they break away from him? Forcing the Stone from these lawless heathens had been his idea. The Scots did not deserve such a priceless treasure. The queen of old might have brought it with her to this land, but she was a mere carrier, a transporter of sorts. Only England merited the crowning stone of Scotland's rulers.

And *he* would be the one to find the Stone. A foul curse left his mouth to mix with the night air now laden with smoke and ash. He should have taken the Stone all those years ago when there had been no doubt about where it had resided. But he had let his lust for a woman override his thinking.

Never again. He hardened his heart against memories of the past. All that mattered was finding the Stone so England could dominate Scotland forever.

Candlelight spilled a golden glow about Scotia's chamber. Ian stretched in his chair next to her bedside, then groaned as every muscle in his body protested the movement. He needed to walk, or to pick up his sword and train. But fear had kept him at Scotia's side through the last three endless and terrifying days.

Leaning forward, he put his hand to her forehead. The fever had abated early yesterday. And still she slept. Ian frowned. He had done everything his foster mother had taught him. Scotia had to do the rest.

He stood and began to pace the room, finding it difficult to contain the restlessness that had overcome him during the night. He would do anything to see that she healed, including stay by her side for three more days, or longer if need be. All that mattered was her recovery. What would he do without her?

He forced the thought deep inside himself. He could not think of that now. She merely needed sleep. She would wake when she was ready, and they would continue their training as usual. He released a dismissive laugh at the thought. "Nothing is ever usual with you, Scotia."

"Ian." Her eyelids fluttered open.

At the sound of her hoarse voice, relief surged through him and he forced back a lump that formed in his throat. He strode to her side. "Scotia," he whispered. He could hardly breathe, his heart pounded so violently. He drew her fingers against his rough cheek. He needed a shave and a bath, but even that had not been enough to lure him away from her side.

She took a deep breath, as if exhausted. "Water."

He reached for the cup that sat near her bedside and helped bring it to her lips. She drank until the cup was empty. "Would you like more?"

She shook her head. "How long have I been asleep?"

"Three days."

Her gaze studied his face. He wished he could hide the weariness that must surely show there. She needed no one else's burdens. She had enough of her own. "Have you been here the whole time?" Her words were slurred.

"Aye." He dragged a hand through his hair, trying to bring it into some sort of order.

She groaned and tried to sit up. "I am feeling better now."

Ian put his hand on her uninjured shoulder and pressed her back down, alarmed at how little effort it took to do so. "Not so fast."

"I am merely tired," she said with a touch of irritation.

She sounded more like her usual self. A smile came to his lips despite the terror that had held him in its grasp and was only now beginning to subside. "Getting out of this bed will only make things worse. Please, just this once, trust me and lie still."

She sighed impatiently. "All right, but I want my armor. All of it."

"Nay." He steeled himself for her reaction. "Not until I

181

am certain your fever has passed and your wounds have healed."

With a frown she tried once again to sit up. This time he let her. He pulled his hand away, but kept it near in case she should falter. Scotia would not believe she could not do something until she tried. One attempt from her would be worth him arguing all day.

She eased herself up on trembling elbows and her face drained of color. Her gaze grew disoriented, then panicked. Her eyes widened and her breathing grew sharp before she collapsed back onto the fluffy heather tick beneath her. "How will I battle like this?" The question sounded as though it had been ripped from the depths of her soul.

"You cannot." Ian took her icy fingers in his once more and held them up to his chest. Even now, the fight had not left her, despite being injured and weak.

Good. That spirit would serve her well as she recovered. The more determined she was to leave this bed, the sooner she would be back to training.

And the sooner he could seek his revenge against the Four Horsemen. He had been trying not to think about his need to leave as she lay sick, nearly dying. But now that it appeared she would recover, he could no longer deny his duty to free the country of the villains that threatened them. Maisie would happily tend Scotia. The older woman had tried to relieve him during the three long days of Scotia's recovery, but Ian had refused, wanting to stay near should she need him. Lizbet would be thrilled to have her playmate back. Even Griffin had shown his concern as he checked on Scotia's progress each morning before leading the new men in several of her training routines.

"The others will be pleased to know you are awake."

Ian let go of her hand. He avoided her gaze as he moved to the window to stare out at the moonless night. Should he tell her about the report he had received from her scouts early this morning? The Four Horsemen had changed their advance. Instead of progressing north in their usual fashion, they had done what he had feared most—turned their attack to the south, back toward his village of Kilninian. Back toward his father, his clan, and his home.

His body tensed, muscle by muscle, in a combination of fury and pain. He would have to leave soon if he were to stop the Four Horsemen before they endangered his clan. But leaving Glencarron Castle would mean leaving Scotia, possibly forever if the battle did not go in his favor.

"Ian," she called from the bed in a weak voice. "What is wrong?"

He drew a steadying breath, then turned to face her, offering her a reassuring smile he did not feel. He should tell her the truth. She deserved to know what had happened. He studied her face. Exhaustion clouded her eyes, but did not hide the spark of vibrancy that always seemed to shimmer just beneath the surface of her being. She would fight them even now, despite her own weakened state. If he told her about the Horsemen, she would leave this chamber to fight them. And without a doubt, she would die.

A crease furrowed her brow. "Ian?"

He set his jaw, remaining silent. She would want nothing to do with him when she learned he had withheld the truth. But what did it matter? Despite the fantasies and longings he had given free rein while she recovered, he had no future with this woman. His life had one purpose and one purpose alone: to kill the White Horseman.

Since Malcolm's death it had seemed enough of a goal,

finally giving the purpose of his life with the MacKin-nons a focus. Revenge against the murderer of his brother seemed a fitting tribute to all Abbus MacKinnon had done for him. He had put his heart and soul into that end. Nothing else had mattered—until Scotia had entered his life and thoughts of warring had turned to thoughts of touching her, holding her, feeling the beat of her heart next to his.

He turned his gaze away from her, away from the look of concern in her eyes. He clenched his fists, trying to control the twist of pain in his chest. God help him, with one simple look she could slice right through years of hardened resistance he had created around his heart.

She touched a part of him he never knew existed, and wished now he had never discovered. It would make his destiny that much harder to fulfill. But he would do it; he had no other choice. He would stay only until he was certain she regained her strength, another day or two at the most.

Scotia had her own obligations to fulfill. She needed to bear a female child to carry on her lineage. When he left, perhaps she would open herself and her heart to one of the new warriors he had brought with him. The twist in his chest tightened until he could bear it no longer. "I must go," he announced as he hastened from the room, leaving a startled Scotia in his wake.

Once in the hallway he leaned against the stone wall, allowing the cold to seep inside him, praying it would act as a balm to the purgatory he had created in his own mind. He should not care if Scotia took another man into her arms. He should not care, but he did. Ian stared into the unlit corridor, seeing nothing but a depth of darkness that truly mirrored his soul. He could not re-member a time when he had been more miserable, despite the torment of his childhood. That seemed a mere bump in his path compared to now.

His destiny left him no choice but to leave. To think he had any other option would be disastrous for them all.

Chapter Twenty-one

"What are you hiding from me?" Scotia demanded. She sat on the edge of the bed, where she had been a prisoner to bouts of sleep and wakefulness for the past two days. She was feeling stronger now and ready to get back to training. "I can see that something is going on just by looking out my window. The men you brought are training with a force that speaks of some known peril."

Something was wrong. She could see the evidence written into the very texture of Ian's face. His eyes bespoke danger, just as the tension in his shoulders and along his chin warned of a heaviness that threat brought to him, or herself, or her people.

Maisie and Burke had both been to see her, yet she had been unable to wrest any information from them, either. "If Ian has somethin' to tell ye, he will do it in his own time," Maisie had said, to Scotia's growing irritation.

She gritted her teeth, trying to hold on to the anger that offered her some safeguard against him. Why would he not confide in her? "Tell me or I will leave this room to find out for myself. I would go now if I could but find my clothing."

"You are still too weak."

"That is your opinion." She straightened her shoulders and tried to show him how much stronger she felt. "Where are my armor and my sword? And why are there guards at my door?"

"The guards are there for your protection," Ian said. "They are keeping unwanted visitors out. It is for your safety alone that they stand near."

She knew he had posted the guards to keep her safe. That was not what had irritated her so. It was the knowledge that she could not defend herself if someone came to challenge her, or even help Ian against the unspoken dangers she read in his eyes. The Four Horsemen had to be the reason why he held back information from her. No doubt he thought he was protecting her, but her whole life had been spent training for the coming conflict with her enemy.

"I will not be confined to this bed forever." She started to stand, but thought better of it when her legs wobbled beneath her. Scotia sighed in frustration. Best to stay seated and argue her point.

To her annoyance, Ian smiled. He had noticed her attempt to stand. "You may leave any time. No one is holding you here." He stood near the window, and occasionally shifted his gaze to the hills and vales beyond her land.

She gritted her teeth and tried to gain her feet once again. If she tried hard enough, she might be able to overcome her fatigue and the trembling of her limbs. "I need my armor and my sword," she gasped as her legs weakened beneath her.

187

Ian shot to her side. Two hands of strength wrapped about her, lowering her gently against the bed. "I will give them back to you when you are ready to return to battle. You are making progress in your recovery. It will not be long now."

The solid wall of his chest pressed against the softness of her own. Her pulse quickened; her senses heightened. After so many days of isolation and rest, his nearness overwhelmed her. Without her armor she felt vulnerable and weak. How she longed for a thin sheet of metal to separate her from the warm feel of his body against her own.

"I am ready," she said, a bit more breathless than she had intended, but it was difficult to breathe when he stood so near.

"Ready for what, Scotia?" She startled at the mix of sadness and regret in the timbre of his voice.

She turned to look up into the depths of his eyes, trying to see in his gaze what she sensed in his voice. But any response she tried to make stilled on her tongue as her senses sharpened. The warmth of his body reached out to her, carrying with it the musky male scent that was only Ian's.

With a will of its own, her body pressed closer against his, trying to identify this new sensation, experience it further, while her mind struggled to control it. "My . . . armor," she said on a shaky breath, trying to fill her lungs not with air, but with the essence of this man who held her in his arms.

A look of pained reluctance crept into his gaze. "To protect yourself against your enemies or me?" He slid one hand up her back, over the thin linen nightrail someone had dressed her in. One of her mother's, no doubt. Callused fingertips slipped over the softness of her skin, leaving his imprint on her in a trail of heated sensation.

He knew her thoughts too well. Scotia began to tremble under the combined forces of pleasure and shock, and no amount of willpower could control the betraying tremors. She needed protection from herself as much as she needed it from him.

That odd reflection of emotion vanished from his eyes as his fingers lightly caressed the wounds at her shoulder. Instead of pain, his touch brought an ease to the area. The wounds had healed over the last several days, thanks to his care.

"I never thanked you—"

Ian held a finger against her lips, bringing tingles of sensation along with his touch. "There is no need for words. I can see your feelings in your eyes."

She lowered her lashes to hide her gaze from him. How could he read her thoughts so easily when she had been taught to shield her inner feelings all her life? What else did he see there? Could he see the war of emotions that tugged between her desire for him and her duty to remain strong, alert, untouched?

She tried to form words that might express her thoughts when his fingers traced the curve of her chin, running across the sensitive nape of her neck as if he were trying to commit each nuance of her to memory.

Then his fingers moved on, to delve further down until his hands cupped the fullness of her breasts. His thumbs brushed the hardened peak of her nipples. She gasped, but did not pull away. Instead, she shut her eyes and gave herself over to the pleasurable sensations he brought out in her, wondering if he would touch her breasts again and hoping she could bear it if he did. No one had touched her like this before. And, heaven help her, she liked it.

No one had ever told her that a touch, this slow caress, could bring an empty ache to the apex of her thighs, or make her breasts feel tight, or fill her with sensations she had no right to feel but no desire to stop despite the fact she knew she should.

Any protests died as she moved her hands down his back to his tight, trim waist, then further down, to his buttocks. The feel of muscle and strength beneath her bare palms made her bold. She cupped his buttocks as he had her breasts, pleased by the groan of pleasure that escaped his lips.

"Is this an invitation?" In one fluid motion he pressed her back against the heather tick and the tumble of covers that made up her bed. "An invitation we can both remember after we . . ." His words drifted off, but the look of sadness and regret came back to his eyes.

What was he telling her? Her mind warred with her body to find a meaning, but her body won over all rational thought, pulling her into the moment, leaving all else behind.

Scotia slid her hands up his back and into the silky texture of his hair, capturing him as surely as he pinned her beneath him. She gasped as her breasts brushed against his broad chest, at the possessive way he caught one of her legs between his own, at the rigid maleness pressed intimately against her thigh.

Lightheaded and disoriented, she tried to control the passion that washed over her. But she could not hold back a moan of pleasure as he pulled her closer, trapping spirals of untamed heat between them. The sensation was both exquisite and consuming.

She wanted more of it.

"If there is to be more between us, you will have to say the words, Scotia." The warmth of his labored breath curled against her cheek in silent invitation. "You have not been well, and I shall not take advantage of that state unless you wish it."

She looked into his eyes, eyes that held both infinite patience and heated desire. Her gaze moved to the lips that hovered above hers, ready to descend if she gave him one small sign of encouragement. She wanted him to continue, but the thought of what came next held her back. She had learned enough from her mother to know this was how babies were formed. Yet her mother had said she would find no pleasure in the deed. How could that be possible when she had found only pleasure in his arms up to now?

A long moment stretched between them while Scotia stared at him mutely, unable to find her voice.

His mouth drew closer until he was only a whisper away. "Say you want this," he said in a soft brogue made rough by the desire he held back.

A mere movement of her body would bring his lips to hers, one movement and she would be lost to his kisses forever. But with those kisses came a deeper commitment. Was she willing to make herself even more vulnerable than she was now for the sake of an heir, someone to carry on her task as Warrior Trainer? All for the sake of a kiss?

With an agonized cry she turned her head away, knowing that the shadows would return to his eyes, shadows she would have put there by her denying them both this moment.

"I understand," he said from beside her. His voice was not hard or angry, but laced with acceptance. He rolled from her and rose from the bed. She did not look up until she heard the door close softly behind him.

He said he understood. How could he when she barely comprehended what had passed between them herself?

Scotia twisted into the tangle of bedding next to her with a soft cry of unspent longing. Instead of her thick down coverlet, a soft woolen fabric pressed against her cheek. She drew back to look at it. His plaid. A single sob filled her, rose, caught in her throat. She could not breathe around the pain as her soul shattered within her.

Why could she not have said the words he had longed to hear, that she had longed to say? She pulled the length of cloth away from the other linens and held it against her cheek, hoping to find solace in the action. None came. She closed her eyes and drew in the scents of mint and musk from the fabric—scents that would forever remind her of him.

For the next two days, Scotia forced herself to get out of bed each morning and afternoon to train in the privacy of her bedchamber. Regaining her strength grew in proportion to her desire to be in charge of her own destiny. Ian had not come to visit her since she had turned him away. She understood why, but that did not make his absence any easier to take. If he would not come to her, she would go to him. But not until she could stand before him as his equal on the battlefield once more.

Each morning she put herself through a series of stretches, working muscle by muscle until the stiffness caused by her injury and inactivity gave way to strong, supple movements. She used her time alone to retrain her body and refocus her mind. In the afternoons, she put herself through a series of kicks and lunges, parries and rolls, using the iron candleholder as her makeshift sword until she fell onto her bed, too physically spent to go on. But even exhaustion could not block out the memories of the moments she had spent melting in Ian's arms.

Instead of finding comfort in his arms, she snuggled up

against the length of plaid he had given her, finding contentment in its presence beside her cheek.

As light crept into her chamber on the third day of Ian's absence, Scotia awoke to find her armor lying atop the coverlet at the foot of her bed. Her shield, sword, brigandine, gauntlets, cuisses, cross-garters and boots. It was all there, freshly oiled and shined. Next to her armor lay new quilted padding and a pleated skirt in the colors of the MacKinnon.

Scotia scrambled to her knees, searching the bed for the length of cloth Ian had left with her. She tossed the bed linens aside in a desperate scramble, knocking her armor to the floor in her haste. Panic gripped her as she threw the linens aside, one by one in her search. The cloth was gone. But who had taken it, and why? She jumped off the bed and stared at the shambles of her room, at the softly pleated skirt on the floor, near her feet.

Someone had taken the cloth to sew her this garment. Maisie? Ian? Scotia bent down and scooped it up, allowing the fabric to rub against her fingers. Beneath the plaid lay her usual tired red skirt.

A new skirt or her old? Someone had wanted her to make a choice.

Scotia pressed her lips together as she clutched Ian's plaid in her hands. What should she do? If she put on the fabric of his clan, would she be marking herself his? She brought the fabric up to rest against her cheek as she had when it was merely a length of fabric. The scents of mint and musk still lingered there, penetrated her mind, bringing forth an image of Ian, his lips hovering above hers. A delicious warmth spread through her at the memory.

It might be an act of lunacy to wear his colors so intimately, but then again she had been skirting the bounds of sanity since the day he had arrived. What was one more irrational action when added to the rest?

She drew her nightrail over her head and tossed it down beside her old red skirt. With a slight tremble in her fingers, she dropped the skirt over her head, tying the drawstring at the side. The fabric settled around her hips in a cloud of softness. With her fingers, she smoothed the plaid into evenly spaced pleats and smiled. The garment shaped to her hips as her old skirt never had, revealing feminine curves she had only recently discovered.

She smoothed her hands over her hips and across her womb. If she closed her eyes tightly enough, she could almost imagine a flicker of movement inside her, or the gentle swell of her belly beneath her hands. A child: a permanent mark upon her body as well as her heart; an everlasting memory of the passion she and Ian shared to cause a child to develop and form.

She opened her eyes. Did she want a child with this man? Could she move past her own fears of motherhood and vulnerability to allow that to happen?

The image of Lizbet came to mind. Dear, sweet Lizbet, whose gentle acceptance proved to her she could be loving despite their less than perfect start. Scotia drew in a slow, deep breath. There were ways to keep a child safe once it was born, as her mother had kept her safe. As all the Scotias before her had kept their children safe from attackers.

Would she feel the same way if she ever carried Ian's child—despite the fact there would always be others like Haldane who would challenge her?

Haldane. He had almost defeated her. She brought her fingers up to the dark pink scars that stood out against the pale backdrop of her skin. Ribbons of color that looked so small and insignificant compared to the enormity of what had caused them. She had let down her guard for Ian and had been attacked when she was most vulnerable.

Two wounds that marked her as a warrior, and two reminders of the moments of madness that she and Ian had shared.

Her pulse quickened at the thought of him. Would she have done anything differently if she knew Haldane would attack her? The answer was immediate. Nay. She would have done almost anything for those moments in his arms.

Why would she risk so much? She would risk everything for him, because she . . . She let the sentiment drift away, not wanting to put a name to it. Yet even as she did, all the reasons for staying away from Ian, all the difficulties, were fading, losing their edges, becoming less clear.

Scotia felt the awakenings of a smile come to her lips, joined by another odd, almost foreign sensation. Joy tumbled through her stomach, sending shivers of delight out across her bare arms and legs.

She had to see Ian, had to somehow communicate that she was ready for a different kind of battle with him, ready to surrender to the force that pulled them together since the day they first met.

Chapter Twenty-two

Feeling as light and airy as the fabric at her hips, Scotia swirled where she stood. A bubble of delight rose inside her as Ian's plaid came to rest against her thighs. She would gladly wear his plaid, his mark, if it meant that the rest of her desires would come to her as well.

She raced back to the bed and slipped into her armor, eager now to leave her room and find the man who had changed her life for the better. Her fingers trembling with anticipation, Scotia plaited her hair. When she finished she picked up her sword and shield, then opened the door.

Two of the men Ian had brought into her service stood at the entrance to her chamber dressed in full body armor. They held their spears in the shape of an X across her door, barring her exit. "Mistress," the taller of the two said.

"At ease," she reassured them, but they did not drop their weapons.

She placed her hand at the cross in the wood and pushed gently against the spears. The men did not yield. They could only stare at her with wide eyes and slack jaws. Scotia frowned. "I will leave this room," she said with more force than she had intended. But her words had the desired effect. Both spears vanished, her way unchallenged.

"Pardon, mistress," the guard on her left replied. "We dinna mean to stop ye. 'Tis just that ye look so different from the last time we seen ye. We are ever so glad ye are well and ready to train us again."

Scotia turned to the other guard. Admiration shone in his eyes as well. "'Tis a wonder that ye be a grand fighter when ye are also such a bonny lass."

Scotia stiffened at his comment. What was wrong with these men? A skirt could not make that much difference in her appearance. Could it? Or was it how she felt in the skirt that changed her image? Baffled by their behavior, she hurried past the men.

As she made her way through the familiar stone corridors of her home, she found herself relaxing. In this castle she was whoever she wanted to be—warrior, woman, mother. A mother. The thought sent a sudden chill across the back of her neck. She did not think she would ever get used to hearing that word in relation to herself. But perhaps in time . . .

Descending the stairs, she heard Ian's voice filtering up to her from the great hall. She could not make out the words, but his voice sounded strained. Any lightheartedness she felt disappeared as she recalled the threat of danger Ian had never confided to her. Her hand moved to her sword, and she was pleased to note her shoulder did not ache at the movement.

As she entered the hall, her gaze sought Ian immediately. He stood with his back to her, facing Griffin. Griffin's eyes widened when he saw her. He smiled.

Scotia nearly faltered in her step at the unusual

warmth of Griffin's silent greeting. She glanced behind her to see if anyone else were there that he might be smiling at. There was no one. Tension flared inside her as she continued her approach. Something was seriously wrong if Griffin could look at her without his usual combative anger.

"Make the necessary preparations. I will join you when I can," Ian said. He turned slightly, offering her a profile view of his face. A frown accentuated the shadows of fatigue and worry beneath his eyes. As if sensing her presence, he turned to face her.

She hoped for an encouraging smile like the one Griffin had greeted her with and was not disappointed. Pleasure and a hint of desire shone in his eyes. "You look enchanting," he said as he came toward her, his arms extended as though he meant to embrace her right there in front of Griffin.

Then he stopped, his hands returned to his side, and his smile faded. The tension once again descended over his face. "Are you well enough to be out of bed?"

"I am feeling much stronger. It is time I resume my obligations."

"As a trainer?"

"Among other things." She drew her sword and held her shield out before her. The ring of metal blade against her metal scabbard sent a chilling reverberation through the nearly empty room.

Ian motioned to Griffin with a slight jerk of his head to leave the chamber. Griffin obeyed without objection. Scotia watched him stride from the room as a sense of impending doom swept over her.

"What is going on?" she asked even as she feared the answer.

"Now that I know you are well, I can no longer put this off." Anguish contorted Ian's features.

Suddenly his words and actions over the last few days came crashing around her in instant clarity. The look of sadness in his eyes when they talked, the kisses they had shared with such heated passion, followed by the regret she had heard in his voice as he left her chamber that day.

He was leaving her, this time for good.

"Ian?" She hated the way her voice trembled, but could muster none of her usual control.

"I must go, Scotia."

The air in the room hung still and heavy as he searched her face. She wanted to turn away from his probing gaze, but forced herself to hold steady. "Why?"

"The Four Horsemen have turned their attack back to the south, toward my village. Griffin and I must leave right away if we intend to stop them."

She was slightly comforted that he would not go into this battle alone. Griffin would help Ian against the four warriors and their army. But even with Griffin, the odds were against their survival. "I can send other warriors with you." It was a desperate attempt, she knew. But if she could not stop him, she would try to save him instead.

"Nay. I will not leave you in danger only to protect myself."

She tried to tamp down a surge of anger by centering her thoughts. But fear and anger, desperation and hopelessness dominated all reason. "You are reckless, Ian MacKinnon, to stand up to those men alone."

"I have to try."

"Perhaps we should just give them the Stone. It certainly has not been protecting our people."

"Have faith, Scotia. Handing it over to these villains

will not save us. The Horsemen will never cease terrorizing our country. Giving them the Stone will only make our troubles worse."

"Aye. You are right."

Ian's jaw tightened. "Is the Stone the reason you will not leave the castle?"

She nodded, bracing herself for the frown of disapproval she was certain would follow. Instead, Ian offered her a rueful smile. "You and I are both trapped by duty in a destiny neither of us wants. And neither of us can turn away from what it is we must do."

She stared at him a moment, trying to find some way to deny the truth. Nothing could alter this reality—there could be no escape for either of them. Perhaps Ian was right to think their lives were predestined. His path was clear, as was her own. Still a part of her refused to accept the cruelty of such a fate.

Frustration and bitterness welled inside her. She staggered backward beneath the force of her emotions before she grappled for control. She had to find a way to will away the pain. Scotia clenched her fingers around the hilt of her sword. Her sword. Her gaze dropped to her weapon. Only when fighting could she plunge herself into an emotionless abyss. She needed to go there now. She raised her sword. "Fight me, Ian."

He kept his gaze fastened on her, his expression bleak. "I must go, regardless."

"Fight me!" She waved her sword dangerously close to his face, trying desperately to turn off the agony that burned at the back of her throat.

"Are you sure, Scotia?" He drew his sword.

"Yes," she said softly.

He swung his sword round and round in an easy motion to warm his wrists for the battle ahead.

Scotia began to walk around him, watching, measuring Ian's movements as he rolled his shoulder, flexed his calf, warming his muscles for the abuse they would soon thrust upon each other.

This was their good-bye, at the end of their swords. Strange, but for once in her life she would have preferred kisses.

Ian's balance shifted forward, and she knew he prepared for the first strike. She would allow him that much since she had challenged him. But it would be the last moment she would yield, to him or any man, ever again.

His attack was sudden. He lunged forward while his sword arched sideways, toward her head. It was a good move, one she had taught him if he wanted to take out his enemy in a swift first blow.

She blocked the move. The two weapons came together, sending sparks flying into the charged air. As quickly as he attacked, he darted back, spun around and attacked from the other side.

Once again, Scotia blocked his strike. This time with her shield. The hit sent a wave of pain through her shoulder, and she gasped at the effect.

Ian dropped his guard and lowered his sword. "Had enough?"

A part of her wanted to lower her own sword and let his compassion seep through her resolve. But not today—not if she was to find the dullness she longed to take over her body. Scotia lunged forward, ignoring the surprised grunt from him as her sword sheared off a section of his plaid that hung at his shoulder. A small piece of cloth dropped to the floor while the remaining heavy material flopped down to hang behind him like a tail. "Never drop your guard, Ian. Not for an instant. Not to anyone."

"A final lesson?" Ian asked as he quickly stuffed the

end of the fabric into his belt to keep himself from tripping. He offered a brief salute with his sword before his blade whistled through the air as it arched toward Scotia's stomach, her knees, her forearm, her head.

"Take it however you will."

He had learned the lesson well. Scotia blocked each strike with her shield and her sword, absorbing each blow into her body, into her muscles, welcoming the fatigue. Her muscles began to feel numb, lame, stunned by his attack, and she decided to turn her swordplay to attack.

A scraping sound came off to her right, but she kept her eyes trained on Ian, allowing no distraction. He briefly glanced to the side where the sound had come from. Scotia took advantage of his distraction. She sliced at him but only caught air. Ian dropped, rolled, and came to his feet behind her, holding a shield in his hand.

Scotia stepped back and cast a furtive glance beside her. Burke and Maisie stood with their heads together in conversation, looking both pleased and apologetic.

The battle continued. Ian used his shield to block, each stroke she made. Their fighting changed, softened until it become more of a dance. They circled each other breath for breath, passion for passion—movements that stoked the fires of need and regret. Motions that could warm a heart as well as chill a soul.

A flash of metal gleamed in the afternoon light of the room. A shiny reflection caught Scotia's eye, and she forgot about battle. Ian's shield, polished to a brilliance like none she had seen before caught her image and entranced her with what she saw. Some part of her realized that Ian had stopped moving as well, but she could not react to anything but the image of herself in his shield.

High color brought a glow to her cheeks. Her hair cascaded out of her plait to fall in waves of unfurled softness about her shoulders. Her face was leaner, more well-defined than it had been before she became ill. And her eyes no longer contained the aged sadness she had seen in them so often in the past. Instead, a gentle acceptance of who she was shone through. She almost laughed at the rightness of her image. She had become all that she had originally feared, both woman and warrior. Neither state dominated the other.

Perfect balance.

The full enormity of her realization brought a smile to her lips. Her gaze moved to Ian's. Her pulse quickened. Her mind cried out to his, *Do not go.*

The tension was obvious in his coiled muscles as he watched her, like a predator stalking its prey.

She did not move, did not say a word. The next move was his.

His gaze moved to her mouth, to the smile she could feel slipping away the longer he remained silent. "I have waited so long to see you smile," he finally said. "A spontaneous grin changes you from beautiful to stunning."

Scotia caught a deep, shuddering breath as he moved toward her. The look in his eyes did not speak of battle or even good-byes. Nay, it said he wanted to devour her.

The beat of her heart sounded in her ears, pulsed through her body, and thrust her forward, into his arms. Their lips came together in a fierceness that spun out of control before it even started. Pulling her up against his hardening body, he parted her lips. She drew his tongue into her mouth. An incomprehensible wildness stole through her, making her brazen and bold. She slid her hands through his hair, holding him tight.

His hand splayed across her buttocks, bringing her into vibrant contact with his rigid arousal. With a silent moan of desperation, Scotia pulled her lips away. She pressed

GERRI RUSSELL

her cheek against his chest, trembling in the aftermath of the most explosive passion she had ever experienced.

"I will treasure this memory forever." Sadness filled his gaze as he leaned toward her once more to place a kiss upon her cheek. Without another word, he left the chamber.

Scotia did not move even though she wanted to bring her fingers up to cover her cheek, to hold that last brief kiss from him against her skin forever. The room before her began to blur, and grief welled up until it pushed her numbness aside, wrenching a strangled sob from deep within her.

Ian was gone. But he would not be alone.

"Burke," Scotia said, struggling to find her voice. "Send Keith Ranald to me immediately."

Ian might feel the need to fulfill his destiny alone; she had no such compunction if it meant keeping him alive. He had brought men into her service, and she would use them now.

"Mistress?" Keith Ranald entered the chamber and offered her a respectful bow before approaching.

Scotia gathered the threads of her composure. She had to stay in control of her emotions. If she did not, she would be lost. "Thank you for attending me."

"'Tis an honor. What may I do for ye?" Pride sparkled in his blue eyes.

"I have a request to make of you and the others."

Keith drew his shoulders up, making him appear even more hearty and robust than he already was. "Anything."

"Here me out first. Dangers lay in this request, and I will respect your decision if you refuse."

Confusion replaced the pride in his expression. "What would ye have us do?"

"Follow Ian. Do not let him know you pursue, until he has need of you."

"But—"

"He and Griffin intend to confront the Four Horsemen. Alone."

"No . . . ," Keith breathed as his hand moved to the hilt of his sword. "To fight them alone . . ."

"Will you follow him?" *Will you keep him safe?* Scotia added in her thoughts.

"If we go after Ian, then yer own defenses will be weakened," he said consideringly. "How can we leave ye exposed like that?"

"Ian's need is greater. My own men will remain here."

After only a slight hesitation, Keith nodded. "'Tis done. We ride immediately." He offered her a terse bow, then hurried from the room.

Scotia stared after his retreating figure. At least Ian had a chance of survival now. The thought, however comforting, did not free her from the painful yearnings of her heart.

Chapter Twenty-three

Maisie and Burke stood side by side as they waited for Keith Ranald to leave the great hall. When just the three of them remained, Maisie made her way toward Scotia on legs that had suddenly turned unsteady and weak. Scotia stood with her back straight, not moving, barely breathing. Maisie watched as Scotia slowly tensed her muscles, as her hand tightened on the hilt of her sword, as the joy that Ian had brought to her face ebbed away, replaced once again with the cool aloofness that had seen her through her youth. She was retreating back into the darkness that had shadowed her life before Ian had come to her.

"Scotia." Maisie placed hesitant fingers on Scotia's arm, trying to offer whatever comfort she might.

Scotia lifted her face. The devastated look in her eyes rendered Maisie speechless. The emotions that had shaped and formed Scotia up until now—the pain, the misery, the withdrawal—reflected in the depths of her eyes. Emotions she had hoped Scotia would never have to experience again.

"I need to get back to training." Scotia made to move toward the door, but Maisie stilled her with a hand on her arm.

"Ye do not need to train. Ye need to talk this out."

"I cannot." Scotia shook her head.

"Ye canna hide yer emotions from me. I see what yer feelin', and it'll consume ye if ye doona talk about it with someone." The strong bearing of Scotia's shoulders drooped ever so slightly, but was enough of a sign of agreement for Maisie to continue.

"Ye cared about that bonny lad, didn't ye?" Maisie asked carefully.

The words brought Scotia's gaze back to Maisie's. "He is gone," Scotia said, her voice breaking.

With those simple words, Maisie knew all the things Scotia did not say: all the fears, all the hurt. How many years had she tried to compensate for Scotia's mother's lack of compassion and caring? She knew the young woman before her as well as if she were her own child. Maisie tried to gather Scotia to her, to offer what little physical comfort she could, but Scotia pulled away.

Scotia's sword and shield slipped from her fingers and a clang resounded in the great hall. When the sound ebbed away, Scotia brought her trembling fingers up to her mouth, as if doing so would hold the pain inside her.

"Do not go back to that cave of darkness ye've locked yerself in for so long," Maisie said, finding her voice. "Let it out, Scotia."

Scotia shook her head. "I . . . don't know how." Tears welled up in her eyes and her throat worked to hold them back. She turned away, shielding her grief from Maisie.

"I want to help. Please let me help ye." Maisie shifted where she stood, not knowing what else to do. Scotia didn't want comfort, not from her.

"Things were changing, Maisie. I feel . . . different." Scotia pressed her lips together as if trying to block the force of her emotions. "Sad. Angry."

"Why?" Maisie prompted.

"He made me feel like a real woman, protected and loved. I had thoughts, Maisie. Thoughts about the future."

"'Tis a good thing." Maisie smiled encouragingly.

"Nay." Scotia shook her head. "Because now I know what it is like to feel feminine, and loved. But all that is gone and I am alone once again. Oh, Maisie. He swept me away in a tide of sensations. I never realized how much I wanted to feel like any other woman—protected and cherished instead of having to always be so strong."

"But ye are strong, Scotia. 'Tis part of who ye are. What is wrong with that?"

"I want more." She flared her fingers across her middle as though she were protecting something there. "I want to be a woman. I want . . . I wanted a baby." The words echoed around the stillness of the room.

"You can still—"

"Nay," she said in a choked voice. "I want Ian to father my daughter. I . . . love him."

Maisie felt tears well up in her own eyes at the tortured sound in Scotia's voice. As though sensing her need for support, Burke moved to her side.

Scotia straightened. "But that will never be." She paused and pressed her lips together, visibly trying to control her tears.

"That's not true." Maisie held her hands out to Scotia.

Scotia jerked back, waving her hands toward the ground where her sword and shield lay. "I am only good at fighting. Hardly the qualities of motherhood."

"Ye'll be a fine mother." A tightness came to Maisie's throat.

Tears spilled from Scotia's eyes. "I shall never know. That part of my life is over before it has even begun."

"There are other men," Maisie offered, even though she knew Scotia would never choose another. She was too loyal, too committed. Once her heart was given, it would be for a lifetime.

Scotia tugged down the edge of her brigandine as she tried to reel in her pain. Despite the changes Ian had wrought in her, Scotia would retreat back into the safety of her armor and castle. There was no avoiding that reality.

Burke reached out, and Maisie felt his fingers close around hers. He seemed to understand her own unspoken need for comfort. This was not the outcome they had worked toward. She drew in a halting breath. 'Twas their duty to see Scotia had a child and continued her line. Yet how could they force her to do so now? Her grief had been laid out before them, stark and unfettered. 'Twould be cruel to insist she find another mate. They had made that mistake with her mother.

Burke squeezed Maisie's hand. She met his gaze and saw a flicker of encouragement in the depths of his tired gray eyes. "Have faith," he said with a gentle smile.

The words helped steel Maisie's resolve. Aye, faith. 'Twas what kept them on their course for the past twenty-five years. Faith in their country, faith in their mistress, and faith in her daughter. Maisie allowed her hand to rest on Scotia's shoulder. To her surprise, Scotia did not pull away this time. Instead, she covered Maisie's gnarled fingers with her younger hand. "Tomorrow things won't look so bad, love." Maisie sent her a weak smile.

Scotia batted the tears from her cheeks with the back of her other hand. "If only I could determine where to go from here."

Burke released Maisie's hand and moved to stand before Scotia, with his back straight and tall. "I realize yer disappointed, lass. We all are. But ye'll move on from this. Ye have no choice."

"But where do I start?" Scotia asked.

Burke's cheeks flushed pink and his eyes flashed, not with anger but with a vibrancy Maisie had long thought dead. Her heart beat a little faster at the sight. "Where ye always start. Go back to yer foundation—back to who ye are." He brought his hand up to rest on Scotia's shoulder. "I've watched ye grow from a wee lass to a strong and independent warrior. I sat back and watched ye struggle when yer countrymen stopped comin' to ye to train, and when the foreigners only came to challenge ye. And I burst with pride when ye won that first battle." Some of the fight left Burke's gaze as he looked Scotia directly in the face. "I've loved ye no matter what happened, no matter yer choices. I've done my duty, Scotia, as if I were yer own father. Now ye must do yers."

He bent down and picked up her sword, holding it toward her. "Now is the time to rise above these difficulties and do what ye were put on this earth to do."

Scotia hesitated as she stared at her weapon. "If I were put on this earth to bear a child to continue my line, then nay, I cannot and will not do that."

"Yer life has other purposes. Those lessons ye should know well."

Scotia nodded her head. "Protecting the Stone and my people. And training those who might someday come to me to learn."

"Aye, lass." Burke smiled.

Maisie continued to study Scotia as her conscience pricked at her to tell the truth, all of it. There were things Scotia should know.

"What is it Maisie?" Scotia asked. "I have come to know that troubled look on your face."

Maisie hesitated. "There is somethin' we should have told you long ago." Scotia waited silently for her to continue. "The reason yer countrymen stopped comin' here to train with ye. Burke and I allowed everyone except the clan council to believe ye had died along with yer mother."

"What?"

"We decided the deception would keep ye and the Stone safe from the White Horseman until ye were ready to stand up to him." Scotia's expression held all the betrayal Maisie expected to see written there. "We loved ye so much. We couldn't bear to lose ye." The sentiment didn't excuse the deception, but it was their only defense. Would Scotia understand that?

"And why do the challengers come to me now, after all this time? Haldane had something to do with it, but he could not have sent them all."

"Three moon cycles ago, we sent your warriors out, encouraging them to spread the word that ye still lived. After all the years of secrecy, we needed to break our silence in order for ye to choose a mate and bear the new Warrior Trainer."

Scotia paled. "That was when the Four Horsemen returned to this country and when foreigners came to challenge me."

"Aye," Maisie acknowledged. "As soon as the news spread to England, the White Horseman came to Glencarron Castle looking for ye."

"And," Scotia prompted tersely.

"We told him ye had left the safety of the castle with the Stone to move among yer countrymen."

The hurt in her soft green eyes shifted to that of guilt and fear. "You endangered the lives of my people all the more. Oh, Maisie . . ."

"Aye," she admitted hoarsely. "But the clan leaders willingly accepted the dangers in order to keep ye safe."

"Neither the council, nor even the two of you, had the right to determine that my life meant more than any other person in this country." Her gaze shifted from Maisie to Burke. "Our people have paid a terrible price." A spark of compassion flared in her eyes, along with steely determination. "They will suffer no more, not because of me. It is time the Warrior Trainer's role took on a new aspect."

"What do ye mean, love?" Maisie asked, fearful of the look she saw in Scotia's eyes.

"Time for me to became more than I am. I might be the keeper of the Stone, but I should also be the protector of my people."

"But what of yer lineage, Scotia. An heir. Ye must have an heir." Maisie looked to Burke for support, but his gaze slid from Scotia's to Maisie's, then off in the distance toward the door. An odd expression crossed his face.

Maisie turned to see Lizbet standing there with her wooden sword clutched in her small hands. "How long have ye been standin' there, child?"

Without saying a word, Lizbet stepped into the room to stand beside Scotia. An expression of infinite gentleness settled over Lizbet's features as she searched Scotia's face.

"Lizbet." Scotia's gaze dropped to the wooden sword in the young girl's hands.

"I need a mommy," the little girl said in the simple yet eloquent way of a child. "I can be your child. Please?"

Scotia gathered Lizbet to her, and drew in a slow, even

breath. "And I need a brave little girl like you," Scotia said with a catch in her voice.

Lizbet buried herself in Scotia's arms with a squeal of joy. With her free hand, Scotia grasped the hilt of the sword Burke held out to her. She could train Lizbet. And even though the blood lineage would disappear, it was a solution she could live with right now.

Scotia shifted her gaze to Maisie. "Things might not have worked out as you or I had hoped, but my destiny is fulfilled, and it is time to move forward from here."

Move forward.

The words held a hopeful sound.

Chapter Twenty-four

The morning mist left a chill in the air that did little to warm Ian's spirit as he headed toward home. His horse picked its way across the rocky terrain of the Highlands. A full day later the image of Scotia, forcing a smile so as not to reveal her grief as he left, stayed with him. He hated to leave her, but he had no choice.

He and Griffin had slept only a few hours last night in their haste to find the Four Horsemen. The empty hours of travel had left him much time to consider Scotia, and all he had learned from her. She had given him so much knowledge in the short time they had been together. But how did it all fit into his life? So far the only answer he had was an empty ache in his chest.

Another day's riding and he and Griffin would be home, back in Kilninian, if they did not find the Four Horsemen first. The thought did not bring the same burning desire for revenge that it had three weeks before.

"Do you think you will ever go back?" Griffin asked, breaking the silence that had fallen between them since dawn.

Go back. "My duty takes me to a place I may never return from."

"It is not your sole duty to see the Four Horsemen pay for Malcolm's murder," Griffin said with a hint of anger in his tone.

"I must stop the White Horseman from hurting anyone else I love," Ian confessed, releasing the darkest secret of his heart. His reasons for revenge had shifted, become more personal. He would stop the man from harming his brethren as well as the woman who had crept past his guard over the past several weeks.

"What happens if the White Horseman kills you first? And even if you are able to strike him down, the other three will kill you. This death wish of yours makes no sense to me."

"Someone must make that sacrifice. I am best suited." *Since I have no one else who cares for me*, he added silently, reminding himself of his initial reasoning. Ian paused— those words were not as true as they had once been.

You matter to me. Scotia's words played over in his mind. He forced the thought away. He had to stay focused on his goal. "If the White Horseman falls, the others will disband."

"What makes you so certain?"

"I am not," Ian admitted. "I had always assumed—"

"Scotia taught us that assumptions get you killed. Did you not listen to her lessons?" Griffin asked.

Ian felt the usual anger tighten his gut. "We do not have time to argue."

Griffin's lips became taut. "Is your loyalty to your clan more important than your life, or a woman who needs you?"

"Scotia needs no one." Ian shifted his gaze back to the trail ahead.

"You do not honestly believe that, do you?"

"I am trying to convince myself that she does not."

Griffin's lips softened into a smile. "Is it working?"

"Not yet." At Griffin's chuckle, Ian stared up at the apricot fingers of sunrise that streaked across the scarlet sky, and focused his attention on a soft echo of hoofbeats. Riders, a dozen or more had been following them since first light. At first he thought he and Griffin had fallen into a trap set by the Four Horsemen, but now he wasn't so certain.

Ian had purposely changed their course to the west a while back, forcing their path into a more open and exposed area near the shoreline, hoping to flush out whoever pursued. The riders had only pulled back, as if to follow them. But who were they?

"Do you hear them as well?" Griffin asked, breaking the silence.

"Aye," Ian replied.

"Should we loop back and try to sneak in behind them?" The narrow path widened onto the smoother surface of a dirt road. Griffin brought his horse up beside Ian's.

"Nay. The horses are weary. The village of Lochaline is ahead," Ian said. "We can rest the beasts there for a while, and then determine whether to pursue." As if understanding Ian's words, the horses picked up their pace, eager for the rest and food that might be ahead. Finally, they neared a rise in the road, and the whisper of frantic voices came to Ian's ears.

He urged his horse to a faster pace, racing over the rise and down into the village below. At breakneck speed, the scene before him became merely a blur of images—spirals of smoke, charred remnants of wood where houses used to stand, people dressed in ragged and singed clothing wandering in states of dazed confusion among the ruins of the village. His stomach roiled at the scent of burning wood. For a moment, Ian saw his own village, his own clan, devastated after an attack by the Four Horsemen.

A wrenching sadness mixed with his rage as he gazed at the ruins. The Horsemen had been here, and not long ago, judging by the ash and smoke that hung in the air. Bringing his horse to a stop, Ian dismounted.

Griffin slid off his horse and came to stand beside Ian. "The Four Horsemen should not have been this far to the north. Something is not right here."

"I agree," Ian said as he strode into the midst of the village.

The noise built as he drew closer, whispers gradually becoming shouts. Two bedraggled men with soot on their faces spun toward them, their swords drawn. "Who are you?"

Unafraid despite their weapons, Ian continued forward, his hands open at his sides in a motion of peace. "Ian MacKinnon of the clan MacKinnon, and he," Ian gestured beside him, "is my brother, Griffin. We mean you no harm."

Instead of relaxing, the men's stances became more rigid and their gazes moved beyond where Ian and Griffin stood.

The sound of hoofbeats thundered, then stopped. Ian twisted around, his sword drawn, ready to attack until he saw who followed them. The Ranald warriors—all eighteen of them. "Why are you here and not with Scotia?" The words sounded harsh, even to his own ears, but he did nothing to temper his tone. These men should be with her, protecting her.

Keith Ranald dismounted and hastened to Ian's side. "We dinna mean to startle ye with our approach. When we saw ye gallop ahead, we thought ye might need our help." He looked up, his gaze passing over the village. "What has happened—"

"Why are you not with Scotia?" Ian interrupted. He knotted his hands at his sides, fighting the need to grab Keith Ranald by the shirt and drag him off his feet.

Keith's gaze returned to Ian's. He flinched at the fire Ian could not keep from showing in his gaze. "She sent the lot of us after ye."

She risked her own safety to save his worthless head. His anger abated, leaving a funny sensation in the pit of his stomach. Why would she do something so . . . so careless?

The villagers lowered their swords and returned them to their scabbards. "Are these men MacKinnons as well?"

"They are of the clan Ranald, friends of the MacKinnons," Ian informed the older of the two village men.

"What happened here?" Keith asked.

The older man, Hector, shook his head, his sorrow a living thing. "The Four Horsemen. Last we heard they were headed to the northwestern isles. We relaxed our scouting troops as a result. Then last eve, they took us by surprise."

Uncertainty crept inside Ian. "We learned they were headed south."

The younger man tried to rub the soot from one of his cheeks, but only succeeded in creating a long black smear across his face. "Say what ye will, Hector, but I was one of those scouts who saw the Horsemen heading to the north with me own eyes. Two of 'em and their army as well."

"Then how do ye explain all this?" Hector's wild-eyed gaze spanned the remains of their village.

The younger man's shoulders sagged. "I should have wondered where the other two were, and why their army looked a bit smaller. But I dinna think about it at the time."

"You only saw two Horsemen?" Ian tossed a worried glance at his brother.

Griffin's brow knitted in thought before he spoke. "Is it possible they could have split up?"

Hector's eyebrows shot up. "Saints have mercy on us if they did."

Ian growled his frustration. "Scotia's plan." She had wanted her warriors to divide the Four Horsemen. But now that her goal had been achieved, the danger to the country had intensified. When the Horsemen were together, his countrymen could at least predict where the villains might strike next. But with the Horsemen separated into two armies, reports would come to villages from all over, causing confusion or a false sense of security, as it had in this very village.

Ian's gaze moved about the village. Smoke curled toward the sky from the wooden remains of several homes. And yet, upon his second viewing, he noticed several buildings still standing.

"How many men did you lose in this battle?" Ian asked.

Hector thought a moment. "Only four," he said with a frown. "Though it seemed like many more at the time of the battle."

Hope crept inside Ian. Could Scotia be right in her assumption that less men would bring less destruction and be more vulnerable to the Scottish defenses?

"Did the Horsemen say anything to indicate where they might head next?" Griffin asked, flexing his hands as though in preparation for a battle.

The younger man's face darkened before his gaze dropped to the charred earth beneath his boots. "The large warrior on a white stallion stormed through the village crying out like a wild banshee." The man shivered at the memory. "The sound was gruesome, inhuman."

"What did he say?" Ian prompted.

He brought his gaze back to Ian's. "He said, 'Give me the Stone and the woman who guards it. The terror will end only when I have the Stone.'"

The woman who guards it. Scotia. Ian frowned, suddenly not liking the progression of his thoughts.

"What direction did they head when they left here?" Griffin asked.

"North."

North. Toward Scotia. And south. Toward his clan.

A fist of fear closed around Ian's heart, making it difficult to breathe. Scotia was alone in her castle without seasoned warriors to protect her. His clan would be attacked.

Two places he needed to be, and at the very same time. But how? He was only one man. How would he ever choose between them?

He clenched his fists at his sides as the image of his hands ripping apart the Horsemen, flesh from bone, filled his mind.

Perch like a bird. The thought came out of nowhere, acting like a salve to his tormented soul. One of Scotia's earliest lessons. *Sometimes a warrior must perch and think before he reacts.* Ian closed his eyes in an effort to block out the disquiet of his mind. He needed to think clearly. To find a solution.

A hand came to rest upon his shoulder. "Are you all right, Ian?" Griffin asked.

With sudden clarity, Ian knew his answer. He opened his eyes and turned to face his brother.

Griffin stared at him with concern. "Ian?"

The two had been lifelong rivals, but this day would

change all that. This day they would join forces and let the past blur into utter insignificance. "Griffin, you must journey on to the clan. You are their hope, and their protection. Take all of the Ranald warriors with you except Keith and four others. The rest will help you to keep the clan safe."

His brother's eyes widened. "And what about this revenge of yours?"

"Avenging a dead man hardly seems more worthwhile than protecting the living."

Griffin's brow shot up. "All the living, or one woman in particular?"

"She is alone in her castle, Griffin. Unprotected except for a few inexperienced warriors. I want to offer what little help I can to keep her safe."

"I know we have had our differences, and for that I apologize," Griffin said, his voice uneven, his gaze troubled. "I know now that you are as good, or better, than any man in Scotland."

"There is no time to explore those dark roads now, Griffin."

Griffin regarded him with something close to fondness. "You are a good man, Ian."

"As are you. Now go." Ian turned the conversation away from himself. "Return to the clan. I trust you to do what is needed for our clan. You have studied with Scotia. You know her lessons. Protect them well. And if there is time, teach the others as she has taught you."

Griffin's expression turned from surprise to sadness before he dipped his head. "I did not learn the lessons well. I fear I let my pride rule my head."

"Sometimes those things that make us weak are also the things that make us strong. Remember that. This is your time to prove yourself, Griffin. Make it count."

Griffin studied Ian's face in silence before a slow and thoughtful grin came to his lips. "I think I finally understand why I disliked you for so long." He sighed, the sound filled with a touch of humor. "You always accepted your weaknesses, where I could not accept mine. It seems so simple now." His gaze changed, filled with remorse. "All those years . . ."

"They matter naught," Ian said.

Griffin pulled his shoulders back, his bearing tall and proud. "I will guard Father, and all the clan, with my life."

Ian smiled. "I know." And he meant the words.

Griffin returned his smile. "Go to Scotia. From the beginning it was obvious Father picked the right man to send to her for training. She needed you as much as you needed her."

Ian's smile faded. She needed his help right now to protect her from the White Horseman; he would not deny that truth. But anything more . . . He could not consider anything more. "God be with you, brother," Ian said, anxious now to be on his way.

Griffin reached out to clap Ian on the shoulder. Their first physical contact that had not come from anger. Griffin did not pull his hand away. Instead it lingered there. His features became pinched, then eased as if he had wrestled with something and come to a decision. "God be with you, brother," he said slowly, emphasizing the last word.

The word brought a flush of warmth to Ian's soul. He put his hand over Griffin's. "Until we meet again."

Griffin nodded, then turned away to mount his horse. Ian watched as his brother, followed by thirteen of the Ranald men, disappeared through the smoky haze of the burned-out village. The MacKinnon clan would be safe in Griffin's care.

The two men from the village watched as Griffin and the others rode away. "They'll need God's mercy and His help to overcome the demons like those that rode through here," the younger man said.

Hector faced Ian. "Are you heading to the northwestern isles to face the Horsemen there?"

"Aye." Ian nodded to Keith Ranald and the other four warriors who had remained with him. Together, they strode to their horses and swung up into their saddles, united by their purpose. They would return to the Isle of Skye to help defend Scotia and her people. But would they be enough to defend a whole castle from even two of the notorious Horsemen? Could they gain the edge they needed to win in battle?

His chances would be better if he had just a few more men. Ian turned to Hector. "Would you and the others be willing to go with me, back to Glencarron Castle, back into battle with the Horsemen in order to end their tyranny, once and for all?"

Hector paled. "Nay. I must try to help those who are injured and rebuild what we can."

"I'm with ye." The young man beside Hector unsheathed his sword. "There are others here who will help put an end to their destruction."

"I am grateful for your help," Ian said. "How soon can you be ready to ride?"

"Not long. We have no supplies to gather, only ourselves and our horses."

Ian nodded as the younger man hurried away. He would return to Glencarron Castle to fight his enemy. But it was not the only reason for going back. He had tried his damnedest to ignore the power Scotia held over him. But no matter how hard he tried to remove himself from his feelings, she pulled him back.

There was no other woman like her in all of Scotland. Ian smiled wistfully at the memory of their first battle. Within the space of two heartbeats he had found himself wrapped in her cords of leather, flat on his back with her sword at his throat. Truly a prize among women.

When the men were ready, Ian turned his horse around and led the fifteen men who had joined him along with Keith Ranald back down the path he and Griffin had traveled a short while ago. Encouraging his horse into a faster gait, Ian scanned the glen ahead for signs of the Horsemen. He and Griffin had seen no evidence of their presence when they had traveled this way before. But they could have missed their approach between the rugged terrain that stretched across the Highlands.

He had to hurry back to Scotia as quickly as possible. He never should have left her. He knew that now. He would have spent every moment of every day for the rest of his life thinking about her, worrying for her safety, wondering how she fared in these troubled times. Why had it taken a threat from the Horsemen to make him see that revenge was not as worthy a goal as protecting those you cared about?

He did care. Perhaps a bit more than he should, given who he was when compared to the enormity of Scotia and her role as guardian of the Stone.

Her role as guardian put her at risk now, not her role as the Trainer. Ian dug his heels into his horse's sides, impatient to go faster. Time was of the essence if he was to get to her before the White Horseman did.

Chapter Twenty-five

A rush of joy filled Ian despite his weariness when the pale gray towers of Glencarron Castle came into view against the backdrop of the morning sky. He and the warriors with him had ridden hard all night to reach Scotia as fast as possible. With a hungry gaze he searched the parapets for a glimpse of her. He cared not whether her face filled with anger or delight when she saw him. Just to see she was safe would be enough for him.

Yet he caught no sight of her reddish-brown hair. Or any of the guards, for that matter. The towers of the castle appeared as deserted as they had when he had first approached her castle. Ian dropped his gaze to the gate. It stood wide open, with no one in sight.

Alarmed, he pushed his horse into a full gallop. The thunder of hoofbeats matched the pounding of his heart. Had they arrived too late?

At the gate, Ian dismounted before the horse came to a full stop. The other men followed suit. Everywhere there was silence. Ian's heart seemed to freeze, but not his feet.

He was running even before the thought to do so formed in his mind.

"Scotia!" The exclamation was part greeting, part battle cry.

He skidded to a halt just inside the door of the great hall with his men at his heels. Their breathing seemed overly loud and out of place in the emptiness of the chamber. "Scotia!" Ian searched the room for signs of struggle, conflict, blood, anything to indicate what might have happened.

"Ye will not find her here." Maisie's voice came from behind him.

Ian spun around, his heart in his throat. "Where is she?"

"Fulfillin' her obligations." A deep sorrow weighed down Maisie's appearance, making her look older, more tired, more feeble than ever before.

"Speak plainly, I beg you." Ian strode toward Maisie and took the older woman's chilled hands in his own. "Where has she gone?"

"To a village nearby to set a trap for the Horsemen."

Ian's breath stilled in his chest. "Alone?"

"Nay," Maisie said as she pulled her hands from his. "She took many of the guards, one of her scoutin' patrols, and Burke."

Ian shook his head as he tried to make sense of this turn of events. "Why?"

Maisie's look darkened. "When ye left, she decided she belonged among her people, not locked inside a castle any longer."

Ian released an inarticulate sound. "Damn her bravery. The White Horseman could be anywhere."

Maisie's brow shot up. "Such concern from a man who passed her love over for the sake of revenge."

"I had no choice," Ian said through gritted teeth. "But I have returned."

"For good?" Maisie's face brightened as her mood shifted from accusing to curious.

"I cannot tell the future, Maisie. None of us can." Ian pushed his fingers through his hair, suddenly feeling restless, filled with the need for action despite his exhaustion. "Where has she gone? Do you know?"

"Aye. She has gone to a small village nestled at the base of the Cuillin Hills just across the isle to the south."

And most likely in the direct path of the White Horseman's approach. "How long ago did she leave?"

"At first light."

"Then there is still hope of catching up to her before she gets herself killed. Why could she not stay here and remain safe?" he cursed.

"She's a warrior, Ian. Even female warriors need to battle when their souls are on fire." Maisie crossed her arms over her chest in a look that dared him to argue.

"When I find her I intend to give her plenty to battle, namely me."

Maisie smiled. "Yer father was right to send ye here, Ian MacKinnon."

Ian narrowed his gaze. "What do you mean?"

"We'll discuss it when ye return. Scotia needs ye now."

Ian nodded. More than anything he wanted to find Scotia and convince her to return to safety. "I shall need a fresh horse."

"There are horses already saddled and waitin' in the courtyard for ye and the men in yer company." At Ian's surprised look she added, "We watched ye approach. That is why the gates were open."

"Then you are not alone here?" He had yet to see anyone besides Maisie.

"The others are here. We are workin' on another of
Scotia's plans." When he opened his mouth to ask her
what that plan might be, she shooed him away with her
hands. "Go. Be gone. Ye have yer own tasks before ye. All
will be explained when ye return with Scotia."

"The White Horseman is on his way here, Maisie. Are
there enough men left at the castle to protect you, Lizbet,
and the others?"

"I've no intention of surrenderin' this place to anyone
until Scotia returns."

"I will leave the new warriors I brought from Lismore
here to help guard the castle. The Ranald warriors will
come with me."

"As you wish," Maisie agreed.

Ian nodded. Then with quick and sure steps he made his
way outside to where the fresh horses waited. The sooner
they found Scotia, the better it would be for all of them.

Scotia wiped the sweat from her brow with the back of
her hand and leaned against the edge of the pit she had
helped to dig. The scent of freshly turned earth surrounded her, and the trench she and her helpers had dug
surrounded the village. They had been working before
dawn to create a fortification that would give them an advantage over the Four Horsemen.

Since her arrival yesterday, she and the clan leaders
had put a three-part plan into place. The trench would
serve as the first obstacle the army would have to overcome. Those who made it across the trench would then
have to make it through the mounded dirt that held
sharp, deadly spears; get past a row of archers; then meet
the warriors with swords before they would ever reach the

women and children Scotia and the other warriors tried to protect.

The arrangement was the best they could do without the protection of a castle. Even if she could lead these people back to her own castle, they would be more vulnerable on the open road then they were here, tucked beneath the trees.

She would triumph over the Horsemen and end their tyranny with the help of these people. The time had come to end the battle over the Stone of Destiny.

The thought of the battle ahead sent a shiver of excitement down her spine. She could honestly say she was not afraid. Had she not trained for this purpose her whole life? And even though she was no longer near the Stone, she had no regrets about her decision to be among her people. Ian had taught her that. If she were ever to expand her sense of her own people, and have them come to know her as a trainer and not just a warrior to best, she had to be among them, experiencing their joys, their triumphs, their defeats.

As she looked out at the grassy fields before her and the hills beyond, her world had never seemed quite so expansive. There were no walls to confine her or boundaries to hold her captive to her duty. Only wide open spaces that seemed to go on forever.

Scotia resumed her work of scooping the soft, loamy dirt into a wooden bucket, then dumping it at the edge of the trench in an ever-growing mound. But even the hard, physical work could not take her mind from those last moments with Ian. The bucket shook beneath her fingers as she filled it once more, and she cursed herself for a fool.

She had to stop thinking of him. How else would she ever move forward? Ian was her past. Scotland's people and their independence were her future.

"Thinkin' about Ian again?" Burke asked from the edge of the trench.

"Not if he were the last man alive." Scotia frowned at her steward. Were her thoughts so easy to read these days?

"Come out of there," Burke called. "The trench is done. The men want to cover it with branches and leaves before it grows dark." Burke's gaze moved across her dirt-streaked knees and fingers. "Give me yer hand. Ye need to rest for a bit." He held out his fingers. She accepted them, then pulled herself out of the depths of the trench by her own efforts.

"Ye've been workin' since first light."

Scotia brushed the dirt from herself. "Many hands will make the work easier and faster."

"The scouts ye have posted beyond the village have yet to report any activity. Surely, there is time to take a short rest."

Scotia shook her head. "We must keep going, until all is complete."

"Then let me help, too." Burke picked up several branches from the piles left around the trench, then carefully spread them over the open area. With everyone helping, it did not take long to conceal the trap, and they soon found themselves back in the center of the village before a great fire. Over the flames, a stag roasted, sending the intoxicating fragrance of richly roasted meat through the village.

Scotia ate sparingly. As had been the case since Ian's departure, she found she had little interest in food or drink. All around her were sounds of the villagers celebrating their success in setting a trap for the Horsemen. The noise eddied and swirled but passed her by, leaving her filled with restless energy. She paced back and forth at the edge of the gathering, unable to remain still for long.

At the snap of a twig, Scotia spun toward the woods, searching the thin row of trees to the south. In the hazy purple light of dusk she saw a young boy who had been gathering branches in the woods running toward the village. His footsteps echoed the sudden frantic beat of her heart. Her muscles tensed, and she reached for her sword.

"Six men on horseback are coming," the boy called out as he skidded to a stop at the edge of the trench. Several leaves that covered the trap fluttered and swirled at the force of his movement.

"Do you recognize any of them?" Scotia asked as she shifted a large platform of wooden planks over the trench for the boy to cross safely into the village.

"Nay," the boy panted. He ran over the makeshift bridge then helped her to pull it back. "But the man who appears to be their leader wears a plaid of red and green and blue and white."

Ian's plaid. Scotia's gaze swung from the boy to the figures riding ever closer. A hush fell over the village.

"Should we get the crossbows?" one of the villagers asked. The men, who had celebrated only moments before, prepared for battle.

"He be friend, not foe," Burke spoke from near her side in a voice that held as much surprise and wonder as Scotia herself felt.

The village once again grew deathly silent as Ian and the men drew close enough for Scotia to see the easy smile slip across Ian's face—a smile that brought out the dimple that intrigued her so much. Until that moment, Scotia had thought she remembered exactly what he looked like, but she had not.

They had been apart only a few days, but she had forgotten the way his linen shirt clung to his wide shoulders and the muscles that lay shadowed beneath. His angular face held an arrogant handsomeness made all the more sensual by that dimple at the side of his finely sculpted mouth. And his eyes—at one time they had been filled with uncertainty. Now, blatant determination shone in their depths, making her catch her breath at the intensity of his look.

Scotia stared at him in mute fascination as the muscles in her throat struggled to say something intelligible to him, to greet him, or chastise him, she knew not which her heart wanted more. So she merely watched him as he approached with no words, only hope.

Until she remembered the trap.

Chapter Twenty-six

Ian entered the village just as dusk descended over the land. He forced his eyes to remain open despite the fact he'd had very little sleep in the past two days. From atop his horse he searched the village for a glimpse of Scotia. He spotted her tall form immediately at the edge of the crowd that gathered near a blazing fire pit.

He knew the moment she saw him. Her eyes went wide, and a hint of a smile pulled at the corners of her lips. A moment later, any pleasure he might have imagined there vanished, replaced by a somber expression. Those gathered near her must have noticed a change in her. The soft rumblings as they talked settled into a silence that left only the whisper of the wind to greet him.

"Good eve," he said as he brought his horse closer to an area strewn with leaves. He urged his horse forward.

"Halt," Scotia demanded.

Ian pulled back on the reins, bringing his mount to a sudden stop, forcing the men behind him to do the same. The animal pranced sideways in protest of the motion. "I wish to speak with you, Scotia."

"Wait a moment." She and the young boy next to her pushed the makeshift bridge over the fallen leaves. "Now, you may cross."

Ian lead his horse over the wood. As he did he heard the soft snap of a branch beneath the plank and knew Scotia and the villagers had prepared a trap against the approaching danger. On the other side of the wooden bridge, Ian brought his horse to a stop. He dismounted without taking his gaze from Scotia.

The men, women, and children of the village stared at him. He nodded his head in greeting, but saw little of them. He had eyes only for Scotia.

She was dressed in her armor, and she had changed from the skirt Maisie had made out of his plaid back into her usual red skirt. She remained still as he approached her. If he were not mistaken, he saw a slight tremor run through her before she set her chin a little higher.

"I thought you were returning to your clan?"

Her face remained expressionless. He had so many things he wanted to say to her, so many words he had rehearsed during his journey here, but none came to him now. He wanted to pull her warm, yielding body against his and tell her how scared he had been when he thought she would have to battle two of the Horsemen alone. But more than anything he wanted to hold her in his arms and never let go. "I had to make certain you were safe."

A flicker of hope brightened her gaze before she caught herself and schooled her features into a bland, expressionless shield once again. "As you can see, I am quite well."

Fear and longing shimmered through him. He wanted to express those feelings now and give them a voice. But as he opened his mouth to speak, he looked around him at the interested faces of those gathered near. An elderly woman clutched a wrap about her thin shoulders, her eyes wide with interest. A young girl of no more than three held her older sister's hand. Together they stood beside him, their gazes filled with curiosity. Burke stood nearby, but at a distance from the rest, simply watching the two of them with a confident, knowing smile. Even the burly men he had gathered together to protect her from the Isle of Rum leaned in toward them, eager to catch whatever words he might choose to say.

"I think it would be best if we found somewhere quiet to discuss the matter." Ian hesitated as he surveyed the crowd. "Alone." He reached for Scotia's arm, but she stepped back, out of his reach.

"Anything you have to say to me may be said here." She crossed her arms over her chest. Her gaze remained unyielding.

Ian noted the high color of her cheeks and caught the spark of determination in her gaze. Surely, something in her current situation agreed with her—be it her self-chosen release from her castle or the revival of her purpose as she now saw it—for he could honestly say she had never seemed more alive than she did at this moment. "Come back to the castle," he said simply. What else could he say in front of all these people?

"Nay, my mother moved herself too far away from her people. I am determined to live among them, and, if necessary, die among them, helping to gain the independence we deserve from the Horsemen and England."

"Do you not think that is what I want as well?" He reached for her hands, taking them into his own. That she did not pull away from his touch sent a thrill through him, but her posture remained rigid. "The situation is different now than it was when you left your castle."

She frowned, and he knew he had pierced through her aloofness. "How?"

"Your plan has succeeded. The Four Horsemen have divided into two groups. One group has turned south toward my village. The other group is headed north toward your castle. I must admit, I did not see the Horsemen and their army on my way here. Even so, that does not mean these good people are safe. Danger is everywhere. We must go back to the castle."

He could feel the tension in her hands at his words. "I wanted them to separate, but I can now see your fears in this course of action as well." She paused, searching his face. "What about your clan, Ian? Who will protect them?"

"Griffin."

She nodded slowly, and a look of satisfaction settled across her features. "He is still reckless, but he is a strong warrior. Whether he admits it or not, his training has improved his skills."

"I am glad you approve."

She dropped her gaze from his. "Does Maisie know about the Horsemen?"

"Aye." Ian traced his thumb across the leather gauntlet that covered her palm.

She drew a sharp breath. "I must think," she said curtly. She pulled out of his grasp, then turned away.

"You must return to your castle. We can formulate a plan of attack there. Keep yourself and these people safe." Ian ignored her grim expression and the curious stares of the villagers. He had to make her understand that her safety was more important than her pride. "I was a fool to leave you."

Her gaze returned to his face. "That may be, but *I* am never twice a fool."

He could see the anger and hurt that flashed across her expressive face, a face that no longer hid her emotions. He had hurt her by leaving with so little warning. Yet, he could not change what mistakes he had already made. Ian put the words he could not say in public into his gaze. "Scotia—"

She turned her back on him and addressed the villagers. "There are two scouting parties currently searching for signs of the Horsemen. With the danger so close, I will need four volunteers to organize a watch for tonight."

Four brawny men from the village stepped forward. "We offer ourselves."

"You have my gratitude." Abruptly, she turned back to Ian. "Follow me." She marched toward a nearby copse of trees. "I will grant you a few moments alone. But only a few."

He would take those few moments and ask for more. Ian nodded to himself as he walked behind her. He would make her see reason no matter the arsenal she threw at him. If only the weariness he fought for the last two days could be denied a while longer. He struggled against the heaviness in his legs and in his thoughts by concentrating on the path before him. He could not sleep until she was safe once again.

Scotia stopped in the secluded shelter of the trees, then turned to face him. "This should be private enough." She stood there quietly, her hands resting on her hips, a finger's length from her sword.

"You will have no need of your weapon with me," Ian said.

"You are bold, Ian MacKinnon." She drew her sword. "You challenged my authority in front of the others. The only way for me to save face is to challenge you to a battle."

"I don't want to fight you again, Scotia." He sat on the ground, leaning back against a tree stump left behind by a woodsman. "I have been riding a horse for two days straight. My back aches, my legs are sore, and right now I am so tired I can hardly stand without the ground feeling like it is moving beneath me. Please, come sit down. We can talk here." He patted the ground next to him.

Scotia bristled and her fingers tightened on the hilt of her sword. "They will expect me to challenge you."

"Then do what they don't expect and come sit beside me."

She lifted hot, angry eyes to his.

He sent her a smile that was every bit as sensual as a kiss.

A long moment later, she sheathed her sword. "How do you do that?"

"Do what?"

"Know exactly how to turn my resolve against me?" She sat down on the soft earth next to him.

He brushed her cheek with the back of his hand and felt some of the tension leave her. "It is a gift."

"More like a curse." She leaned back, away from his touch, and stared off into the distance. "So why did you come back this time?"

He allowed her to retreat from his touch for now. "The White Horseman is desperate to find the Stone of Destiny. He knows you have it hidden somewhere. The villagers in Lismore seemed to believe he searched for you among the citizens of Scotland."

"Aye. Maisie and Burke told him I was among my people three months ago. That's when they started to terrorize the country, ransacking each village for me and the Stone." She turned away, searching the distance, her face suddenly pale and sad. "It is my burden to bear, just as my ancestors did before me."

He took her hand and laced his fingers with hers. "Will you let me help you?" He reached for her with his free hand and drew her head down to his own shoulder until the silken smoothness of her hair rested against the warmth of his plaid, which lay draped across his left arm. "Let me bear your burdens for a while, Scotia. Together we can determine what to do."

"I should not—"

"Shh," he interrupted her. "We do not have time for arguments, only accord." He gently rested his head against the top of hers, finding contentment in her closeness. When he felt her relax beside him, he knew she had surrendered to the moment.

Scotia stared down at their intertwined fingers and tried to ignore the comforting thrill of his touch. In spite of her unspoken protests, he had taken her hand in his and broken through all the barriers she had erected around her heart since he had left her.

That he would leave her again, she had no doubt. Had her mother not warned her of that trait in men long ago? Was that not why the Warrior Trainer never married? Make no commitments, her mother had told her. Accept a male into your bed to father your child and send him away before he weakens your spirit and your mind.

Scotia brushed her thumb across the top of Ian's hand. Odd, she did not feel weak right now. She felt stronger when he was beside her than she did on her own. A fact she would never admit to him. The man would find some way to use that knowledge against her when she least expected him to. Scotia smiled to herself. She could still beat him in a battle of swords, and as long as she had that skill she would at least have some power over him.

Scotia shifted her gaze from their joined hands to the lush hills covered in a sea of grass and heather. The foliage had turned a brilliant purple against the fading light of dusk. The tension over the threat of attack had not left the villagers, but they did not stop their nightly routine of gathering together at the end of the day to celebrate the goodness in their lives. Voices mixed with the ethereal sound of the bagpipes, wrapping the end of the day in serenity.

Scotia snuggled against Ian's warmth, content to be near him and share, even from a distance, the traditions of this small village.

Ian reached up and removed the pin that secured his plaid at his shoulder. A moment later, he pulled her more fully against him, then spread the tail of the fabric across their legs and bodies, enveloping them both in a cocoon of warmth against the encroaching night.

"Are you feeling more at ease?" he asked in a soft, beguiling brogue.

"Aye," she replied.

"Then tell me about your past." She tensed at the request, but he soothed her with the soft hush of his voice. "There is nothing to fear here with me. Please tell me, Scotia, why you seek revenge on the White Horseman, because I know it is more a personal vendetta than you have ever acknowledged."

"It's a long story."

"It will be a long night."

Scotia couldn't argue that fact. "To tell you the story I must start at the beginning."

He nodded and waited for her to begin.

"Ever since the Stone of Destiny first arrived in this country with my ancestors it has been moved from place to place in order to keep it safe. It has moved from the Isle of Iona to Dunnad, to the fortress of Dunstaffnage, to the Abbey of Scone, where it was nearly captured by Edward the First. But a quick-thinking abbot substituted a lump of common sandstone for the true Stone. That was the prize Edward the First thought he took from our country. The people of Scotland always knew that England had a false stone. What they did not know was where the real Stone went next."

"Glencarron Castle."

"Aye. My mother took the Stone back to our holdings on the Isle of Skye, where she had chosen to live and train." Scotia released a weary sigh. "The ruse almost worked. No one except the White Horseman doubted England's easy success. He tried to convince the English king of his suspicions that the Stone was false, but the king paid little heed to the White Horseman's ravings. All seemed peaceful for a time until the White Horseman returned to Scotland, this time with an army of his own."

"That was twelve years ago?" Ian asked.

"Exactly. The White Horseman and his army headed for Glencarron Castle. After a monthlong siege, he finally breached the walls of the castle and fought his way to my mother." Scotia closed her eyes as the aching memories swelled inside her. In her heart she heard her own agonized cry as the arrow pierced her mother's armor. "He killed her."

Scotia shuddered at the recollection, but somehow, in the shelter of Ian's arms, the image did not seem as painful as it had in the past. "He thought he killed me as well when he put an arrow in my back."

Ian's body tensed, but she continued. "That was when Maisie and Burke forced me to flee. When we returned we found that the White Horseman had torn the castle apart in his desperation to possess the Stone. When he could not find it, he assumed the treasure had somehow been secreted out of the castle during the siege and hidden among the Scottish people for protection. Maisie and Burke allowed him to believe that falsehood."

"Why?" In the silvery darkness, he sat up and searched her face as though instinctively sensing her sorrow over the pain her people had had to endure because of that lie.

"I was only ten and three at the time of my mother's death," she said in her own defense. "Maisie explained that she and Burke only wanted to protect me until I matured. With their secret, Maisie and Burke allowed the Warrior Trainer to slide into the realm of legend."

"An effective deception," Ian admitted. "For I believed you did not exist until my foster father bade me to go to you."

"Effective until they determined it was time I bear a child and continue my lineage. So they sent out the word of my survival along with my men as they protected our country. But instead of suitors, foreign mercenaries like Haldane came, wanting to challenge me for my lands and title."

"Be that as it may, all those events are behind you now."

"How can you say that?" She gaped at him with a mixture of derision and disbelief. "The Horsemen are more of a threat than they have ever been before. And . . ." She was stunned into muteness by the warm and sensual look in his eyes, no longer remembering the words she had been about to say.

"I will protect you."

The husky sincerity of his voice snatched her breath away. Even so, she could not allow herself to fall into that trap again. "Perhaps, until you determine it is time to leave me again. All men leave. It is what they do." Her mother's words played through her mind.

He took her chin between his thumb and forefinger

and lifted it, forcing her to meet his steady gaze. "What makes you say such a thing?"

She had no choice but to stare into the dark intensity of his gaze. She saw anger there, as well as an earnest desire for the truth. "My father left me. Lizbet's father left her. You will leave, too, when you tire of—"

"Tire of you?" His eyes turned smoky, unpredictable, dangerous. "One taste of your sweet lips and I have not been the same man since." His gaze dropped to her lips. "Tire of you . . . My desire for you is insatiable."

Scotia's entire body began to tremble as his lips descended to hers. "Nay."

"Unrelenting," he whispered as his mouth traced a hot trail across her chin, then up to her ear. "Beyond reason."

Scotia caught a deep, shuddering breath before he pulled her into a protective embrace and trailed a line of scorching kisses down the sensitive skin of her neck to her shoulder. The warmth of his breath stirred her unbound hair as his mouth began retracing a path back to her lips. One kiss and all thoughts of denying him vanished. By denying him this moment, she would be depriving herself of something almost more vital to her existence than the air she drew into her body, air that mingled with his as they came together in a kiss both poignant and possessive.

His tongue traced a hot line between her lips, coaxing, urging them to part, and then insisting. The moment she yielded, his tongue plunged into her mouth, stroking and caressing, demanding even more of herself than she offered him now. He would consume her, body and soul. Could she give him that much of herself and still remain whole? Had her mother not warned her against this very thing?

Ian slid his hand across the outside of her left thigh and beneath the hem of her skirt, his callused fingertips sliding over the softness of her skin, bringing her flesh to life. Heat and desire coursed through her loins, loosening her will to resist, turning her flesh warm and pliable to his touch. Up, up, he moved his hand over her thigh, around to the roundness of her bottom.

Scotia began to tremble more violently under the combined lash of both pleasure and shock. An empty ache began to form inside her until she could no longer deny what she wanted, what she needed from him. "Love me," she whispered against his lips, ready to give herself over to the sensual Eden that beckoned.

Chapter Twenty-seven

Ian looked down at Scotia. Her eyes were tightly closed. He forced himself to lie still against the seductive arch of her body. "Open your eyes, Scotia."

Dusk gave way to night, claiming their mingled breath in a swirl of misty air. Scotia threaded her fingers possessively through his hair. Her allure was undeniable, but he had to know for sure that she truly wanted him and not just an heir.

He hesitated just inches from her lips. The slightest shift in either of their bodies would bring them back in contact again. "Scotia, please, look at me," he said, not bothering to disguise the need that pulsed in his voice and in his blood.

Slowly, her green eyes opened and the haziness there faded.

"I want nothing more than to lose myself in you. But before that can happen I want you to know who you are choosing. Look at me, Scotia. Really look at me before you decide."

Wariness crept into her gaze. "What do you mean, Ian?"

He braced himself for the rejection he knew would soon follow. "I am no one, Scotia. I do not know anything about myself other than what the MacKinnons have given to me with the gift of their name. If you choose me now, you will choose me forever, because if a child comes from this union, I will not abandon you or it."

"Oh, Ian," she reached up to brush her trembling fingers against his cheek.

He could not resist the gentleness of her touch. He turned his face into her palm, branding it with a hot, fevered kiss. "Say you still want me," he whispered, exposing his weakness, making himself vulnerable, knowing even as he spoke the words that she would surely reject him now. How could she not? When she could choose her mate from among Scotland's finest, why would she settle for him?

He closed his eyes as he fought his growing desire. He waited for her to pull away, out of his arms. He waited to feel the emptiness that was always a part of his soul, an emptiness that seemed to vanish whenever she drew near.

Gentle as a butterfly's wings, her lips touched his. In a flutter of sensation, she caressed his lips, warmed them, then made him long for more of the same. No one had ever kissed him so sweetly, so innocently. She eased away and he could hear the ragged pull of her breath. "Your bloodline matters not."

He opened his eyes, desperate to read what he could in her gaze. Naked desire stared back at him, mixing with his own gratification. She would not reject him, at least not this night.

She brought her hand up to his chest, atop his racing heart. "I do not want to put off this moment any longer. Who knows what tomorrow will bring. The Four Horsemen have caused enough chaos in our lives. Let us grasp this moment for what it is. We will worry about the rest later."

Worry about the rest later. She kissed him again. Snippets of sensation flickered through his mind—rigid muscle met voluptuous softness, the scent of mint mixed with heather, the beat of her heart mingled with his own breathlessness. Harmonious, arousing, intimate.

He released her mouth, fighting his burgeoning desire. Recklessness had seen him through the majority of his life. He would not make one more mistake on top of the rest that would condemn another innocent to the kind of torment he had endured growing up.

"Marry me, Scotia."

Her eyes snapped up to his, dark and unreadable.

He met her gaze honestly, fully aware of the enormity of his request. Perhaps no other Warrior Trainer had married in the past. But he could not let that stop him. "If you want me to make love to you, to leave my seed and the potential for life inside you, then those actions will be sanctified by marriage. For me, there is no other alternative."

Fear and sadness slipped into her gaze. She would refuse him. "I . . . I cannot marry you." The words sounded as though they were ripped from her throat. She rolled from him and surged to her feet. "No man can have me in that way, Ian. The Warrior Trainer must never marry."

Ian stood, not bothering to hide the hunger he knew was clearly written on his face. Without taking his gaze from her, he drew the tail of his plaid up, then secured it at his shoulder.

Time suddenly seemed to stand still around them. His blood throbbed through his veins, slowly, powerfully, as it never had before.

She caught a deep, shuddering breath and stepped toward him, so close he could feel the heat of her body reaching out to his own. "Ian, do not do this," she pleaded in a voice no stronger than a whisper. "We can be together without marriage."

"Marriage is not the only solution here. He reached inside his sporran and pulled out a red length of cord.

Scotia's breath came fast and shallow as she stared at the cord in his hand.

It was obvious by her reaction she knew his intent. Handfasting was as legally binding in Scotland as a marriage performed by a clergyman. Except that with handfasting, the terms were either for a year and a day or a lifetime. The choice would be hers. "I wish to bind myself to you, be it just for tonight, if that is all the time we have, or for a year and a day." He tried to keep his voice level and calm. "Place your right hand in mine." He offered her his hand. He did not touch her, merely waited for her to choose, to commit to his offer.

A breathless moment passed and then another as she remained still.

He kept his hand steady, but his confidence faltered. The silence became heavy, almost stifling, drowning out the noises of the night, of the villagers, of all things except the beating of his heart.

Then her fingers twitched, and his heart seemed to freeze. She inched her hand slowly forward until it slipped, trembling with anticipation or fear, into his own. "If we live past the coming conflict with the Horsemen, then I will take you for a year and a day. That is all I can promise for now."

It was more than he had ever hoped for.

Scotia felt a flare of warmth move through her as Ian's strong fingers closed around her own. In the space of a heartbeat, all her reservations melted away. The shell of protection she had built around her heart vanished, and she felt as though she had been holding her breath for years, waiting for this moment. Only now with her hand in his did the air flow through her, sweet, fragrant, and free.

Ian wanted her as his wife, however temporarily. Their lives would be joined. The thought brought as much fear as exhilaration.

A soft chuckle sounded from beside her. Out of life-long habit, Scotia's hand fell to her sword.

"Easy there, love," Burke said from where he and the other villagers had gathered around the private alcove of trees. She wondered, startled, when they had joined her and Ian. She had been so absorbed in Ian and his words that the whole village had managed to catch her unaware. A sliver of uneasiness pulled at her. Had her mother not warned that she would lose her focus if she gave her attentions to a man?

"Burke," Scotia breathed, avoiding the unwanted reminder from her training. "Why are you over here?"

"We all saw the two of ye standin' close with a red cord in yer hands." His grin moved from fatherly to content. "We thought ye might be . . . well, we came to see if ye needed a witness or two."

She did not know how to respond.

"We would be grateful since Scotia and I are to be handfasted," Ian said over her hesitation, but a spark of uncertainty returned to his gaze. Yet that brief glimpse into his soul said more than the whole of his words ever had. She remembered their conversation on the stairs after Griffin had attacked her, and the memories he shared about his life with his clan, and finally the words he had spoken while she lay fevered and dying in her bed—all those times he had shared his own vulnerability without her realizing it. Until now. She saw for the first time a chink in his armor that covered a wound that went far deeper. Slowly, she extended her hand to him.

Burke nodded his approval and took the red cord from Ian. "Then allow me to do the honors."

"Before we proceed, I have a request to make of you, Ian." Scotia paused, as though searching for the right words. "If something were to happen to me, I ask that you take care of Lizbet."

"Nothing will happen to you, Scotia. Not while I am here to protect you."

"You and I both know what it means to live the life of a warrior. Nothing in our lives is ever certain."

"Lizbet will be cared for as if she were my own," Ian agreed smoothly.

Scotia signaled to Burke to proceed, but Ian pulled out of her grasp.

"First we must remove your gauntlets," he said, ignoring her right hand to take up her left. Shivers of sensation worked their way up her arm as he gently slid the leather protection from her hand in a motion that was more caress than task. Her pulse quickened when he repeated the motion with her right hand, but instead of releasing her, he slipped his fingers around hers, holding her tight.

"Now we are ready," Ian said with a nod to Burke.

The older man twisted the red cord around their wrists three times before he tied a knot. Scotia stared down at their bound hands. Ian had chosen a red cord to bind himself to her. Red. The color represented courage, strength, and passion. The last thought sent a surge of heat through her body that culminated in her belly.

"It gives me such pleasure to witness this moment, my dear," Burke said with a catch in his voice. "But I'll be warnin' ye now, ye'll have to marry once more in the chapel when we get back to the castle or Maisie'll have my hide."

Ian's smile bordered on possession as he gazed at Scotia. "Only Scotia can decide the fate of our future. Maisie will have to wait."

The tone of his voice exuded confidence, and she almost let herself believe the fantasy of the moment. She did not want to think of tomorrow, or of what obstacles lay ahead of them. The only thoughts she had were of Ian in her arms.

Burke cleared his throat and glanced up to address the villagers gathered in the intimate setting. "With this cord, I bind two lives into one." Burke shifted his gaze back to the two of them. "Scotia and Ian, with the Lord and these good people as yer witness, yer lives are joined. May the next year find ye bound in spirit as ye are now bound in life."

When he finished speaking, Ian lifted her bound hand to his lips. He brushed a kiss, featherlight and airy, across the back of her hand. "I pledge you my life," he said quietly, but with steely resolve.

But not his love. She drew her shoulders up, trying to ignore the ache in her chest the omission of those words had caused.

A cheer rose up from the crowd. A moment later, the skirl of bagpipes drifted once more upon the night air to wrap the village in a seductive serenade.

The beat of a drum sounded along with the bagpipes. Scotia studied her husband. She knew what came next. They would remain bound to each other until they consummated their marriage.

"Come to me, Scotia," Ian invited huskily.

A small voice inside her urged her to remain where she stood, that she could not give herself over to the passion between them. It was the voice of her mother setting limits upon her again. Another voice reminded her that she and Ian had joined their lives, however temporarily, and that appeasing her passion was her due, if she wanted it.

And heaven help her, she wanted it.

Drawn to him by a will stronger than her own, Scotia held her breath and took the two steps that separated them.

Ian's arm tightened around her possessively. His smoldering gaze dropped to her lips, and Scotia felt her body ignite at the same moment his mouth swooped down, capturing her lips in a kiss of demanding hunger. His hand urged her forward, even closer, to mold her pliant body against the rigid contours of his. With a silent moan of desperation, she slipped her free hand up his chest, her fingers clutching his broad shoulders, her body arching into his. A shudder shook his powerful frame as she fitted herself to him, and his lips crushed down on hers, parting them. His tongue drove into her mouth with a hungry urgency and she became lost in his heated magic.

"To the cottage!" A second cheer arose from the crowd. Before she or Ian could object, they found themselves lifted into the air by four of the village warriors.

The jarring movements of those who carried them into the heart of the village caused the cord that bound them together to cut into her wrist. They stopped before a small crofter cottage. The door stood open, as though in anticipation. A heartbeat later, she found herself whisked inside, along with Ian, and deposited atop a floor covered in luxuriant pelts. Over the thunder of her heartbeat, she heard the door close softly as the warriors departed, leaving the two of them alone.

She knew what came next.

Scotia swallowed roughly as she surveyed the room. There was no other furniture. A small fire burned in the hearth across from the door. The flames added a soft, gentle heat to the air as well as warming the room with a rich, golden hue. Scotia took a deep breath, trying to calm herself, but a sudden fit of trembling gripped her and doubts assailed her mind. What if he found her lacking or undesirable? She had no training in the art of seduction, only battle. *Nay*, she told herself as she tried to steady her nerves. *I must not give in to my fears. Fears are to be conquered, not fed.*

As though reading her thoughts, Ian took her other hand in his. "There is nothing to fear." A smile touched his lips. Scotia found herself drawn to them. His lips were full and soft, and in that moment, she wanted to feel them on her mouth, her body. She longed to run her own lips along the strong line of his jaw, to twine her fingers through his hair.

To experience all she desired, she would have to remove her armor. The last time she had tempted that fate, she had nearly died. But now she had her men to keep her safe, give her time to redress, should the need arise.

Other needs drove her now. Her need for Ian.

Without hesitation, he reached for her belt with his free hand and unbuckled it, then placed her sword on the fur pelts that covered the floor. Again, her trust overrode her fear. Before she had come to know Ian, she would have grieved at the loss of her sword. Now, she welcomed the release from its weight and from its purpose as her mind turned from her duty as a trainer of warriors to her duty as a lover.

"You are beautiful, Scotia," he whispered against her cheek as he placed the lightest of kisses along her jaw. When his lips touched the corner of hers, she turned her head to receive his kiss.

Her body responded immediately to his caress.

Warmth pooled in her belly and arousal flared as she drew him more deeply into her mouth. With her free hand, she trailed her fingers down his shoulder, across his back, until she unwittingly urged him closer against the softness of her body, fitting the evidence of his arousal tightly against her thigh.

Deftly, Ian unlaced the leather cording at the side of her armor, freeing her from confinement. With fingers that caressed as they moved, he eased the armor over her head, then tossed it aside. Silently he continued until her padding, cuisses, cross-garters and skirt joined her armor on the floor. A moment later, her shift whispered across her skin until is settled lightly atop the cord that bound them together in marriage.

She stood naked before him, bathed in the golden firelight and the warmth of his gaze.

"You are a warrior with no equal, Scotia," he said, his voice as caressing as his touch.

No equal. At the words, her gaze dipped once more to the red cord that connected them both physically and symbolically. She wanted an equal, a partner, and someone she could trust. That man stood before her now.

"You are wrong, Ian. *You* are my equal, my husband, and a man I have every right to explore." And explore him she did. With her free hand she disrobed him, until his clothing joined hers upon the floor. Her gaze traveled across his wide, strong shoulders to the light sprinkling of blond hair that spread across his chest. She followed the narrowing line down, across the rippling flatness of his stomach to the most male part of him. At the sight of his arousal, a wild, almost uncontrollable heat flared inside.

"Untie our hands," Scotia said, surprised by the urgency in her voice.

"Not yet." He pulled her to him. She gasped, then

closed her eyes, overcome by the startling sensation of his skin against her own. He brushed his lips across hers before he slid his mouth down her neck, across her shoulders, then further down until he reached her breasts. He nuzzled them slowly for endless moments before his lips closed over her taut nipples, first one, then the other. She moaned softly as he increased the pressure of his warm and languid caress, pulling her into a dark, whirling storm of pure desire and need. She tangled her hand in his hair, feeling the thick, cool silk slide through her fingers. Her legs felt weak beneath her as she drew in the heated, musky scent of his skin.

"Ian," she called, uncertain what it was she asked for, but she knew she longed for more of this dizzying arousal.

His mouth left her breasts, and still she trembled with the vibrant awareness of his body so close to hers. With a physical effort she forced her eyes open and looked at him. What she saw made her heart ache. In the glow of the firelight, his face was hard and dark with passion, and yet there was as much tenderness in his eyes as desire.

A sudden yearning took hold of her, fired her desire and her boldness. She slid her hand over the rigid muscles of his chest, watching as they flexed instinctively in passionate response to her touch. His reaction—heady, earthly, erotic.

She trailed her fingers over his arms, his neck, and shoulders, following each touch with her lips. His skin was like satin, and heat radiated from him, spreading through her, pulling her into a place without thought, without time, where all she knew were the waves of sensation and fire cresting through her body, and the desperate need for more.

And, for the first time in her life, feeding her senses became more important than controlling them. Casting aside her normal discipline, she hungered for the wild in-hibitions he drew out of her. Free from restraint, she wanted to touch him, to feel the full length of him against her skin. An incoherent sound of anticipation es-caped her. She claimed his lips, expressing all at once her need for him and her capitulation.

Powered by need, she kicked out her foot, trapping Ian's legs and bringing them both down to the furs. In a movement as reckless as her desire, she reached for the hilt of her recently abandoned sword and brought the weapon up to slash through the cord that bound them to-gether. Their commitment was still binding, with the cord or without.

Free of her bond, she caressed Ian's back and hips and buttocks, savoring the firmness of his muscles beneath her hands. She claimed him as her mate, even if he would only be hers for a short while, even if their joining would not give her the child she so desperately longed to con-ceive. Each touch, each kiss sent all rational thought fur-ther from her mind until she could only feel something wild and primitive building inside her, racing through her veins, seeking an unknown release.

Ian must have felt it too if the rapid rise and fall of his chest were any indication, but his response was not filled with the same breathless urgency that pulsed through her. Instead, he took his time, brushing her hair away from her neck with agonizing tenderness to kiss her neck, her shoulder, her collarbone, her breasts. With each sweet kiss, the reality of the world faded until there was nothing left but the two of them and the shadows of the small chamber.

He slid his hands to her waist, holding her captive, a sweet prisoner, as he cradled her body against his own. And nothing had ever felt more right. His hands moved down to cup her buttocks, the roughened texture of his palms flaring against the satiny softness of her flesh. He closed his eyes and breathed deeply into the tumbled mass of her hair, as though savoring her scent.

"With you, I feel whole," he said in a whisper of sound.

The words sank inside her, warmed her. Before she had time to adjust that to flowering sensation, he trailed his fingers along the lean muscle of her thighs, to her inner thigh and deep inside her core, bringing her passion to new heights of rapture. She gave a soft cry.

He responded with a single savage groan as he rolled her onto her back, eased his hard thighs between her legs and filled her body with promise and heat.

A sharp gasp tore from her throat at the pain that came as quickly as it eased. Only then did Ian begin to move, slowly at first, then deeper, filling her more fully with each thrust of his hips. The fire that had smoldered like embers in her belly burst into flame. The heat of it filled her, consumed her, as she sought whatever it was he tried to give her. Helplessly, she moved her hips against his.

Scotia felt as if she teetered on the brink of oblivion, filled with sensations too intense to bear in silence. She could hear breathless cries of pleasure she knew must be hers, but she could no more control them than the mounting waves of honeyed fire that tightened her muscles and arched her back.

Heat spiraled inside her, growing stronger and stronger, until all sensation shattered around her, propelling her into the awaiting abyss. A groan escaped Ian. She held on to him, pulling him with her over the edge of forever.

Every inch of her body, every fiber of her being filled with a warmth and pleasure she never dreamed possible. In his arms she felt not only safe and protected, but also cherished and consumed. Nothing had ever seemed more natural than having Ian within her, having his hands caress her body, having his lips upon her own.

Careful not to separate their bodies, he pulled her alongside him, resting his chin at the top of her head. "Rest for a while. You will need it. We have waited too long to reach this place for me to leave before we are both fully sated."

His hand came up to feather the lightest caress across her belly. "Do you believe its possible that I have given you a child already?"

Scotia's swirling senses halted with a sickening plummet. Passion gave way to the reality. A child. It was what she had wanted. It was her obligation to provide the next female Warrior Trainer.

Yet now, in the shelter of Ian arms, she realized that she wanted more than that from him. Not only did she want him to father her child, she wanted him to love her. Closing her eyes, Scotia struggled to control her frayed emotions. He had failed to speak those endearing words of love to her. Was she so unlovable? Her mother had always made her feel that way.

"Let me up," she whispered.

"What is wrong?" Ian shifted her in his arms until he faced her, breaking their intimate connection. A surge of tenderness swept across his features. "The first time is always painful. The next will not be that way. I promise."

How could she endure the glory and splendor of their lovemaking again, knowing it would fulfill her passions but never bond them as a man and a woman should be? "Ian, I—"

A knock sounded on the door and the moment dissolved between them. "Scotia. Ian." The voice was that of Burke's. "I'm certain ye'll have my hide for the interruption, but the scouts are just now returned with urgent news about the Horsemen. 'Tis important."

A look of regret passed across Ian's face before he turned away from her to grab his shirt. They dressed in a silence that no longer felt intimate, only charged with the tension of their unfinished conversation and the possible threat of attack. When his shirt and plaid were back in place, Ian brought his gaze to hers. He waited while she fastened her sword at her side. "Ready?"

She nodded, and he opened the door.

"What do you have to report?" Scotia asked.

The torch Burke held in his hand illuminated the doorway and spilled a yellow-gold glow into the room. Scotia knew the moment she saw the overly bright look in his aged eyes that something had happened. Burke sent a skittering glance at Ian before looking away. "One of the scouting parties has returned." He hesitated.

"Go on," Scotia encouraged. "What has happened?"

"The scouting party encountered the White and Red Horsemen and their army as they came up from the south. Only two of the six men are still alive."

A dark shiver passed through Scotia. The battle had begun. "Where are the men?"

"Being tended to by the village healer. They were both badly injured."

Scotia nodded and took a step toward the door. "I will go to them."

Ian followed by her side. "I am with you."

Burke held up his hand, stalling their movements. "There is more." Again, he shot a furtive glance at Ian. "Another scouting party reports that the Green Horseman is dead, that the Black Horseman has turned back toward Scotia's castle, and the Black Horseman has a prisoner with him. The scouts say he is still alive but tied to a scratch plow and badly beaten."

Ian's body tensed. "Who is this man?"

A muscle moved spasmodically in Burke's throat. "Griffin."

Chapter Twenty-eight

Griffin grimaced as he struggled against the bindings at his wrists. The rope did not give. Instead, the motion pulled the oxen's yoke that circled his neck and the scratch plow that dragged behind him in the ground deeper into his shoulders.

"How does it feel to be a beast of burden?" the Black Horseman taunted from atop his horse as he prompted Griffin, bearing the weight of the plow along in the darkness, back toward Scotia's castle.

Griffin stopped walking. "Why don't you just give me a sword so we can settle this like men?"

The Black Horseman reined his horse to a stop. "Why? So you can kill me the way you killed the Green Horseman?" The Black Horseman kicked out, connecting with Griffin's face.

Sticky warmth flowed from his nose and over his lips as pain exploded in his head. Only the plow at his back kept him standing as it caught his weight by jamming into his back. The plow skidded against the ground, leaving a thick groove in the dirt. He spat the blood away from his lips.

A sharp bite of laughter punctuated the air. "You might have managed to stop us from killin' your clan, but you'll be the one to pay for their survival."

The Black Horseman raised the lash he carried. "Now, my beastly warrior, keep movin'!"

Griffin looked to his left, then his right. All around him the Horseman's army watched with derisive triumph gleaming in their eyes. Griffin straightened his body as best as he could. "Nay. I am not going anywhere. If you wish to kill me, do it here."

"I don't wish to kill you. We need you as bait. Cooperative bait." The lash came down, over and over, until Griffin could not help but gasp at the pain.

The lash stopped.

"Now keep walking," the Black Horseman commanded.

Unable to do anything more, Griffin shuffled forward.

The Black Horseman spurred his horse into a walk beside Griffin. "We must go to the White Horseman. He will be interested in the news you *shared* with us."

Griffin gasped for breath as he staggered forward. He had shared nothing about Scotia, the Stone of Destiny, or Glencarron Castle. His own father had offered the information in order to spare Griffin's life. Griffin's unschooled reaction to his father's betrayal had only proven Abbus MacKinnon's claim.

Griffin's breathing grew painful when he thought of what his father had done. Why save him, only to betray Ian and Scotia? It made no sense. The moist night air felt good on Griffin's face, and he breathed deeply, hoping the air would act as a salve to his lacerated chest as they continued to push through the darkness.

Soon the rhythm of his feet drowned out all thought,

all feeling, as he followed the Black Horseman. What seemed a lifetime later, Griffin looked up to see Glencarron Castle beneath the soft glow of the moon's light. A surge of anticipation awakened the warrior sleeping inside him. The battle would begin soon. A battle that would decide his own future as well as those he had come to love.

Griffin struggled to stand, tall and proud, preparing to fight whether he was tied to a plow or clutching a sword, just as Scotia had taught him.

Amidst the light of fifty torches, Scotia and Ian led the entire village and all their warriors through the darkness, following the obvious trail one group of Horsemen and their army had left behind. The disrupted brush would have been clue enough that he headed toward Glencarron Castle. But he also made no effort to conceal the tracks left from the horses or the deep grooves cut into the soil by the heavy plow Griffin carried.

Scotia sat atop her horse. She surveyed the mounted warriors who fanned out in front and behind the group, braving the darkness of the night. Warriors and villagers alike carried torches as well as some sort of weapon, be it a sword, a spear, an ax, or a crossbow. A surge of pride welled inside her. They were all prepared to do what they must to survive a midnight attack. With Ian among them, she felt the odds were greatly in their favor.

Her gaze strayed to the man and horse to her left—her husband. Scotia smiled to herself, surprised at how easily the word came to her. Despite the tension Ian must be feeling, his posture was not rigid, as most men's would have been given the same situation. Instead, he sat his horse with an air of nonchalant control. It was a look that warned all who gazed upon him to proceed with caution. A look that said he had a purpose in mind and nothing would keep him from that.

If she were wise she would heed that warning, but she could no longer put off the question that had haunted her since they had departed from the village in haste. "Do you wish you had gone on to the aid of your clan instead of coming back for me?"

"That question serves no point other than to torture us both." He glanced her way, then turned back to the dark landscape ahead. "I made my choice. And I would make the same decision all over again if it meant keeping you from harm."

He had chosen her protection and safety over the lives of those who had raised him. What had she done to deserve that kind of devotion? Was there more than his claim to keep her safe behind his decision to remain with her?

She wanted to believe there was a deeper meaning, but most likely it was only her own desires clouding her thoughts.

Desires and kisses and irrational yearnings—never had she known such a world existed until a few hours ago. Moonlight caressed the masculine sensuality of his body. He was strong, supple, and hers for a year and a day. Her cheeks warmed against the cool night air.

Scotia forced herself to turn away from the tug of Ian's presence. Near him, she found it harder and harder to remember she served Scotland as guardian of the Stone, as a trainer of warriors. But was that all she could be? Was there no room in her life to serve the roles of wife and mother? Could she let go of centuries of obligations and duties to think of herself and her own happiness? If her own mother had been so horribly wrong about sex with a man, could she also be wrong about marriage? It was something to consider.

Feeling the enormity of her decision, Scotia shifted her gaze to the stars. She had found answers to her troubles in the heavens before. Perhaps she would do so again.

The night seemed to sparkle all around her, as if the air had been freshly washed and cleared of all that had come before this moment. She drew a breath of the sweet air into herself. New beginnings. Fresh chances. Would such a thing be possible for Ian and herself? Hope glimmered inside her despite all the odds against them.

She stole another glance at the fierce yet gentle man beside her. Perhaps if they made it through the coming battle, they would have that second chance.

The remainder of their journey passed in silence. Scotia used the time to run a thousand different possibilities through her mind. Had the Black Horseman rejoined the White and Red Horsemen? Did they head for her castle, or did they wait in secluded darkness, ready to spring a trap upon those who drew near? Would she and Ian find themselves trapped between the two groups before they could attempt to rescue Griffin? Did Griffin remain alive?

She knew from personal experience the White Horseman could be as cruel as he was cunning. And what about those she had left back at the castle? Were they as safe as she had assumed they would be?

She shivered, fear suddenly making her limbs feel heavy and weak. Age-old terror now seemed fresh and vibrant, coursing through her with the same intensity it did twelve years past. Scotia tensed, every instinct within her fighting the memories she had yet to let rest. She was older now, wiser, and stronger. Any match between them would be on equal ground this time.

The thought acted like a tonic to her system, revitalizing her body with not only strength, but determination. She drew herself up in her saddle and kept her gaze trained ahead of her, both watchful and prepared.

This time she would be ready to fight.

When dawn gave way to the morning light, and the crenellated towers of Glencarron Castle came into view, Scotia's determination faltered at the stark reality before her. Even at a distance, she could see the deep groove in the earth they had tracked all night continued right up to the gatehouse.

The pounding of her heart drowned out all else as she scanned her castle, searching for clues as to what had happened in her absence. The outer bailey walls were undamaged, but the portcullis stood open, suggesting that at least one of the Horsemen had found his way inside.

But more distressing than the open gates was the fact that neither her guards nor any of the Horsemen's army were anywhere in sight. Desperate to discover the fate of her people, Scotia kicked her horse into a run, speeding toward her home.

Ian followed beside her, his presence a welcome comfort. As they reached the gatehouse he slowed his horse, forcing her to lag behind him. The unconsciously protective gesture warmed her icy spirit and she allowed him to take the lead. They dismounted. The warriors and villagers who had traveled with them gathered behind them.

At the sight of red droplets of blood against the rock-strewn ground, Scotia stumbled, then caught herself. The smell of blood, with its cloying, metallic sweetness, came to her nose and raked the back of her throat. She bent down to touch the sticky substance. Her finger came up wet. "It is fresh." She was unable to say anything more. A wave of guilt and powerlessness crept upon her before she could stop it. She should have put a stop to the fighting years ago. If she had only known. . . .

Ian's hand settled upon her shoulder. Gently he turned her to face him. Understanding and compassion reflected in his gaze. "It is what we do now that matters. Come," Ian said, as though reading her thoughts.

Rising to her feet, Scotia drew her sword, ready to battle whatever evil stood in her way. No one harmed her loved ones and got away with it.

"Prepare yourselves for anything," Ian warned the crowd that stood loosely grouped behind him. "Stay together. There is safety in numbers." He reached for his sword as he brought his gaze back to Scotia's. "Is there any way I might convince you to stay out here and allow me to fight this battle alone?"

"Never," Scotia said in a tense voice. "This is my battle as much as yours." She would put an end to anyone who threatened her family. Maisie, Lizbet, even Griffin—she loved them each in a special way.

Ian nodded, and a glimmer of admiration reflected in his gaze before he turned away. "Then stay near me. I want you in my sight at all times."

She opened her mouth to object, then stopped herself at the realization he only wanted to see her safe. Warmth filled her at the thought. She wanted the same for him. "Agreed." Together they stood a better chance of succeeding in battle than they did fighting alone.

Yet as they headed toward the open gate, Scotia paused.

Ian slowed to a stop beside her. "What is it? What is wrong?"

"I had a thought. It might be nothing, but I cannot shake the feeling that this is all too easy. The trail here was so deliberately set."

"What are you thinking?" Ian asked.

"I find it difficult to believe the Horsemen would come so close to the village of Cuillin, yet not attack. Then, when we learned of Griffin's capture, the Black Horseman left blatant clues for us to find, even in the dark. When we got here, the trail of blood made us assume it was Griffin who had been injured or killed . . . and yet . . ." Scotia hesitated, reasoning things out as she talked. "Why would he go to such extremes to see us come through the front gate of the castle unless—"

"It is a trap," Ian answered.

Scotia nodded. "We need to find another way inside— something that will give us the element of surprise."

"The tunnel in the cliffs," Burke said from behind her.

Scotia turned to look into Burke's gray eyes. In fragmented bits and pieces her memories coalesced. The arrow arching toward her. Her feet refusing to carry her forward. The evil grin on the White Horseman's face. A young girl, her hands red with her own blood, guided over the jagged rocks below to a boat that had taken Maisie, Burke, and herself to safety that fateful night.

The tunnel.

For years, even thinking about entering the tunnel brought on an irrational fear that left Scotia fazed and weak. She had not been near the place for years, not since she had rigged it with a system of thin ropes that triggered bells inside the castle walls. A shiver of dread tried to creep across her flesh, but this time she was ready for it. No more. The man did not merit her fear. "Follow me. I will show you the way inside. But we must act quickly, before they discover our change of direction and trap us beneath the castle with nowhere to go."

With Ian by her side, Scotia lead their small group of warriors down to the shoreline, up the rocky cliff, and into the tunnel. The soft sound of the surf hitting the rocks muted the sound of their footsteps as they made their way up the rocky passageway. She stopped the group along the way to disengage the ropes of her warning system.

The cloying scents of earth and salt hung heavy on the air as the group continued on. Finally they reached the end. With as much stealth as possible, Scotia gathered her small army into the cramped chamber at the top of the tunnel. The few torches they had brought with them turned the darkness into a hazy light, illuminating a door off to the left.

When the others crowded into the narrow space, Ian leaned into the small wooden door. "Ready?" He met her gaze squarely, with no hesitation.

"I am ready," she replied, and raising her sword, she prepared to meet whatever surprises awaited them.

For a brief moment, Ian's expression softened as he leaned toward her, to brush his lips against hers. "To the future," he whispered against her cheek before he pulled away. Then, with his sword poised, he gave the door a mighty heave. Wood splintered as it hit against the stone wall. Together, they charged into the open air—and came to a swift halt. Ten men with bows drawn and aimed at them stood atop the garden wall.

"I see our honored guests have finally arrived," the White Horseman jeered as he towered over them, a hulking barbarian.

Chapter Twenty-nine

Scotia searched the garden area. The Black Horseman and the Red Horseman stood behind their leader on the wall. Behind them a sea of soldiers spilled across the rest of the garden area, crushing beneath their boots the fragile sprouts her gardeners had sown so carefully. So many men—too many.

Scotia's gaze snapped to the White Horseman's face, to the wrathful intensity that burned in his eyes. This time she could not stop the shiver of cold fear that moved through her. The old, familiar terror she had felt the night he had slain her mother began to hammer in her mind, bringing a tremor to the fingers wrapped tightly about her sword.

"Impossible," she breathed above the sound of the villagers murmuring and shuffling behind her.

"Nay, it is possible indeed. I set a trap to push you into a better trap. Brilliant of me, would you not say?"

Scotia could feel a bead of moisture dampen her temple as she realized her mistake. She had judged the White Horseman's actions by her own thinking. And she had allowed her own fears to overshadow the lunacy of this man. A stupid error. One that could cost them their lives.

"Do not blame yourself." The White Horseman's voice grated against her taut nerves. "I would not be so foolish as to insult your intelligence by believing you could fall for so obvious a trap as that first one I set." His mouth quirked into a terrible smile. "You are the mighty Warrior Trainer. The very same clever young girl who led me to believe you were dead for the last twelve years, or this day would have come much sooner indeed."

Scotia tried to bury her emotions deep within herself, refusing to let them betray her again. She had to stay on the edge of her control. "Your ploy will not work."

"It already has." A triumphant look beamed from the White Horseman's face.

Ian took a step forward, but Scotia stilled him with a hand on his arm. "Nay, Ian." Fear slipped past her guard and into her voice. "He will kill you without a thought." Her plea must have penetrated the haze of his fury because he stopped, but his sword did not come down.

Scotia trembled despite her attempts to stop. Her breathing came in rapid bursts as the years since their last meeting melted away and she saw the White Horseman as she had then. He was still a hulking figure, his muscles honed by brutality instead of training. Villainous and ruthless.

Drawing on years of training and practice, she inhaled a slow, calming breath and forced the memory away. There were differences in this man now, just as there were differences in herself from that time so long ago. The morning sun brought out the deep lines of age that had settled near his unearthly pale eyes. His eyes had changed the most. Instead of steady and strong, they now appeared overly bright and unfocused as his gaze darted between Ian and herself.

The White Horseman smiled mockingly. "Are you going to stare at me or give me what I want? I am not a patient man. Any further delay on your part will only cause your friends an earlier death." He jerked his head to the side, and her gaze followed. Rows of his army stepped aside to reveal three battered prisoners.

Instantly, Scotia's fear dissolved into rage. Griffin, Maisie, and Lizbet were tied to stakes that had been driven into the soft earth of the garden. Their hands were secured behind them, their legs bound as well. Angry red welts showed on their faces and arms. Lizbet hung limp against her bonds. Scotia's heart cried out to go to her. The poor child had already suffered enough at the White Horseman's hands.

Maisie glowered at her captor's back, ready to slay him with her gaze if given the chance.

Then there was Griffin, whose body appeared swollen and bruised. Blood oozed from cuts on his face and legs. From beneath the swollen blue lids of his eyes, Griffin offered her a look of outraged sympathy. *I am sorry*, he mouthed, though no words came forth.

Scotia looked back to her enemy. She once again tried to subdue her anger without much success. "How dare you treat them this way."

The White Horseman curled the hand that held his sword into a white-knuckled fist, and a feral gleam sparked in his light eyes. "I'll dare that and more until you give me the Stone."

Beside her she could feel Ian tense. She turned to him. His fingers curled tightly around the hilt of his raised sword. His aim, the White Horseman's heart.

As if sensing the danger he faced, the White Horseman brought his blade against Maisie's throat. "One move from you, Ian MacKinnon, and she breathes no more."

Ian's face became a mask of control, but icy fury burned in his eyes, so cold, so deadly, that Scotia could almost feel his wrath chill the blood in her veins.

"Where is the Green Horseman?" Scotia asked, knowing the answer, yet stalling for time while she scrambled to formulate a plan.

"I killed him," Griffin cried out hoarsely, struggling against the bonds that held him captive. "He and the Black Horseman attacked our village. But this time we were ready for them."

"Quiet!" shouted the White Horseman. "Or you'll die first."

Griffin's news that Ian's village had been spared and the Green Horseman killed brought with it a first ray of hope. Though three Horsemen still remained, the doubt Griffin's deed placed in their minds might be the weakness she sought to find.

A warrior never fights with anger, revenge, frustration, or arrogance, she reminded herself.

She drew silent strength from the earth beneath her feet and allowed the calming surf below to turn her anger into energy.

"One warrior matters little in the overall plan to dominate Scotland."

Even as the White Horseman made his claim, she could see a glimmer of uncertainty pass across the other warriors' faces. And where there was uncertainty, there was vulnerability. Scotia forced a laugh in a deliberate attempt to bait him. "You think the Stone will enable you to do that?"

The White Horseman's face grew red with anger. "The

legend surrounding the Stone is proof of that. The Stone has brought great success to those who possess it. When I carry the Stone into battle for England, I shall never lose. How easy it will be to dominate Scotland after that."

"Nay," Maisie cried out. "Do not give it to him. I beg ye, Scotia. Keep it safe. Our lives are insignificant when compared to the Stone." Her plea became a strangled gasp when the White Horseman pressed his blade against her throat, drawing a ribbon of blood.

Ian growled.

Scotia steeled herself not to react. It was what the Horseman wanted, was it not? To see her tremble with fear as she had when she was younger? "Obviously, we are at a stalemate." She widened her stance, assuming her fighting posture. "I have something you want, just as you have something I want. If you kill Maisie, you will never see the Stone, let alone possess it."

His jaw went rigid, but the hand that held the sword at Maisie's neck relaxed.

"Perhaps we could negotiate terms if the MacKinnon would lower his weapon," the White Horseman snarled.

Scotia kept her gaze trained on her enemy. "Lower your weapon," she asked Ian, hoping he could hear the new-found confidence in her voice, that he would trust her enough to do as she asked.

She could feel his questioning gaze upon her, but his weapon remained aimed at the White Horseman. "One charge and I will have him before the archers can stop me."

She fought the urge to turn to him, to allow her gaze to linger over him as a wife would look at her husband, to reveal to him both her fears and passions. Yet she could not. To do so would expose how much he meant to her and bring him certain death. Nay, she had to treat him as she would any other warrior in her army if she was to keep him safe. "Lower your weapon," she repeated with a sharp, authoritative voice.

He finally obeyed, and Scotia breathed a thankful sigh.

"If we are to *negotiate*, as you put it, we will do so in the courtyard near the keep upon equal ground." Scotia braced herself for his refusal. To her surprise, he did not offer her one.

"After you." He waved his hand toward the small door that led to the inner bailey. His men parted, making a path for them.

Scotia frowned. "I am not so foolish as that. Again, we will negotiate. You send half of your men, then I will send half of mine."

The White Horseman's eyes narrowed upon her. "Why should I agree to something so ridiculous?"

"Because I have the Stone." She had no choice but trust he would do as she asked. But if he betrayed her, she would be ready for that as well.

His face darkened, but he lowered his sword from Maisie's throat. "Agreed." He turned away. "Move the prisoners!" he shouted.

"Leave them here," she countered, her voice bold. "They are not going anywhere in their present condition."

That brought a jeering smile to his face. "You're right about that. All right. Leave 'em behind, but with an armed guard."

It was one more guard than she wanted, but Scotia conceded the point. One man would not be difficult to eliminate when the time came to set them free. It would also mean one less man to face in the courtyard. With as much indifference as she could muster, she addressed Ian. "Take the first group into the courtyard."

He gave her a beseeching look that spoke his confusion at her actions. She offered him the slightest warning shake of her head. She was not sure what he saw in the motion, but after a brief hesitation he turned away to gather half the group of villagers and warriors. Once the task was complete, Ian followed the Horsemen's army through the small door and into the courtyard beyond.

Scotia watched them go with a new sense of determination, which Ian had placed inside her with his one brief gaze. To everyone else it meant nothing. To her, it said *I trust you.*

That determination remained steady as the second group made their way through the doorway. When everyone else had left except herself and the White Horseman, Scotia cast a final glance back at the prisoners. As she did, a motion to her left caught her eye. She saw Burke peek out from the door of the tunnel. She allowed herself a small smile of satisfaction. Her steward would see to the guard watching over Maisie, Lizbet, and Griffin. In short order, the three of them would all be free.

Encouraged by this second ray of hope, she pushed through the door into the courtyard with the White Horseman at her side. Just as she had hoped, Ian had spread the two groups around so they were not all clustered in one place.

"Now that I have agreed to this little arrangement, where is the Stone?" the White Horseman growled from behind her.

Scotia sheathed her sword, then turned to face him. "Leave the others below and come with me." She did not wait to see whether he followed. Her plan was to draw him away, up the stairs that led to the west tower. She hoped that by removing their leader, his army would flounder when the inevitable battle broke out. Nothing else would end what the Four Horsemen had begun.

At the top of the stairs, Scotia looked behind her, past

the White Horseman to the people below. She saw nothing but confidence on the faces of her people. They knew what they had to do. She sought out Ian. She should have known he would be watching her progress. Yet his expression was completely unreadable. She had no idea what he could be thinking. In that moment she realized she had become accustomed to reading the emotions he so readily displayed. Their absence made her feel bereft and alone as she continued up a second set of stairs to the newly altered round tower above.

"Quit stalling," the White Horseman thundered behind her.

"If you want the Stone, then it is here you must go." Scotia reached the top of the tower and spun to face her enemy, her hand rested lightly on the hilt of her sword. If needed, she could draw the weapon before the Horseman could advance on her.

A murderous gleam lurked in his eyes. "Give it to me now." His voice rose to a bellow that drew every eye in the courtyard to them. He searched the small tower. "Where is it? I see no shrine or housing for the Stone up here. If you thought to trick me, you will pay for the misdeed with your life."

"It is no trick. The Stone is here, and in plain sight, where it will be safe from you and your kind forever."

"Where?" He drew his sword, but not before she drew hers.

She dropped into her fighting stance. "It's in the wall of the tower. Third stone from the left beneath the crenellation that faces due west. If you look closely you will see that the Stone is darker than the others that surround it. The etchings that cover the surface will prove to you that it is indeed the real Stone of Destiny."

When he saw the Stone, his eyes widened with triumph, then anger. "You put such a priceless artifact in the wall of your castle?" He backed away from her, toward the Stone. "It is sacred and blessed."

"It is worthless stone compared to the value of human life." Scotia kept pace with him. She would hand over the Stone in an instant if it meant keeping her people safe, alive. But if the Horseman gave her an opening to attack and drive him from this world instead, she would gladly take it.

He stopped before the darker stone and kneeled down beside it. "The Stone of Destiny." His voice filled with awe as he traced his fingers over the etchings of a Latin cross on the surface of the Stone. It was the opening she searched for.

She lunged. Her blade penetrated the chain mail that covered his sword arm. His fingers went slack, and his sword dropped to the wooden floor with a clatter. The same moment the White Horseman howled in pain, the battle broke out beneath them in a thunder of sound, like a storm rising from the west, refusing to be tamed.

Chapter Thirty

The moment Scotia headed up the stairs to the tower with the White Horseman, Ian prepared to act. He feared for her, as he clutched his sword, ready to send the signal for the battle to begin. He opened his mouth to issue the order when the very same cry he intended erupted from behind the inner bailey wall.

Ian spun to the gate across the courtyard. Familiar faces, members of his own clan, rushed into battle against the remaining Horsemen and their army. Behind the first charge of men came Abbus MacKinnon. Without hesitation, Ian fought his way to his father. When Abbus's gaze alighted on his son, his gruff expression shifted to a smile. "Ian, my boy. Let's show these Englishmen what a Scot is made of."

The clash of battle sounded all around them. Ian saluted his foster father with his sword, glad to have his support as well as his clan's. "I will have to leave that task in your capable hands, Father. Right now Scotia needs my help."

Two of the Horsemen's warriors charged for them. With a quick thrust of their swords, the assault ended, leaving his foster father and himself isolated for a brief respite.

"How did you know to come here?" Ian asked.

"We followed the Black Horseman when he took Griffin captive. I told the Horseman to come here if it was the Stone he was after."

Shock ran through Ian. Whatever explanation he had expected, it was not that. "You put Scotia and her people at risk."

"I did it to save yer brother. I'd already lost one of ye to the Horsemen. I couldn't lose you or Griffin as well." Abbus strode toward the fighting. "Ye've got a woman to save, and I've got a battle to win." His father's voice boomed above the din of the conflict.

With a brief salute, Ian darted back toward the tower where Scotia had taken the White Horseman. Ian had nearly reached the stairs when a flurry of fire arrows shot past him, landing in a haystack left from the winter's store. With a whoosh of sound, the dry hay caught fire. Tongues of greedy flame soon covered the hay, sending a plume of gray smoke billowing across the battlefield.

Given a different situation, he would have stopped to put out the fire. But he had to get to Scotia before it was too late.

His throat was raw. His lungs burned from breathing the acrid air as he raced up the stairs. He took each step more swiftly than the last. He ignored the rising crescendo of battle around him, concentrating on the tower that held both the woman he loved and the man he despised.

* * *

Fear and despair gripped Scotia as plumes of angry gray smoke rose from the courtyard below. The castle was on fire. Her people were in danger from the flames as well as the Horsemen's army. Scotia gripped the hilt of her sword with all her strength. She was a warrior, a protector, and a liberator of her people. There was no time for fear. Only action.

Blood from the cut she had inflicted on the White Horseman's arm seeped through his chain mail shirt like a splash of crimson paint. It was not a deadly wound, but it would give her the edge she needed to destroy him.

Anger blazed in his icy cold eyes as he scowled at his wounded arm, then at her. "How dare you strike me?"

"I dare to kill you."

"Do not be so foolish."

From below, cries of triumph mixed with shrieks of agony, each sound compounding the next. Ian and her people were striving to rid themselves of the men who challenged their freedom—she would do the same with this evil man.

"Listen to them," the White Horseman taunted above the roar of the battle. He picked up his sword. "They fight against the unconquerable. Just as your mother did."

"Is that what you think?" Scotia forced her mind to clear. She had to concentrate on the task ahead of her, just like her men below. "You think you cannot be beaten?"

He drew himself up. His actions did not frighten her. Not anymore. In fact, his effort to make himself look more menacing only gave her a bigger target to strike.

"Nothing and no one can stop me once I have the Stone. You will die, too, unless—"

"Unless what?" she asked, edging closer to him.

A spark of amusement entered his eerie eyes. "Unless you hear me out."

"You choose to bargain with me now that my sword is pointed at your heartless chest?"

He smiled. "I am not so heartless as that. Some say I can even be quite generous."

"Forgive my distrust, but I find that hard to believe."

He laughed, the sound more grating than pleased. "Give me a chance. Hear what I have to say. It might interest you."

"What could you possibly have to say to me?"

"Very good, my dear. I can see in your eyes that spark of anger. That anger can make you an even greater warrior than you are now. Let me take the Stone away from here, then join me. Fight at my side against your countrymen. I will teach you the things your mother never did."

Scotia could only stare in startled shock at the audacity of his words. "Join you? Bring more harm to my countrymen? Never."

His smile slipped and a sneer took its place. "There is an edge to you, Scotia. A dark edge. Come with me, fight with me, and I will help you find that darkness you try to hide from yourself and others."

Scotia went still as memories from her youth came back to her. At first there had been sadness, but that soon shifted to rage, a rage that nearly consumed her after her mother's death. She had felt alone, abandoned, and inadequate because she had not been able to do anything to stop the man before her from killing her mother. Instead of fighting him, she had run to Maisie for comfort.

Scotia felt that rage build inside her again, felt her fingers digging into the hilt of her sword, but a voice inside her whispered and she knew to heed its warning. With a long, deep breath, she forced the furious emotions deep inside her. Aye, she had felt rage, anger, even despair, but her training had saved her then as it would now. Through discipline and training, as her mother had taught her, she had learned to shift the dark emotions from bad to good.

Scotia squared her shoulders and swung her sword before her. "There is no darkness in me. Not anymore."

He charged forward, but Scotia was ready. Their swords collided with a clash. When they did she kicked out, catching the White Horseman in the stomach and sending him staggering backward. Twelve years of anger and frustration went into that kick, igniting her senses, consuming her fears.

"We are so alike, you and I—angry and filled with hatred." His blade arched toward her in what would have been a disemboweling sweep. She blocked the move, then spun away.

Scotia remained steady, her emotions in control. His words were meant to distract her. "There is nothing similar about us."

"Oh, but there is." His gaze became oddly intent. "Had I known what an asset to my cause you would have been, I would have taken you with me years ago instead of leaving you for dead."

"I never would have gone. Death would have been preferable." The intensity of his gaze made her uneasy. Something had suddenly given him more strength, energy, and prowess. Her hand tightened on her sword. She would kill him, by any means. She just needed an opening. Balancing on her feet lightly, she waited for the right moment to strike.

That moment came a heartbeat later. He struck a blow with such force the momentum caused him to stumble to the left. She reacted, aiming for his extremities—his forearm, his knees, his upper arms, and his legs, darting in and out, sneaking past his guard, until she left slashes and nicks across every part of him.

A blatant arrogance dominated the features of his harsh face. "You would have gone." His sword flashed again, high in the air, deadly, lethal, filled with his own rage.

"What makes you so certain?" Before he could bring his blade down, Scotia sent all her strength and will to survive into her foot. It connected with the White Horseman's knee; she felt the bones smash beneath her boot.

The White Horseman screamed in agony as his legs went out from under him. He hit the wooden timbers hard, forcing a rush of air from his lungs. His sword tumbled from his hand and clattered to a rest against the stones of the tower wall.

In an instant, Scotia's blade was at his throat. She gripped the hilt of her sword with all her strength. Nothing would stop her from grasping this moment. From seeking justice for all the atrocities this man had forced on her country, on her mother, on herself. She lifted her sword, poised to strike.

"You would have gone . . . ," he wheezed, "because you are my daughter."

Scotia gazed at her enemy incredulously. "Nay." Her throat tightened in response to the White Horseman's confession while her grip loosened on her sword. Such a thing could not be possible. Her sword grew awkward and heavy in her hand. *You are my daughter.*

The White Horseman took advantage of her momentary lapse and rolled away. He gained his feet with a grimace of pain, then drew his dagger. He did not come after her as she had expected. Instead, he turned toward the tower wall and began to hack at the mortar which secured the Stone of Destiny in place.

"It is only too true," he panted. "Have you never seen

your reflection? We are related, you and I. The color of our hair is the most obvious similarity, but there are others." He turned his back on her to scrape viciously at the mortar cementing the stone in the wall.

He turned his back on her. Only an insanely confident man would do something so foolish. That act in itself lent credence to what he had said. Scotia shivered violently at the memory of her image in Ian's shield—reddish-brown hair, high cheekbones, a slightly rounded nose, full red lips. Features so similar to the man before her.

The warrior in her told her to take advantage of the situation, to end this conflict for her people right now. Yet if she did, she would never have the answers to the questions she longed to know about her father. "How is that possible?" Her voice quavered, a sign of her restraint.

He turned to study her with appreciative eyes. "In the usual way. Your mother and I—"

"Enough." Scotia took a step back from him, trying to clear her head. The vile, disgusting man was her enemy. Nothing more. "You killed my mother." Aye, her mother. She had her mother's soft green eyes.

"Such a nasty thing that was, but necessary." He shrugged and turned back to examine his progress in retrieving the Stone.

She tensed. "You tried to kill me."

"I thought I had." He paused his digging to cast her a caustic grin. "I should have predicted your survival. But I was still young, inexperienced in the arts of war." He spared her a mocking glance. "A mistake I will not make again."

Scotia ignored his threat. He wanted her fear and her confusion. She could see it in his eyes. "And when you learned I was alive—"

He gave a soft laugh, interrupting her. "I came for you, but those two ancient retainers of yours lied to me. The woman has since paid for her deception." Any humor in his face faded.

At the reminder of his abuse of Maisie, Lizbet, and Griffin, Scotia's anger started to rise again, but she forced herself to control it. Giving in to the need for revenge would accomplish nothing. She had to wait until the perfect opportunity presented itself. It would. It had to. Or she would make one of her own. "Why do you want the Stone so badly? You are English. It means nothing to you."

His hand fell away from the Stone, but he remained hunched beside it. "It is the ultimate symbol of power and good fortune. I spent my youth studying ancient texts about the Stone of Destiny and learned that your mother's line had first possessed the artifact. It only made sense that she would somehow be its keeper."

He shifted his position to face her. His dagger remained steady in his hand, but she was a painful pace outside his reach. She should kill him now, but for better or worse, she had to know more. "Go on."

"Suddenly curious?"

"Nay." She lied. "Just trying to learn how your twisted mind works."

"The same way as yours." He turned his back on her again and started digging at the edges of the Stone once more. Chunks of mortar fell away. "Which is why I know you are no threat to me until you hear what I have to say." He laughed in the silence that hung between them. "Want to hear more?"

"Aye," she said tersely.

The sound of his blade scraping the mortar hung in the background as he continued his tale. "I made my way to Glencarron Castle the first time to train with your mother. She accepted me as a student even though I was

English. I spent the next several months trying to seduce her with my charms. But she was unimpressed."

The sound ceased as he turned to face her again. "Why do women never know what is good for them?"

Scotia frowned. "Why do men always tread down roads they should not?"

He shrugged, though his face was wreathed in a smile. "I was angry with her one night. When I tried to get her to reveal the Stone's location, she refused. So I took something else instead. Her body."

He paused, waiting for Scotia's reaction.

She gave him none. "Continue," she said, though she had a sharp suspicion where his words would lead.

"I took from her body what she readily denied me. At the peak of my pleasure she nearly skewered me with her sword, then tossed me into the night."

Her mother's words flooded back to her: that distraction could cost her, that pleasure had no place in the Trainer's life, that love made a woman weak. It all made sense now. Her mother's own distraction had brought down her guard and had allowed this man to take something that had not been freely offered. Suddenly Scotia was ice-cold and numb, as she closed herself off to his mocking smile and the vindictive glint in his dark eyes.

Forced joining. That was what her mother had based all her lessons upon. But her mother was wrong. So very wrong. Ian had proven that to her time and again with his gentle, sensual seduction. All her life Scotia had accepted what her mother had told her as the truth. All because of this man. The numbness began to recede, seared out by the anger possessing her soul.

"I had no idea you were a product of that night until I returned to Glencarron Castle with a small contingent of men. We stormed the gate and made our way inside the great hall. I was prepared to force her to hand over the real Stone, not the fake one King Edward had taken back to England with him as a prize. I had thought to harm the members of her household until she gave me what I desired. But the moment I saw you, I knew you were the advantage I needed to make her change her mind."

Chunks of mortar and sand sprinkled upon the floorboards as he rattled the Stone, trying to wrest it from its hiding place. Her grip on her sword became steady once again, as her intentions solidified in her mind. "You might have used me to your advantage once, but I am wiser and more experienced now."

As the sound of the Stone scraping against the rocks that held it in place increased, so did the tension in the air between them. The White Horseman simultaneously pulled on the Stone while narrowing his gaze at Scotia. "Put that sword down. Does the fact I am your father mean nothing to you?"

A momentary pang of regret crept through her resolve. The man was her father; but he was also vile and ruthless. And he had to die or no one in her country would ever be safe from him. She took a step forward. "You might have been responsible for my birth, but you are no father to me."

Suddenly Scotia realized all too clearly what Ian had been trying to say to her on the night of their handfasting—the reason he wanted to bind himself to her, despite the fact he did not love her. To father a child was easy. To guide that child through life with discipline and love was the true measure of a man.

"Scotia."

Scotia closed her eyes against the sound of Ian's voice in her imagination. All she had to do was think of him and he appeared so vibrantly alive in the depths of her mind. She drew in a slow, even breath, trying to focus her thoughts.

"Scotia."

She half-turned toward the wall walk that connected this tower with the others. "Ian." A surge of tenderness swept through her. Framed by the doorway with his blond hair tousled, his muscles flexing, and his sword boldly before him, he looked like an ancient warrior rising out of the mists.

"Isn't this touching?" The White Horseman's mouth curved into a lethal smile as he staggered to his feet with the heavy Stone clutched against him like a shield.

Fear tightened Scotia's chest at the realization that she had just given away her feelings for Ian in her words, her actions.

Ian looked to her, then the White Horseman. Scotia's muscles locked with tension. Did Ian see what she feared? A resemblance between them? Or did his speculative look mean something else entirely?

The White Horseman pulled her from her thoughts. "Perhaps we are not so much alike after all, my dear. I learned long ago that attachments only get in the way." He turned to Ian. "Allow me to rid you of this handsome distraction." The White Horseman held the Stone of Destiny to his chest with one hand, his dagger poised to strike Ian in the other. Just a flick of his wrist and he could send the weapon arching toward Ian's chest before either of them could stop it. "Perhaps in your grief, you will decide to join me yet."

A sudden cold sickness settled in the pit of her stomach. "Nay. Take the Stone. Do not harm him." The words were more challenge than plea.

The White Horseman gravely studied Ian's face before

he shook his head. "No," he said. "I think I will enjoy killing this Scot far too much for even you to turn me away from the deed."

Anger and hatred replaced her fear. "What will it take for you to spare his life? I will do anything you ask, even go with you if that is what it takes."

The White Horseman's brow wrinkled in thought. She used his hesitation against him. She cleared her mind of all thought until all that remained was her goal.

Protect Ian.

With the slightest effort, she shifted her weight to the balls of her feet. She let herself feel nothing as she prepared to kill her father.

Chapter Thirty-one

Ian's skin grew clammy and wet. He had looked death in the eye before and had never been afraid. But now, a fear both hideous and painful gripped him. It was a fear not for himself, but for Scotia. He knew what she planned to do. He could see it in the positioning of her body. Her weight had shifted to her toes, ready to strike.

Before he could stop her, she sprinted forward, a burst of energy set in motion.

The White Horseman's eyes flared as his head snapped toward Scotia.

In that beat of a moment, Ian surged forward. He was closer to their enemy. If he pushed himself to the limit, he might reach the target first. A cry began deep in the pit of his stomach. *"MacccKinnnonnn!"* The war cry of his clan, a sound as old and untamed as the hills that gave it birth. The warning poured from his throat as his stride swallowed up the wooden planking beneath his boots. He hit the White Horseman hard, his momentum carrying him forward, pushing them toward an opening in the crenellations, toward certain death.

Even death would be a welcome price for Scotia's safety.

Ian's gaze moved to hers as he fell backward with the White Horseman. Her eyes filled with wild, panicked fear. Ian tried to reassure her, to let her see in his eyes a fraction of the peace and serenity that filled him now.

The White Horseman screamed in rage as he tumbled through the open space with the Stone still clutched to his chest.

"Ian!" Scotia cried. The word echoed all around them, filled with horror, grief, and longing. She pushed forward, the motion slow, slower than the rate at which he fell.

"I love you," Ian said, the words filling him with an awesome sense of wonder, power, and satisfaction as he hit the edge of the tower and the vastness of the sky rose up to greet him. The emptiness at his core vanished, replaced with a fullness, a completeness he never dreamed possible.

His gaze captured hers as he gave himself over to the pull of his destiny. And he wished he had kissed her one last time.

His body lurched to a stop.

Blinding hot pain radiated across his midsection as his belt cut into his flesh. He sucked in a gasping breath and tried to fight the sudden dizziness that assailed him. He twisted toward the castle's ledge. Scotia, braced against the castle wall, clutched the leather of his belt in her bloodied hands.

The White Horseman fell past Ian, past the castle wall to his death.

Ian kept his gaze on Scotia. Tears rolled down her cheeks. "Don't you dare die on me, Ian MacKinnon." Purple veins stood out at the sides of her neck as she struggled to pull him back to safety.

The muscles of her arms began to tremble beneath his weight. The pain in her injured shoulder must have been agonizing, yet she bore his weight. He loved her all the more for her efforts even though they were in vain. "Scotia, I am not afraid to die. Save yourself."

"You cannot tell me you love me, then disappear from my life." She set her teeth and pulled, hard.

His body inched toward her. He could not let her suffer on—he would do what he could to help her. He grasped her hands with his and planted his feet against the walls, giving her as much leverage as possible. As she drew him back, he walked up the wall, speaking words of encouragement and promise. But he doubted she heard anything, so intense was her concentration. His body inched upward with excruciating slowness, each moment bringing him back to the woman he loved.

When the edge grew near, he stretched his fingers until they gripped solid rock. The rough texture bit into his palms as he hoisted himself over the tower's edge. He collapsed onto the floorboards, panting, trembling, and filled with relief. "We . . . did . . . it."

Scotia dropped to the ground beside him, her body shaking. "Praise the saints. I thought—" Her voice clouded with tears.

"As did I." He wrapped his arms around her, pulling her close. "Thank you," he whispered, feeling his breathing slow and his heartbeat returning to normal.

She remained silent. Curled against the warmth of his body, her tremors slowed, then stopped, as did his own.

"Scotia?"

She shifted in his arms to face him. "Hmm?"

"This battle is not over yet."

"I know." She studied his face. Her glorious green eyes

were strong and clear once more. "Before we go back into battle I want to ask you something."

"Anything." He brought a finger up to brush a wayward tendril of hair from her cheek.

"Will you say that to me again?" she asked.

"*That?*"

"Did you only speak the words because you thought you were going to die?" A raw ache sounded in her voice, and he instantly knew what she wanted to hear.

He cupped her face with his hands. "I love you," he told her with all the joy in his heart. "I love you." He bent his head, covering her mouth with his in a slow, sensual kiss. "I love you."

She kissed him back, holding him fiercely. What started out as a slow, gentle celebration of life became an urgent plea. With an effort, Ian dragged his mouth from hers. "As much as I am enjoying this moment, we really must stop now before I am hopelessly lost."

"You have the same effect on me." She pressed her face to his chest and drew a shuddering breath.

"Our duty is not yet complete." His gaze shifted from Scotia to their swords. Their weapons lay on the wooden planking inches from them. "Come," he said as he stumbled to his knees. "We must yet fight."

He held out his hand to help her up. She put her fingers in his. With his free hand he retrieved her sword and handed it to her before grasping his own.

"Do you wish to see him?"

Scotia nodded. Together they moved to the side of the tower and peered down at the crushed body of the White Horseman, the Stone he had desired above all in his life now weighing down his chest in death. Waves slammed against the rocks, shifting his broken body with their advance and retreat. Soon, both the man and the Stone would be lost.

Scotia stepped away from the tower's edge. When she did, the wind picked up the ends of her free-flowing hair, setting it into motion about her face and shoulders. Her cheeks held a rosy flush and a soft glow breathed life into her timeless green eyes. With the backdrop of the wild Scottish hills behind her, she looked as though she had stepped out of legends of old and into this very moment.

"Ready?" He took her hand in his.

A shadow crept over her face.

"What is it, Scotia?"

Her fingers shook ever so slightly as she raised her gaze to his. "Nothing. Let us proceed."

They made their way down from the tower. Each step brought them closer to the nightmare the White Horseman had left behind. When they entered the courtyard, Ian released Scotia's hand.

Fire had devoured the bakehouse, the stables, and the stacks of hay not used during the winter. Flames of red and orange swept hell across the outer perimeter of the courtyard. Smoke and ash hung heavy in the air, but not thick enough to hide the bodies of the dead and dying. The sounds of battle rang in the clash of swords, the shouts of men, and the cries of the wounded. The castle could be rebuilt, but the lives taken this day would never be regained.

"Before we fight here, we must release Griffin and the others."

Scotia nodded and followed him to the gate leading into the garden. Inside the confined area, Ian squinted through the thick haze of smoke.

"Ian?" a familiar voice called out, and a dark shadow appeared from behind the door, sword in hand.

GERRI RUSSELL

"Griffin?" Ian felt a chill course through him, but he kept it carefully under control. His own fears would not help to heal his brother's swollen and bruised face and body. "Are you all right?"

Griffin lowered his sword. He started to smile, then grimaced instead as the muscles in his face rebelled against the action. "It takes more than a beating to stop a MacKinnon."

Ian could only be glad for that. Despite their differences, Griffin was still his brother, his family. "How did you manage to free yourself?"

"Burke remained hidden until all the others left. He cut us free after surprising the guard."

Ian nodded. He narrowed his gaze to search the smoke-filled garden. "Maisie and Lizbet, where are they?"

"We are here." Maisie and Burke, with Lizbet huddled between them, stepped out of the tunnel opening and hastened toward him.

"I was so worried," Scotia cried as she folded all three people into her embrace.

Ian smiled faintly as he stood gazing at the four of them. "Are you harmed?" Ian asked the older woman. Anger seethed through him as he search her tired gray eyes for signs of distress. The slashes in her clothes and the welts on her face and body indicated that she had been whipped. Repeatedly. Damn the White Horseman for his villainy. At least they would suffer at his hand no more.

"I am well." Maisie hugged the little girl beside her. "Lizbet, however, will have none but Scotia comfort her."

Scotia dropped to her knee and lightly caressed the young girl's battered face. "Lizbet, the White Horseman is dead. Soon this will all be over."

"I want you to stay with me. I feel safe with you," Liz-

296

bet cried as she buried herself in Scotia's arms and held on with all her might.

"Scotia would stay with you if she could," Ian interceded, "but her duty calls her elsewhere right now."

The young girl lifted her chin. Tears pooled in her brown eyes—eyes that held an unspoiled innocence despite the horrors she had lived through in her young life.

"You must be brave, as Scotia is brave," Ian said softly.

Lizbet stopped crying, and with an effort straightened her slight shoulders.

"That is better," Scotia said. "There is something I need you to do for me."

"What is that?" Lizbet asked.

"You must help Maisie and Burke to save the castle. Find a way to contain the fire."

Lizbet nodded. "What about you?"

"Ian and I must help the warriors who battle in the courtyard." Scotia patted the girl's cheek and sent her after Maisie and Burke, who had begun filling buckets of water from the garden well.

"I will go with you," Griffin said. As he drew his sword, a steely resolve settled in his eyes—a look Ian had never seen there before. Much had changed in Griffin since they had last parted.

"I would welcome your help," Ian said.

"As would I," Scotia agreed.

Together, the three of them headed out the gate and into the fighting now obscured by thick and heavy smoke.

"Griffin," Ian shouted above the sound of swords clashing. The soft whiz of arrows arching through the air shattered the spaces between the clang of metal and the moans of the dying that raised a chorus of grief over it all. "Go to Father. He is here. Protect him."

Griffin's face brightened at the realization their father had come after him. "Where is he?"

Ian nodded toward the melee. "I last saw him at the front gate."

Without hesitation, Griffin turned and strode away.

The smoke in the courtyard began to ease. As those who fought became more visible, so did he and Scotia. Two warriors charged toward them. "Fight with me back to back," Scotia shouted.

She had barely taken her position when the two men reached them. Both fell easily to the ground, only to be replaced by two more. Ian drove his sword through one man's body just as an arrow whizzed past his head, but strangely he felt no fear. He channeled the heat and power of battle sweeping inside him into a cool efficient weapon, as Scotia had taught him.

He pressed against Scotia's back, finding comfort in her presence there. Together, they moved deeper into the fray.

"What is our plan?" Ian shouted.

"Two Horsemen remain as the core of this army. If we take them down, the ranks will dissolve." Scotia searched the wild, twisted fighting for the Black and the Red Horsemen. She and Ian moved as one, farther into the crowd until the fighting closed around them, enveloping them in its midst.

With a renewed vigor, Ian pressed his attack, clearing a path through the fighting until he saw both warriors ahead. The Black Horseman battled with Griffin while the Red Horseman clashed swords with one of the Ranalds. The Red Horseman's thrusts came more slowly. The tip of his sword dipped slightly, exposing his body. The man was growing weary, as was Keith Ranald.

The Black Horseman lunged at Griffin, barely missing

his thigh. Griffin stumbled in his retreat, but managed to spin out of the way.

"They are both growing tired," Scotia said.

"We must intervene." Ian started forward.

Scotia's hand on his arm held him back. "Not while they are engaged. It would not be honorable. There are other ways to aid Griffin and Keith. Watch."

Scotia rolled forward, hit the ground, then came to her feet between the fighting warriors. She held her sword at the ready. The motion startled them all. The Horsemen's blades grew still. "I will let you live if you take your army and go in peace from this castle and this country—go back to England where you belong."

The Black Horseman grinned at Scotia. "This land will be ours once the White Horseman gains the Stone."

"The White Horseman is dead. The Stone is lost in the Sea of Hebrides."

"You try to fool me," the Black Horseman growled, but panic flickered in his eyes. "We will succeed."

"You have already failed."

The Black Horseman peered about him, and the arrogance in his stance lessened. His gaze hardened as he turned back to Scotia. "We must prevail where our leader did not." With a slice of his sword, he left Griffin behind to challenge Scotia.

"Then you leave us no choice." Scotia blocked his strike and quickly returned the blow. It sent him to the ground.

A small, sardonic smile tugged at the corners of his mouth. "My leader waits for me."

"Then go to him." Her sword came down, its job complete. No sooner had her blade swept free of the body than the Red Horseman charged her. Ian swept forward and drove his sword through the Red Horseman.

Without anyone to command them, the army gradually fell into chaos and then rapidly retreated. Cheers from Scotia's men followed them out the gate. The battle was over.

Slowly, the tension that had driven Ian for days left him, leaving only exhaustion in its place. He strode toward Scotia. Her shoulders were rigid, her back straight as she stared at the fallen men scattered across her courtyard. She stood listening to the retreating footsteps of her enemy with her bloodied sword in hand. He knew so intimately the thoughts that crossed her mind. "It is never easy, the life of a warrior."

The clang of the iron portcullis as it closed behind their enemy reverberated through the entire castle. The sound set her into motion once more. "We must see to the wounded and bury the dead. I will also need a contingent of men to barricade the tunnel through the cliff. I want it sealed at the garden gate and along the shoreline."

"Scotia—"

"Please, Ian." Tears shimmered in her eyes, and something more—a subtle shift in the way she looked at him. With fear? Uncertainty? It was as if she no longer knew what to say to him or how to feel.

Scotia stepped back, putting more distance between them. "Help me with these things. There is no time for talk or tears." Despair crept into her voice. He reached out to pull her to him, but she moved even farther away. "Nay, Ian. I cannot allow myself to feel sorry for the things that have happened this day. Too much remains yet undone."

He did not press her for more, allowing her to maintain the thin thread of control she held over her emotions. She looked pale and stricken and heart-wrenchingly beautiful. He had to let her set the pace, to come to him when she was ready to move beyond this moment and into their future.

Scotia walked back through the charred remains of the courtyard, where several men had already begun work to rebuild the wooden stairs that led into the keep. Thankfully, the stairs were the only part of the keep damaged in the fire.

Abbus came to stand beside Ian. "You would let her walk away from you so easily?"

"It is not what she walks away from, but what she walks toward that gives me hope." Ian turned to gaze at the man who had given him so much over the past years.

Abbus gazed thoughtfully at the burned timbers. "Toward destruction?"

"Nay. Toward our future, together." Ian allowed himself a small smile. "Father, there is something I must tell you."

Abbus's bushy brows arched over his knowing eyes. "What is that?"

"I cannot lead the clan. Scotia is my destiny now." Ian marveled at how easily the words had come to him, how easy it was to relinquish his past.

Abbus smiled in that fatherly way he always did when one of his sons finally did something right. "She was always yer destiny. From the moment ye were left at the base of our door. I knew ye would be the one to fulfill the prophecy her mother created while I trained under her."

"You trained with Scotia's mother?"

"Aye," he nodded. "Myself, the Ranald, and the White Horseman." At Ian's frown, he added, "Scotia's mother somehow knew the spin her own destiny would take."

"How could she know?"

Abbus shrugged. "Perhaps because of the Stone. I never thought to question her. 'Twas from me that she garnered the promise to send her daughter 'a man alone in this world' when she came of age."

His foster father's words whirled across his mind. "You lied to me about my purpose with the clan?" Ian said tersely.

"Aye, my son. But I never would have sent ye if I dinna think ye were the right man for the task. I had hoped the two of ye would eventually marry," he said with a slight shrug.

"We did. Last night."

Abbus clapped Ian on the back. "Congratulations, my boy."

"No congratulations are due yet. She has not promised herself to me forever. Only a year and a day."

Abbus's grin widened. "Well, then ye'd best get to the task of changin' her mind."

Ian watched Scotia as she drove iron nails into the freshly cut planks of wood with more force than was necessary. He would not change her mind. She would have to do that herself.

And when she did, he would be waiting for her.

Chapter Thirty-two

Ian placed the torch against the burial pyre that held the body of one of the Ranald warriors. Night had fallen, and the sky filled with millions of stars that welcomed the warriors as they went to their eternal reward. The air had turned crisp, and a light breeze teased the flames that devoured the warrior's remains. In his mind, Ian repeated the ancient Celtic blessing that would send the great warrior on his way. Despite his will to keep going, moving steadily until the work was complete, he swayed on his feet.

"You are exhausted." Scotia's voice came from behind him.

"Aye." He turned to face her and had to refrain from pulling her to him. "I have slept little in the last three days."

"Then you must retire now. The others and I will finish what remains to be completed. You have already done twice as much as any other man here."

"I would do the same, a thousandfold. These are my

people as well as yours. Just as we united in marriage, our countrymen united in battle."

"Our marriage was a mistake. You could never love me if you knew—"

"Scotia—"

"Nay. Say no more. I had thought on our way back here that there was hope for us." She shook her head in true remorse. "Now, things are different."

Ian narrowed his gaze on her, searching for a way to reach her before she did something they would both regret forever. With every breath he drew he believed she loved him.

Scotia averted her gaze. As she did, her unbound hair brushed her pale cheek, then fell in a wild tumble about her shoulders in luxuriant waves. He remembered another head of reddish brown hair, and he knew the reason she had changed her mind. She did not fear him. She feared the taint of her own blood.

He knew the feeling all too well.

He brought his arms around her and held tight as she struggled against him. When she finally stopped, he waited until she brought her gaze to his.

Fragile love stared back at him from the depths of her green eyes. He smiled to himself as he faced her. "Listen carefully to me, Scotia, because I am not going to let you do this to us. You gave me your love without hesitation the night of our handfasting, and I will not let you take it away, all for the sake of your wounded pride. The harder you try to deny that there is something between us, the harder I will fight you, and without the use of our swords."

She struggled within his arms, but without the same intensity as she did before. "I—"

"I shall haunt your dreams each night," he interrupted,

"just as you have haunted mine since the moment I first saw you. You will lie awake in your bed wanting me, knowing that I am lying in bed wanting you. And finally, when you are ready, you will come to me because you will have no choice."

She flinched, but did not move. Instead of the anger he had expected, her eyes reflected pain. "It is not possible."

He continued as though she had not spoken. "And when you do come to me, I will be waiting with open arms."

Scotia drew a shaky breath. He ignored her attempt to speak, driving his point into her heart as best he could. "I hurt you when I left. I understand that now. But I swear on my life I will never leave you again. I have spoken to my father, and I have relinquished all rights to lead my clan."

Surprise filled her eyes.

Ian laughed. "Father had no arguments for me when I gave him the news. He said leading the clan was never my destiny—you were. And if that is so, Scotia, I am here to embrace that destiny with all my heart and soul."

"There are things about me you do not know," she said in an aching whisper.

"Perhaps those things will not matter to me."

She shook her head. "Nay. You would leave me for certain if you knew the truth."

He released her abruptly. "Love bears all things, Scotia. When you realize that, you will come for me. And I will be waiting," he said before he walked back toward the keep.

She would come for him, he told himself. She had to.

Hours later, Scotia headed straight for her bedchamber and the steaming bath that Maisie had no doubt left for her there. The thought of soaking away the grime and blood in the heather-scented water was more than she could resist. Without hesitation, she took off her armor, dropping it on the floor next to the tub. She pulled her shift over her head and paused at the sudden realization of what she had done.

Scotia eyed the pile of discarded garments. A hysterical sob rose up inside her. For years she had been frightened, terrified even, to remove her armor. Now, with Ian nearby, she did not even consider her actions, merely threw off her garb without a second thought. The chill air of her bedchamber skittered across her bare flesh. Did she feel so at ease with him and his presence in her household that she no longer felt the need for such extreme measures of protection?

Scotia tore her gaze away from the reminder of how much he had changed her life as she slipped into the heated water. Weary from exhaustion, she leaned her head back against the copper tub, wanting nothing more than to forget the events of the day. The images of the battle would eventually fade from her mind. Even the final conflict with her father would soon recede into the realm of unreality.

But she would never be able to forget the expression on Ian's face when he charged the White Horseman and sent him to his death. The primitive anger, the revulsion that etched itself across his features spoke louder than words his feelings for his enemy.

Knowing the truth of who had sired her, how could he ever look at her again with love in his eyes? She had committed to him for a year and a day. As a warrior she would honor that commitment. Savoring each day, each moment, storing them all up for the time when they would be apart. Because even though she wanted a lifetime with him, he would never willingly join himself to her forever if he knew the blood of that horrible man flowed within her veins.

How could he ever love her?

Scotia closed her eyes, trying to clear her mind of everything, but images of Ian pressed in on her instead. She saw Ian battling with her for the first time, staring up at her from the floor with genuine surprise in his eyes; Ian dancing with her in her great hall; Ian gazing up at the stars with her and sharing stories of his past; Ian holding her tight, demanding she hold on to life when she was so sick; Ian standing before her covered with soot and blood proudly proclaiming: *I shall haunt your dreams each night, just as you have haunted mine since the moment I first saw you. You will lie awake in your bed wanting me, knowing that I am lying in bed wanting you.*

He had been wrong about one thing: even away from her bed she would think of him. With a sigh of regret, Scotia finished her bath, then changed into the soft linen nightrail she had worn when she was ill. She crept into her bed and pulled the covers up tight against her chin.

For what seemed like hours but was probably more like minutes, Scotia stared at the unadorned ceiling of her room and waited. But even sleep refused to claim her. Finally, she pushed the bed linens back and got out of bed. The only way she would ever be able to sleep was if she worked herself into blessed exhaustion. And she knew just how to accomplish that.

Taking the candle with her, she stopped at the pile of discarded clothing and armor to retrieve her sword, before quietly slipping out of her bedchamber and down the stairs. When she stood at the doorway of her training chamber, she paused to clear her mind as she always did. But the serenity that usually filled her did not come.

Edgy and off-balance, she stepped into the room, ready to begin a grueling routine. Halfway across the room she froze at the sight before her. On the floor near her feet lay Ian's sword with his plaid coiled around the weapon. Her heartbeat thundered in her ears as Scotia knelt beside the cloth. A pang of longing tugged at her heart. With trembling fingers, she lifted the edge of the fabric up to her face and pressed her cheek into the woolen warmth. Ian's minty scent lingered there. She closed her eyes against the tears that threatened, but they spilled past her barricade anyway.

He had known she would end up here, in her training chamber this eve. And he had left his sword and his plaid for her to find, to give her a reason to come to him if she could not do so on her own. The sweetness of his words came back to her: *When you are ready, you will come to me because you will have no choice.*

Defying all logic and reason, she was ready to go to him. The question was would he be ready to receive her when he knew the truth? Suddenly, it seemed paramount that she find out.

Before she could think about what she was doing, Scotia slipped her nightrail off and wrapped Ian's plaid tight around her body, allowing the length of the fabric to drag on the floor. With a sword in each hand, she hurried down the corridor before she could change her mind.

After a breathless moment, she placed her hand on the door to the bedchamber he had taken for the night. The door swung open with a slight creak of the hinges. She paused in the doorway and drew a shaky breath. The light of a fire in the hearth cast a reddish glow about the room. The light beckoned her forward, toward the bed.

Halfway across the room she paused to lay their swords down upon the floor. There would be no need for weapons between them tonight. She stepped across the swords and continued toward him. Ian lay on his back, one arm draped over his face, the other flung across the bed. His breath came softly within the quiet of the chamber, slow and even. He had kicked off the covers to reveal one naked foot, one long, lean thigh, and the exposed planes of his chest lightly furred with crisp blond hair.

Scotia swallowed, transfixed by the sight of his big, muscular body. He was hers, her husband, for the asking, for the taking. But would she be brave enough to take what she wanted now that she knew who she truly was? Could she take the last step and bare herself to him?

"If you would take one step forward, you could nestle in my arms." He stretched his hand out to her as if doing so would have the power to keep her with him.

She took the last step that separated them and caught his hand in her own. She brought his fingers to her lips. "Hold me, Ian."

His opposite hand snaked out from the bedside. Before she knew what had happened, she found herself beneath him, the softness of her breasts colliding with the unyielding strength of his chest. A moment later he shifted her on her side and cradled her in his arms, tenderly brushing his lips against her forehead. She trembled in response, and his arms tightened around her. "I would hold you forever if you would only let me."

With an effort, Scotia dragged herself back from the mindless swirl her senses had become the moment he touched her. She had to tell him the truth. Now. Before this went any farther. She propped herself up on one elbow and gazed into his eyes. "Ian, I must tell you something, something that could change everything between us."

He continued to rain kisses across her jawline and down her neck. "What could you possibly say that would change the way I feel about you?" His mouth left a scorching trail of kisses across her shoulder and down her arm. "I like your choice of garments this evening. Very fetching." He slipped one hand inside the opening at the front of his plaid to caress the rounded softness of her hip and thigh. "You wearing my plaid makes me want you all the more."

"Are you sure you would want me if I told you my father was the White Horseman?" Scotia shuddered from the combination of her confession and his bold exploration of her body. Without a pause, his hand slid along the side of her breast, his fingers splaying wide in a bold, possessive caress.

"I know," he said in a gentle voice. "I heard him say so on the tower."

Startled, Scotia pulled back to stare into his face. "And still you can touch me like this?"

He cupped her face in his hands, stroking his thumbs over the soft curve of her mouth. "One thing you have taught me since my arrival here is that it is not your background that matters or what makes you great, it is who you are inside. Does that rule apply only to your students and not to yourself?"

Her lips trembled beneath the caress of his thumbs. His words penetrated her soul, her very being. "You do not care?"

His brown eyes smoldered with unleashed passion. "Only for you."

She turned her face into his hand and kissed his palm with all the sensual sweetness his words had brought into her heart. A groan tore from his throat. His mouth sought hers, claiming her in a kiss that was both urgent and gentle. He parted her lips for the demanding invasion of his tongue.

Helplessly lost in the stirring sensation his kisses always brought, she slipped her arms around his broad shoulders. He pulled her against his full length, clasping her against his thighs while his tongue began to plunge into her mouth, then retreat, only to plunge again in an unmistakably suggestive rhythm that sent desire coiling through her loins.

"Ian?" she whispered against his lips.

"Aye," he murmured huskily as his hands moved up to release the tie of his plaid, revealing her body fully to him.

She pulled away from his kisses, but kept her lips close, almost desperate to reclaim her connection with him. She had to speak the words she longed to say, and speak them now while she still could. "I wish to change the terms of our handfasting agreement." She reached for his right hand with her own, and gently threaded her fingers through his.

"What do you wish to change?"

The warmth of his fingers wrapped around her own. "The length of our marriage."

"How long?"

"Forever."

"Not long enough."

Scotia smiled her agreement. His reply made her ache with a sudden yearning to possess him, body and soul. She withdrew her hand from his and trailed her fingers across his broad, muscled chest and the sprinkling of hair that teased her fingers with its texture. "I love you," she whispered, bringing her gaze back to his.

He opened his mouth to speak, but she silenced him with a kiss, taking control of their lovemaking in a desperate desire to prove just how much he meant to her. Her fingers feathered the lightest of caresses against his jaw, his throat, his chest. And where her fingers stopped,

311

her kisses began. The taste of his skin went straight to her head, making her bold, freeing her inhibitions, compelling her to continue what she had begun.

Her lips reached greedily for the hard bud of his nipples, sampling them with slow swirling probes of her tongue. When he shuddered beneath her assault, she shamelessly nipped, then kissed her way across his torso, around his navel, then lower still. When she pressed a warm, moist kiss at the base of his swollen flesh, his head fell back onto his pillow with a sound that was half moan, half plea.

In that moment she realized she had as much power over his body as he held over hers. Delighted by the discovery, she took another taste, then another, breathless at the urgent hunger she could bring out in him. She played the seductress, surprising him with tender erotic caresses that had him twining his fingers in her hair and whispering "I love you" on a disbelieving breath.

She continued her assault until his hands became almost urgent upon her shoulders, and the heat of his body flowed beneath her fingertips with a hunger that matched her own.

With a shift of his weight, he pressed her into the bedding, and his body hovered above her. He kissed every part of her. The passion of his kisses heated her flesh, seduced her spirit, until she felt as though she were drifting beneath him in a hot, wet, shimmering mist.

His adoring hands trailed his kisses, caressing her battle hardened body until her flesh trembled her ultimate surrender. She was his, now and forever.

As though sensing her thoughts, he smiled down at her, bringing his hands to her hips, and with slow exquisiteness he entered her, spreading a smooth voluptuousness through her. Her body arched. Pleasure engulfed her.

His fullness surrounded her. They became one. Slowly, deliberately he stroked her and hot torrents of ecstasy grew stronger and stronger, until she plunged headlong into a vortex of colliding sensations. In that moment, she drew him deeper inside her, opening herself up to him, until his life force pulsed at the very soul of her being. Scotia clamped her legs around him, savoring the warmth of his seed within her.

They lay together, their limbs possessively entwined, neither willing to break the bond that had been forged between them. Her body still heavy with pleasure, she listened to the sound of his heart thundering beneath her ear, content to know that all of it belonged to her now.

"I have so much to thank you for," she whispered softly. "You risked your life to save mine. You accepted me for who I was. And," she dropped her gaze to the flat plane of her belly, "you gave me a precious gift this eve."

He brought her gaze back to his. "A gift?"

She smiled, unable to restrain the joy that tumbled through her freely. "A baby."

A grin lit up his face and brought out the dimple at the side of his cheek. "How can you be certain? These things take time."

"I just know."

His grin faded to a somber smile. "Then that does not leave me much time."

"Time for what?" she asked, confused by the sudden turn in the conversation.

His gaze moved beyond her to where she had set their swords upon the floor. "I have yet to best you in a sword fight."

She inched closer to his chest and let her thigh slide suggestively over the top of his. "I may never let you win."

Ian caught her by the shoulders and rolled her beneath

him as a new urgency blazed in his eyes. "Has it never oc-curred to you, my love, that I may never want to win?"

As his lips covered hers, she surrendered to the stormy splendor of his kiss, thrilled by the thought that their battle would go on forever.

Epilogue

Nine months to the day after that final battle with the White Horseman, Scotia's contractions started at midnight. And from the first hint of pain, Ian was at her side, refusing to leave her.

He brought a cool, lavender-scented cloth up to her temple, brushing away with infinite tenderness the sweat upon her brow as the pressure in her pelvis threatened to tear her apart. It was a battle she had no idea how to fight. She tried to relax, to let the child do the work, but instead of relief, her efforts only brought on a new wave of pain. "Our daughter is in a hurry to be born," Scotia panted.

"If the force with which she tries to enter the world is any indication, the Warrior Trainer line will be well served by her birth." He drew her hand to his lips and pressed a kiss at its center. A wave of pure pleasure moved through her, countering the pain as her belly tightened again. Over the last several months, Ian's expression had softened, becoming more at ease, no longer darkened by the shadows of the past or duties that remained unfulfilled. Only love and anticipation filled his gaze now.

315

She should feel nothing but happiness and anticipation as well, on the day their daughter would enter this world. Yet as she stared into Ian's soft brown eyes, she held one small regret close to her heart. She might have succeeded in providing a new Trainer to take her place, but after centuries of protection by her ancestors, she had been the one who failed to keep the Stone of Destiny safe. The churning gray-green water of the sea was the Stone's protector now.

"What are you thinking about, my love?" Ian asked, watching her face closely.

"Nothing."

His expression became thoughtful. "I can guess what saddens you. And I have something that might ease at least some of your pain." Before she could question him, he slipped his hand from hers and left the room. He returned a moment later with a large object wrapped in the folds of the MacKinnon plaid. "Remove the cloth," he said, holding the gift out to her.

"Ian." She hesitated with her fingers atop the woolen cloth. "I do not understand."

"You will." He gave her a reassuring nod.

With hesitant fingers, she pulled the fabric away and tears misted in her eyes. The Stone of Destiny. "Ian," she whispered brokenly. "How? Oh, I cannot believe this."

"Griffin and I finally located it yesterday morn beneath the waters at the shoreline," Ian said as he placed the Stone on the floor near her bedside. "We have been looking for it every day for these last nine months."

"I had no idea." Scotia wanted to slide her arms around Ian's neck, to show him how much this gift meant to her, but another contraction pulled at her, leaving her powerless to do anything more than grip his hand. "You have . . . given me so much. What have I . . . to give to you?"

He pressed a possessive kiss to the back of her hand with

a reverence that touched her very soul. "You have given me something I always craved, but never expected to find."

"And what is that?" She looked up at him with her heart in her eyes.

"A family."

Scotia could not comment, as another contraction stole her breath and her focus. Their daughter would wait no longer.

" 'Tis time." Maisie moved to the end of the bed along with Lizbet. Maisie prepared to receive the child while Lizbet stood by with clean linens.

As the contraction eased, Scotia caught the young girl's gaze. "Your sister is in a hurry to meet you." Lizbet responded with an eager smile. As part of their family, Lizbet would train alongside any daughters Scotia and Ian had, carrying on the tradition of guarding the Stone and training Scotland's warriors together. No longer would the burden fall to just one warrior. The thought brought with it a sense of peace Scotia had never experienced in her lifetime. Her children's lives would be different. For that, she was extremely grateful.

"Yer doin' well, love," Maisie said in a soft, soothing tone. Scotia barely heard her as a deep, heavy tightening took control of her body and the need to push overwhelmed all else.

A moment later, the healthy cry of a baby resounded throughout the bedchamber, followed by Maisie's startled gasp. Silence fell over the room as Ian's gaze moved from her face to the child, then back to her again. An amused smile brought out that dimple she loved so well.

"What is it?" Scotia asked, around the sudden pounding of her heart. "What is wrong?"

A look of exquisite tenderness came over Ian's face. "Our daughter . . ." He hesitated.

After wrapping the babe in the fresh linens, Maisie placed the child in the lee of Scotia's arms. "Yer daughter, my dear, is a son."

A *son?* Scotia's gaze moved to the tiny infant in her arms. So small. So beautiful. The room suddenly seemed cast in a sunlit haze as the light of morning stretched out across the room, turning the baby's abundant blond hair into burnished gold. From the color of his hair to his firm yet stubborn chin, to the tiny dimple in his left cheek, the baby looked like Ian.

"We have a son, Scotia. A fine, strong son."

Scotia shook her head, still not believing what her heart told her was true. "But the Warrior Trainer only has daughters—that's all they've had for centuries."

He gazed at her uncertainly. "Does it grieve you to know you did not have a daughter?"

"Nay," Scotia mused, "I am merely unprepared for this. All my life. . . ." She gave a soft chuckle. The baby nestled against her body, seeking the warmth and comfort of his mother. "What shall we call him? We can hardly call him Scotia, as we had planned for our daughter."

"Might we call him Malcolm?" Ian asked, his tone suddenly solemn.

Scotia smiled. "It would be fitting." Ian tenderly touched his son's tiny hand. His fist opened and he wrapped his perfect fingers around his father's large one. A look of utter satisfaction rode Ian's features as he brought his gaze back to Scotia's. "Do you know what the birth of a son means?"

Scotia nodded, and a heartfelt smile came freely to her lips. "That our daughters *and* our sons will train together."

The sound of Ian's joyous laughter filled the room. "Who could ask for anything more?"

An Afterword from the Author

I have interwoven fact and fiction so closely in *The Warrior Trainer* that I believe a few clarifications may be in order.

Scotia is a true historical figure. The first records of her come from Egypt, where she was known as Meritaten, a pharaoh's daughter. She was given in marriage to a Greek linguist who came to the Egyptian court to teach the Pharaoh Akhenaten the Greek language. In Greek, her name translated to Scotia. Scotia's husband, Niul, found the Stone of Destiny on the Plains of Luz on his way to Egypt.

Scotia and Niul took the Stone with them when they returned to Greece. They had many children, one of whom was named Scotia, after her mother. The second known Scotia married a Greek king named Milesius. During this time, Scotia became known as a warrior woman and a master of the martial arts. When her husband died in battle, Scotia decided to lead her people, the Milesians, to the Isle of Destiny as was prophesied to Niul's descendants by a Hebrew Prophet named Moses.

With her two sons, numerous followers, and the Stone of Destiny, they arrived off the shores of Ireland, named after the local Queen, Eiré. The Milesians and Queen Scotia were victorious over Queen Eiré, but both queens died in battle. Scotia's people eventually took the Stone and moved north to a remote country known as Albania. They renamed the country Scotia, after their dead queen, and the new rulers were called Scoti.

The Stone of Destiny was moved several times after its arrival in Ireland. When the Stone was located on the Isle of Iona and at Dunnad, it was used to inaugurate the High Kings. In the sixth century, the Stone was moved to a fortress named Dunstaffnage. In the ninth century, the Stone was moved again, to protect it from Viking raiders. At the Abbey of Scone, it was used for the inauguration of the Scottish kings. At this point in history the Stone of Destiny became known as the Stone of Scone.

In 1296, Edward I of England stole the Stone and placed it under the throne in Westminster Abbey, where the English kings were crowned. Some say the Scots knew Edward was coming, and that the monks of Scone hid their precious stone, replacing it with a lump of common sandstone. The real Stone was said to be composed of black marble, with intricate carvings in the shape of a seat. The current Stone, weighing 336 pounds, is of sandstone with a single Latin cross carved on its surface. It has been theorized that the original stone remains hidden in Scotland and is kept safe by a secret society.

On Christmas Day 1950, four Scottish students took the Stone from Westminster Abbey in order to return it to Scotland. In the process of removing it from the Abbey, they accidentally broke it in two. The two halves of the Stone were smuggled separately through roadblocks and across the border, where the Stone was passed to a senior Glasgow politician who arranged for it to be professionally repaired by a stonemason. The Stone was then left by its temporary custodians four months later on the altar of Arbroath Abbey. And again, rumors circulated that the Stone had been copied and a false Stone returned.

In 1996, the Stone of Destiny was returned to Scotland in preparation for the 1999 reestablishment of the Scottish Parliament. Today, it has a place of honor within the Throne Room of Edinburgh Castle, where it is on public display behind armored glass, surrounded by a sophisticated security system. However, it still remains the property of the English Crown and will be returned to Westminster for any future coronations.

In *The Warrior Trainer*, I took creative license in making the Stone of Destiny much smaller than it is so that it could easily be moved by a single person.

I also took the liberty to give Queen Scotia a daughter in addition to her two sons, who are not mentioned in the story. This daughter, the Warrior Trainer, would carry on her matriarchal duty by training her countrymen as warriors, and by protecting the most valuable symbol of Scottish independence, the real Stone of Destiny.

Since it has been proven time and again that real life is often stranger than fiction, I hold on to the firm belief that Scotia's story, and her lineage, could have continued just as I imagined.

CONNIE MASON

To Tempt A Rogue

Kitty O'Shay has been living outside the law for years. Dressed as a boy, she joined the notorious Barton gang, robbing banks and stealing horses with no one the wiser of her true identity. Except their newest member: Ryan Delaney. He is the only one who sees through her charade.

Ryan has infiltrated the Barton gang, hoping to find some information on a dying man's missing illegitimate daughter. Little does Ryan know he'll find her *within* the group. Stealing Kitty away is easy; controlling his desire for the maddening vixen is not. Ryan thought his biggest problem would be convincing Kitty to visit the father she'd never known—until he realized he was in danger of losing his heart to the beauty.

Cornered Tigress

JADE LEE

When the white man arrives, the storm clouds make him appear an ugly baboon growling at the rain. But Little Pearl's missing master owes him money, and Little Pearl owes the Tans. They had saved her from abject poverty and disgrace, set her feet on the Taoist path. And so, barbarian or not, Captain Jonas Storm is welcome. In the alien depths of his eyes, Little Pearl sees the impossible promise of paradise. Even with the shadows growing in the Empire, Heaven is within reach—and this barbarian could take her there.

ERINSONG
DIANA GROE

An Irish princess. A Viking warrior. His people's raids on her country should make them bitter enemies. But when he washes up on her beach with no memory of his life, Brenna finds herself drawn to the handsome stranger. His kind words and gentle touch make her long for his hands to caress her body the same way they run over the gleaming wood of his ship. But even their desire can't deny the secrets of the past. And as they travel through the land of Erin on a quest that could change the course of history, long-ago betrayals and treachery threaten to destroy the haven they've found in each other's arms.

PAMELA CLARE

Surrender

"[*Surrender* is a] lush historical romance...believable characters, scorching chemistry and a convincing setting."
—*Publishers Weekly*

"Riveting, exciting...Pamela Clare delivers what readers want."
—*New York Times* Bestselling Author CONNIE MASON

Iain MacKinnon has been forced to serve the British crown, but compassion urges him to save the lovely lass facing certain death at the hands of the Abenaki. He has defied his orders, endangered his brothers, his men and his mission, all for a woman. But when he holds Annie's sweet body in his arms, he can feel no regret. Though he senses she is hiding something from him, it is too late to hold back his heart. In love and war, there are times when the only course of action is...*Surrender*.

- -

LEIGH GREENWOOD

Texas Tender

He is the most beautiful man Idalou Ellsworth has ever set eyes on. When he appears at her front door, she is struck speechless at the very sight of him. Folks in Dunmore, Texas think her bossy, too focused on rescuing her family's failing ranch to be interested in courting. But in Will's company, she can't think of anything but him. And when the devil-may-care cowboy takes her in his arms, she understands, as never before, the pleasures of being a woman.

Everyone deserves a break from the daily grind...

Enter to Win a Complete Spa Day Package at a Spa Near You!

Spa Package Includes:

**1-Hour Massage Treatment
Facial Restorative Treatment
Gourmet Spa Luncheon
Spa Manicure and Pedicure**

Plus your choice of either a Seaweed Slimmer Body Treatment, Sea Scrub, or Couture Haircut

To enter, send an e-mail to: gerri@gerrirussell.net

Or send your name, address and phone number to:
**Gerri Russell
6947 Coal Creek Pkwy SE #282
Newcastle, WA 98059-3159**

Winner will be chosen from a random drawing
on May 1, 2007. Only one entry per person please.